They kept me company at night, they formed a protective shield between me and the outside world. Hidden behind them, not one soul had all of me, not one person had wormed past the black tangle of deception. For that's what I was best at. Deception by omission. With my inner circle, I lied by omission. With my clients, I lied by distraction, seduction, and the false front I'd grown so good at portraying. I was good at lying. I'd gotten so good at it that I'd lost the truth in everything. Lost the ability to shift through my own bullshit. Lost the ability to know if I was lying to myself. And in that break, I'd lost the ability to police myself.

I started out this twisted game with three rules.

Don't leave the apartment. I stayed inside apartment 6E for three years before I broke that rule. Just once. Then twice. Then... I've lost count by now.

Never let anyone in. I broke that rule with two people, both of whom met grisly ends.

Don't kill anyone. Two years ago, that rule seemed realistic. I know myself better now.

Now, I will have new rules. New restrictions. They are all designed to keep me safely inside, when it'd be best for everyone involved if I am out. You see, there are a lot of people in prison. And they aren't able to run far.

IF YOU DARE

A DEANNA MADDEN NOVEL

A. R. TORRE

REDHOOK

www.redhookbooks.com

Copyright © 2015 by A. R. Torre
Excerpt from *The Girl in 6E* copyright © 2014 by A. R. Torre

Redhook Books/Orbit
Hachette Book Group
1290 Avenue of the Americas
New York, NY 10104
www.HachetteBookGroup.com

Printed in the United States of America

RRD-C

First edition: November 2015

10 9 8 7 6 5 4 3 2

Redhook is an imprint of Orbit, a division of Hachette Book Group.
The Redhook name and logo are trademarks of Hachette Book Group, Inc.

The Hachette Speakers Bureau provides a wide range of authors for speaking events. To find out more, go to www.hachettespeakersbureau.com or call (866) 376-6591.

The publisher is not responsible for websites (or their content) that are not owned by the publisher.

Library of Congress Cataloging-in-Publication Data

Torre, A. R.
   If you dare / A.R. Torre.—First edition.
      pages ; cm.—(A Deanna Madden novel)
   ISBN 978-0-316-38669-2 (trade pbk.)—ISBN 978-1-4789-0652-0 (audio book downloadable)—ISBN 978-1-4789-6177-2 (audio book cd)—ISBN 978-0-316-38671-5 (ebook) 1. Psychological fiction. I. Title.
   PS3620.O5887I3 2015
   813'.6—dc23
                                                                                       2015026681

To girls with broken hearts and vengeful souls.

Go forth and raise hell.

PART I

CHAPTER 1

Past

"YOU KNOW I love you." Jeremy spoke softly against her ear and Deanna stirred, rolling over in bed and pulling the blanket over her head. He tugged on the edge of it but she held it tight. She had strength in her tiny frame and he smiled. Pulled harder and finally broke it clear, her face unveiled when the dark gray sheet was yanked down.

He lived to see her face. The delicate planes of it, the way her nose turned up slightly and her full lips parted in the moment right before she spoke. The arch of her eyebrows, the thick length of her lashes, the piercing amber of her eyes. Storms grew in those eyes; lightning flashed and heat smoldered. He could experience a lifetime in those eyes and never find his way out. Could kiss those lips for centuries and continue to crave the taste. Could dig his hands into the thick mane of her hair, pull her head back, look down into that face, and stay in that moment for the rest of his life.

She wouldn't allow it. Wouldn't allow him more than a passing glance. She was quick, furtive, her beauty hidden behind a flip of her hair, a sharp retort, a sudden burst of overwhelming sexuality. She wouldn't let him stare, wouldn't let him devour, wouldn't let him study. She gave him thin shards of herself and watched closely, with the expectation that he would cut himself and let her drink his blood. And therein lay the problem.

There was a strong possibility he was in love with a psychopath.

CHAPTER 2

Present

WHEN I COME to, the apartment is dark and I am on the floor. I prop myself up with an elbow, then a hand, looking around and trying to find my bearings. Slide far enough right to see the clock: 10:12 p.m. I look to the door and wonder if it is locked. Contemplate checking, but am too tired. My head feels odd, like it weighs a hundred pounds and is wrapped in cotton candy, my brain barely able to think through the mess of it all. I want to sleep, and can't really summon the will to stand, so I crawl on my stomach, along the dark floor, and into bed. Wonder, in the half moment before I fall asleep, where Jeremy is. I start to lift my hand to the pain at my nose, start to try and remember...

I don't notice when my hand hits the floor.

CHAPTER 3

Past

LILY LEANED AGAINST the counter and tapped her fingers on the granite. "Fancy place," she said mildly.

"Not too fancy." Jeremy took four steps in and spun, falling back on the new couch, the leather smacking upon impact.

"Fancier than Prestwick Place."

"Anything would have been." Twenty-three Prestwick Place had belonged to their grandmother, inherited by their parents, passed down to Jeremy. Prestwick had burned to the ground nine months earlier. He rubbed a wrist, then realized the gesture and stopped. "I had to set out pots every time it rained."

"No pots here." His sister glanced up to the ceiling. "And... this belongs to your girlfriend?"

"It did. I close on it next week."

"She just had an extra house lying around?"

"I didn't ask. It was cheap, the insurance check came, I took it."

"Doesn't look cheap," Lily said.

"I think she cut me a deal."

From the other room, Olivia tore in, socked feet sliding

across the wood floor, hands spread out for balance, blond hair settling into place when she stopped. "There's two bedrooms," she said breathlessly. "Is one mine?"

He couldn't help but laugh. "Sure. Go ahead and claim it. Just don't stick a NO BOYS ALLOWED sign up."

His niece wrinkled her nose as if he'd said something wrong. He probably had. Dealing with a ten-year-old girl was like handling a grenade. One wrong joke and she exploded. "I'm a little old for that," she sniffed.

"My apologies." He glanced at Lily, who bit back a smile.

"Olivia, there's a basket of socks on the dryer. Go match them up."

"Quarter a pair?" She raised her eyes hopefully at him.

"Ten cents."

"Deal." She cheerfully held up a fist and tapped it against his, then bounded out.

"Damn, you're a cheap ass." His sister plopped down on the love seat, their heads close together.

"Have you seen that stack of socks? I'll go broke in the time it takes you to grill me."

"Am I that obvious?"

He smiled. "You're that dependable. This is the first time you've gotten me alone in a while."

"So spill and I won't pull out my instruments of torture." She rolled over and propped her chin on the arm of the love seat. "Tell me about the mysterious girlfriend who you've kept secret for a year."

"She hasn't been a secret."

"Then why haven't we met her? You brought that teacher

by on your second date, yet I haven't even seen a picture of this one."

A picture. He needed a thousand of those, yet had only a handful. He mentally moved that up higher on the to-do list. Capture her on film, since he couldn't seem to do it any other way. "Here." Reaching down, he dug in his pocket, pulled out his cell, and flipped it open. Scrolled through a hundred pointless pics till he got to the one he looked at ten times a week. The one that had been his wallpaper till she'd threatened to cut him open unless he changed it. It was a great one, her in his sweatshirt and nothing else, scrunching her face at the camera while she lifted a soda to her lips. Her hair was in a messy bun, pieces of dark falling around her face, her cheeks flushed. It had been taken on a Sunday morning. She'd taken off work and they'd piled into her bed. Streamed cartoons on her laptop and split leftover Chinese takeout. After the food she'd fallen asleep, her head on his stomach, her hand on his thigh. He'd been rock hard when she stilled, her hand stopping its lazy trail up and down his thigh, her teasing touch driving him crazy. He'd been so close to reaching down, was fighting the urge, trying to focus, prolonging the pleasure as long as he could, when her hand stopped, his breath catching as he shifted slightly. Waited. Ran his hand slowly down her back, his touch a question. Then he leaned forward to see her face. Wheezed out a frustrated breath when he saw her slack features, her closed eyes. Shut his own eyes and focused on the soft puff of her breath against his abs. Willed his cock to go down, for the ache to subside, for *Family Guy* to work its asexual magic and kill his dirty thoughts.

A hundred shards of memory were tied to that image. He handed the phone over. "This is her."

His sister pushed up on her elbows and grabbed the phone. Her eyebrows raised when she saw the image. "She's cute. *Really* cute." She sat up fully and examined it closer. "Hmmph. She wasn't too socially awkward to bounce around naked in your sweatshirt. What's she do again?" The question was spit out casually, as if she hadn't asked it ten different ways over the last year.

"Web design." The first time he'd answered the question to anyone. The first time he'd lied about her. He hated it; the words crawled off his tongue and left a sour aftertaste, a strange sensation in his world that was normally so clean and simple. But what could he say? Tell the truth? His sister was already harboring reservations. To reveal that his girlfriend was a cyber-sex queen wouldn't help a thing.

"Must pay well." Tones of suspicion in the words, heard as easily as she had heard deception in his own.

"I don't ask. Not my business." *Or yours.*

"Well, what *do* you ask? Have you met her family?" The question was asked with such hostility that he was grateful for the correct answer to be both truthful and Lily-acceptable.

"No. They passed away when she was in high school."

"Oh, please. *All* of them?"

"Yes." His quiet tone wiped the snide look off of her face. "You can google it if you want. Her mother killed her entire family, then herself."

Her neck bulged when she swallowed, like a pelican forcing down a fish. "Seriously?"

"Yeah. I think that's where her social anxiety comes from." It wasn't exactly a lie.

She laughed abruptly, the sound high and sharp and inappropriate. "We're not gonna kill her, J."

Again, the truth fell out easier. "She's not worried about that."

"'Cause she's never gonna see us?"

The ugly cut of sharpness was back in her voice, this time tinged with...hurt? Great. His sister, who spits nails out with her breakfast, had her feelings hurt. He reached over and plucked the phone back. Ignored her pout and worked it back into his pocket. "It's that important to you? The meet and greet?"

"I *am* the most important person in your life." She slid back onto her stomach.

"Ummm...no," he deadpanned. "Brian, Kent, James, Yen. All ranking higher. Plus Olivia. You're looking at spot six or seven, easy."

"Watch it," she warned. "I have no issue taking your beer buddies out of the picture. For the sake of competitive rank alone."

"You know I'm kidding." He stared up at the ceiling. "I'll talk to her. See if I can convince her to a dinner." He wouldn't be able to. No way. He had absolutely no control over that woman.

"I'll cook," she offered. "Whatever you guys want. She'll be well fed if nothing else. And the girl can stand to eat. She does eat, right? More than just those diet dinners you deliver?"

He grinned. "She eats. And she's fine. Don't say anything about her weight."

"She's got to toughen up sometime. I don't want you dating a shrinking violet, J."

A shrinking violet. Jeremy doubted that there was ever a moment that Deanna had been considered that. He tried to picture a meeting of the two women, one that didn't end in combustion, but failed. "She's not a shrinking violet. You don't have to worry about that."

"Oh. My sweet brother." Lily sighed. "You've always been clueless when it comes to your women."

Had he? His sister's track record in being right trumped his tenfold. But in this she was wrong. He knew one thing with Deanna, that she wasn't meek or mild.

In everything else he was clueless.

CHAPTER 4

Past

"THANKS FOR THE place." When Jeremy whispered against my neck, it made the tiny hairs on my skin tickle. I rolled away, his arm bringing me back, turning me to face him. I scooted down on the bed, so my head was at his chest and he moved to his back, our readjustment complete.

"You bought it. Nothing really to thank me for. Thanks for taking it off of my hands." Yes, thank you for purchasing the home I bought for you from me. Thank you for letting me take that hundred-thousand-dollar loss. Thank you for not dying, and for being here beside me. Thank you for not asking questions and for loving me despite all of this.

He laughed softly and it was almost like a cough, the exhale of humor causing his heart to change tempo, to skip a beat under my ear. I moved my hand down his ribs, then back up, this time underneath his shirt. "You know...it has a bedroom. With a real bed. One off the floor."

I smiled in the dark. "You too highfalutin to sleep on a mattress on the floor?"

"I'm just saying. Maybe you could visit. Spend a night. Help me break it in. Mark your territory so none of the bikini model neighbors get any ideas."

I'd love to spend a night at his place. I had flipped through the pictures online a hundred times, could imagine the feel of the wood floors underneath my bare feet, the sink into the huge jetted tub, the glow of the Sub-Zero fridge when I opened the door late at night. But I couldn't. I slowed the movement of dragging my fingers across his abs and contemplated rolling over. If I had turned away, he'd ask why. Push. And I didn't feel like talking. I felt like staying in the peaceful moment, his heartbeat in my ear, his hand on my back rubbing a soothing pattern. I closed my eyes and wondered at the time. Wondered how much we had left. Soon, it would be nine and Simon would lock the door. But that was at least an hour away. A hour to pretend, for that short time, that we were normal. That I wasn't pushing him out the door to prevent an incident where I might try to kill him.

Once he left, I'd get online. Work for a few hours, then close down the webcams and play. I'd found a new website the week before, a black site where crime photos are posted. A hundred new pics every hour. It's become my midnight snack, my mental feeding ground that I devour in the final moments before sleep. Dr. Derek would flip a shit if he found out. Dr. Derek can kiss my ass.

"What are your plans next week?" My eyes opened at his question.

"Next week?"

"Yeah." His fingers brushed gently across the top of my head, threading into my hair and sliding down, the movement heavenly, and I closed my eyes, enjoying the sensation.

"Nothing." Always nothing. The life of a shut-in doesn't really involve plans. "Why?"

"Just asking." A pause before the response, and something in that pause. A decision had been made in those milliseconds. My eyes wanted to reopen, but I held them shut. Let the moment pass.

Our dance of avoidance. We've gotten quite good at it.

CHAPTER 5

Past

THERE WAS A stranger, leaning up against the wall, when Jeremy walked down the sixth-floor hall. The girl had a cell phone out, thumbs furious against the screen. She glanced over once, then back, a second glance that would have, at one point in time, pleased him. But now he had Deanna, had no need for this girl, her hair a loud shade of blond, her jeans tight, eye makeup dark and obvious.

"Hey," she called out, right around the time that he'd raised his hand to the door of 6E. He gave her a nod and knocked. He didn't need to knock; he could've just turned the knob and pushed in. But he liked the question, liked the grin Deanna gave when she swung it open, didn't like any possibility that he was uninvited. Plus, he'd seen her cam before, didn't need a reminder of her job by walking into a live version of the show.

"Hey," the girl repeated, louder this time, pushing her body off the wall and ambling toward him. "Got anything for Evans? 6G?"

He shook his head without checking the list. "Sorry." Reached up and knocked again. Willed Deanna to hurry up. Could see, in his peripheral, the girl crawl closer.

"That's the weirdo's apartment, right?" She giggled and stepped close enough for her cheap perfume to reach him. "I'm Chelsea." She stuck out her hand. Short, dark purple nails flashed in the vicinity of his crotch. Unavoidable. He shifted Deanna's package to the other arm and slid his hand into hers. "Jeremy," he mumbled.

And at that moment, the door swung open.

CHAPTER 6

Past

THE STRANGE BITCH had a grin stretched across her face and was looking up at Jeremy, every tooth in her mouth peeking through sticky glossed lips at him. His eyes darted to mine and he smiled, his grin lopsided and easy, his hand pulling from hers as he stepped forward and kissed my cheek. "Hey, babe." His breath was warm on my cheek, his hand firm as it pushed at my door. The forward step of his foot carrying him across my threshold, a whoosh of hot air floating through the open door and hitting my bare skin. A hundred other details that faded as I focused on her.

The hand, the one that had gripped my boyfriend's hand, lifted higher, past a peek of tan stomach, in front of a tight blue shirt with Betty Boop's face stretched over an impressively perky set of double D's. Her arms crossed and the breasts became even bigger. "Is there something I can help you with?"

"Just being friendly," she drawled, her eyes dropping and sliding over my bra and thong set. A perfectly tweezed eyebrow raised. "Cute outfit."

I didn't respond, my shoulder hitting the door frame as I

stared back at her, comfortable. "You just move in?" My snoop-
ing of our hall had drastically reduced since I got a life. Still, I
couldn't have missed a move, the loud noises of furniture bang-
ing and scraping down our thin hall.

She waved a dark-tipped hand down the hall. "Staying in
6G for a while with my brother."

6G. Simon's place. Brother. My eyes dragged over her hair,
skin, eyes. They seemed clear and clean, no evidence of drugs
present. Her lips moved, the white glimpse of her straight teeth
making another unwelcome appearance. I studied her features and tried to conjure up Simon's face. Tried to recall if,
behind the unmaintained exterior, he had been blessed with
the genetic makeup this girl carried. I didn't see it. They were
too different. She clean. He dirty. She attractive. He disgusting.

"I'm Chelsea."

Chelsea. *Of course she was.* I felt the shift of Jeremy behind
me, heard the slide of cardboard as he moved my mountain of
boxes enough to fit in the next addition. Heard the slice of his
box cutter as he ripped apart and broke down one of the empty
ones. "Have a nice day, Chelsea." I shut the door as she started
to respond.

"Have a nice day?" Jeremy mocked my response from
behind me.

I turned to face him. "Too sweet?" I asked, tilting my head and
surveying him. His legs were spread slightly, a box cutter still in his
grip. He raised a wrist to wipe at his mouth and his bicep flexed.

He shrugged and the blade flashed against one of my cam
lights. "Just was a little tamer than I was expecting. I figured
you'd drag her in here and jump on top of her."

"Is that what you wanted, Mr. Pacer?" I stepped forward and watched the casual flip of his thumb as he retracted the blade, his eyes narrowing slightly as he caught me watching it. "Deanna...," he warned.

"I'm fine." I stepped closer and unhooked my bra. Took one more step, reaching a hand out and tugging the box cutter free, his body tensing. I didn't look at it, held my own breath until the moment I tossed it off to the side, the hit and skitter of metal indicating its harmless slide to the far side of the room. I exhaled, the tension leaving his limbs as he returned his attention to my face, a drugged arousal clouding over him as his gaze dropped to my now-bare breasts. "But I'm gonna need you on the bed. Now." I shoved on his chest, and he staggered back in the direction of my bed, a smile returning to his face.

I pounced on him.

Unzipped and pulled him out.

Silenced his mutters of time with my mouth as I straddled his cock and sat down atop it.

And sometime, right before I came, I forgot about the box cutter.

CHAPTER 7

Past

"YOU'RE INVITED TO family dinner this Sunday. My sister wants you there."

My fork stopped halfway to my lips, a wrap of pad thai noodles slipping free in the gap of time. I looked at Jeremy and noted the way his eyes slid from me. He wet his lips and—for the first time in recent memory—I didn't want to grab his shirt and kiss said lips.

"Your sister wants me there?" An interesting choice of words. He set down his fork and sat back in the chair. Lifted his chin and looked at me straight on.

"Yeah."

"What about you? What do you want?"

His shoulders lifted but nothing else moved, the casual gesture not matching with any other line in his body. His neck was stiff, his jaw set, his eyes now boring defiantly into me. He was physically prepped, as if for battle. It was a ridiculously hot look. I set down my own fork. "You don't care?" I mimicked him, sitting back in my chair, the metal of its back ice-cold against my bare skin. I should have pulled on a sweatshirt. Or turned up the thermostat. Something so that, right now, I didn't look like a shivering pussy.

"I don't care." He said the words dully, without emotion, but I saw the darkening of green, the way his hand tightened on the thigh of his jeans. Something was going on.

"You look like you care."

"It'd be nice for you to meet my family. For us to be normal."

When the anger came it burned, hot and red through my chest, a hundred emotions pushing out in veins that were too skinny to handle them all. *It'd be nice for you to meet my family.* It'd be nice for him to meet my family too. Would be nice to *have* a family to introduce. How dare he shove that in my face? How could I sit there, with his family, and not think of my own? Not compare every hug, every *I love you*, every child, mother, and father, with my own? *For us to be normal.* Yeah, J. I'd like to be normal too. I'd like to sit across from my boyfriend and get angry and not think about cutting open his stomach. I'd like to walk outside and not try to kill someone. I'd like to pick a boy-friend because of choices, not because he's the only fuckin' person in three years who hadn't run screaming or died beneath my hands. I closed my eyes and tilted my chair back, felt the lift of the feet, the hover, and gripped the table's edge for balance. Counted to ten like Dr. Derek taught me. Envisioned a white expanse before me, all distractions, all thoughts fading, mut-ing, in the white. I wondered, with the tilt of my world back, if I needed to do a curl. Roll my body into a ball and let my fanta-sies run wild. Distract myself from the stabbing pain of memo-ries that his flippant statement just brought on. I'd never curled in front of Jeremy before. Dr. Derek said it would freak him out.

Suggested the white method instead. The white method sucks.
It gives me no release, no break, is the equivalent of unpopped
ears when coming off a flight, my desire to hold my nose and
blow out my world an intense itch. I gripped the table's edge
and heard, across the span of white, him speak.

"Is that too much to ask?"

I pushed against the table's edge and let myself fall.

CHAPTER 8

Present

I'M EXAMINING MY face in the bathroom mirror. Today started out late, a killer headache keeping me in bed until almost noon, two Vicodin barely taking the sting off. When I finally crawled out of bed, I showered, then pulled on a baby-blue camisole and matching thong, blow-drying my hair on the floor by my bed, checking e-mails as the hot air did its thing. When I flipped on the bright lights and climbed onto the cam bed, hooking my laptop in and stretching out on the comforter, my face was off camera, my waist and hips on full display, my fingers busy as they logged into different sites and sent my live feed into every corner of cyberspace. When I propped up on one elbow, panning out, and smiled for my viewers, I didn't understand the image on the screen. I leaned closer to the cam and flinched in surprise, jerking out a hand and ending the stream, my body rolling off of the bed, my feet quick as they hurried to the bathroom. And now, my hand clenched on the edge of the medicine cabinet mirror, I stare into my reflection and at the broken, bloody mess that is my nose. Did I do this? Knock myself out again with another dramatic fall to the floor?

Lose control trying to get out of my locked door and headbutt the steel? I've never done that before, never caused any more damage than a few broken nails and occasional bruises.

I need to go out, buy makeup. I can't cam like this, not without enticing a thousand fans to storm to their feet in chivalrous support. One will probably call the cops, report the jealous boyfriend that they will assume is responsible. I don't normally wear makeup, nothing more than mascara and gloss, which gives me the innocent look all the men love. But mascara and lip gloss will do nothing with this. This is concealer- and foundation-worthy. Concealer, foundation, and whatever other magical items girls who wear makeup covet. I'll go to the drugstore. Just a quick trip, nothing will happen. I *have* to go. I can't work without it, and can't expect Jeremy to pick out makeup for me. I'll hop in FtypeBaby and go, be back within the hour. I grab my keys and stop, looking down at my outfit or, rather, lack of one. I am lacing up my tennis shoes when the knock comes. I finish lacing and try to invent a reason for being dressed, something to tell Jeremy when he asks. I pull open the door and stare into a woman's face.

"Deanna Madden?" The woman's mouth is too big for her face, her lips chewed, a big chunk of lip skin missing from the right side of her smile. She wears eyeliner but no other makeup, the result of which is slightly trashy. She doesn't smile. Neither do I. Behind her, a black man in a suit shifts on the cheap carpet.

"Yes." I curl my toes inside my socks and dig my nails into the door frame. Wonder idly if her eyeliner is waterproof. If I strangle her, will her eyes water? Will the liner run? I need more of her voice in order to properly imagine it gasping for help.

"I'm Detective Boles; this is Detective Reuber. We are with the Tulsa Police Department. May we come in?"

Detectives. Police. Words I've waited years to hear yet *today* is the moment. How odd. I blink to buy time, and it is too short. *May we come in?* "I'd rather you not." No, you may not come in. I will not let you set foot into this place. I lost my virginity here. Touched for the first time here. Seduced here. Contained crazy here. Killed here.

"We just have a few questions. They'd be easier to handle inside." Oh, so TheOtherOne can speak. I flick my eyes to him. Notice the calm chew of his jaw as he works a piece of gum. The steady stare of his gaze as he meets mine. The lift of his chin that speaks of more authority than his cheap suit.

"No." I lift my own damn chin.

The woman glances down the empty hall. "Ms. Madden, these questions are of a personal nature."

"I don't really let people in."

"We can take this down to the station if you'd prefer that."

I hesitate for a long moment, my eyes darting from the woman to the man. The woman to the man. They have guns, both of them, the precious weapons hanging casually from their belts. Bulletproof vests also, the bulk of it most obvious on the woman. Then, against my better judgment, I open the door and step back. "Come on in."

CHAPTER 9

Present

SHE HAS SOCIAL anxiety. That's what they'd been told.
Detective Brenda Boles looks into Deanna Madden's eyes and
calls bullshit on that right then and there.

The girl stands, one hand on the knob, the other on the
frame, and stares at them, her eyes darting from her, to David,
to her. Her back hunches a little forward, her hands are braced
on the door as if to hold herself back. Her eyes show no sign of
fear, or stress. Instead they are wary. Confident. Smart.

Brenda has locked eyes with a thousand suspects before.
And she can tell you, in that moment, right there in the hall,
without a word between them, without a question asked, that
this girl is guilty.

CHAPTER 10

Present

I'VE HAD A grand total of five visitors into my apartment. One was Jeremy, his surprise at my setup interrupted by my promptly launched attack. Then there was Marcus. The other three have been a variety of maintenance workers, whose presence was necessary at some point or other in the last four years. Their visits were short and sweet, but the reactions were all the same. I'm sure, to an unsuspecting individual crossing over my threshold, my apartment's setup would be a bit of a shock. The right side is relatively normal, a bed, some books. If you look further right it starts to get odd, five stacked rows holding over a hundred cardboard boxes, arranged by size and contents, all of the items that an enterprising recluse might need. But it's the left side of the apartment that really gives someone pause, when their eyes slide back, past the kitchen that divides the two spaces, past the small round table, past the large lone window that tests my sanity. The left side is pink. Pink walls, pink bed frame, pink bedspread, pink dresser and side tables. Posters break up the space and bring in more colors, pillows plump up the bed and make it inviting, the ensemble another level of

WTF when you see the giant steel framework that surrounds the entire bedroom set. The framework supports eight high-def cameras, over 10,000 watts of lighting, sex toy attachments, laptops, extension cords, and ethernet cables.

I hold the door for the detectives and wait for a reaction.

The woman stops first, an unexpected halt that causes the man to collide into her. He apologizes, she sidesteps, and then he stops. I lean against the door frame and wait, wondering how long this entire production is going to take.

"Wow." The woman speaks first. She holds out a weak finger in the direction of the pink bed. "What's...what's up with all this?"

"My work." I shut the door and walk to the round table. Perch on the edge of it and cross my arms.

TheOtherOne steps to the left and crouches, lifting the edge of the pink bedspread. Like I'd have hidden something there. Give me a little credit.

"Step away from that please," I snap. He looks up and hoists himself back to standing.

"Just looking around, Ms. Madden."

"Look all you want with a warrant in hand."

"What kind of work do you do?" EyelinerCop raises a thinly plucked brow and I wonder how she'd take to constructive criticism. Pluck that brow any more and she'll have to find a new way to spend her free time.

"I work online. Webcamming." I expect a blank look and am rewarded; the majority of people having no clue about the webcam business. The woman rubs her forearm and I notice the chill bumps. Smile to myself. Stay in my seat, leave the thermostat where it is. Sixty-four degrees should keep this visit short. I am dressed for success in my sweatshirt.

"Webcamming...?" She raises her eyebrows and I say nothing. She wants to ask a question, she can go right ahead.

The man coughs. Of course he knows what it is. I keep my eyes on her and see, in the peripheral, him lean forward. "It's in the adult industry."

If her eyebrows get any higher, they'll hit her hairline. She looks down and shifts her purse higher on her shoulder. Oh... so it makes her uncomfortable. Interesting. I've seen so few reactions to my work. The man turns, and it catches my attention, his feet moving the wrong way, toward my real bed and the library of cardboard boxes. "What's in the boxes?"

I lift a shoulder. "Stuff. Supplies."

"Supplies?" This woman really needs to learn how to ask a fucking question. I take the bait this time, no real reason not to.

"Food and toiletries. Lightbulbs for my cam lights, laundry detergent..." I stand and step around to the back of the table and hope they follow me. "That kind of stuff."

"Why so much of it?" The man tilts his head, reading a label, carefully written in Sharpie on the side of a box. "You've got to have a year's worth of stuff here."

I swallow. Open the fridge and pull out a few waters. Search my future words and look for pitfalls. "I don't get out much. I prefer to do any shopping online. That means I have to buy in bulk."

Now EyelinerCop is looking at the boxes, and the pit in my

stomach grows. "Even floss? You buy *floss* online? Isn't that a bit...excessive?" She turns to me.

I set their water bottles on the table. "Did you have something to ask me? Because I need to get back to work."

"Is that a safe?" The man's voice is sharper, and the water bottle crackles from my squeeze. "What's in the safe?"

CHAPTER II

Present

I DIDN'T SKIMP when it came to the safe. It's big, not big enough to hold a body, but possibly could, if the person was chopped into parts. It currently holds two guns, twenty-one knives, my gas mask, leftover fentanyl, and an assortment of other weapons. It also holds a small scrapbook, one that used to sit on our family's coffee table. I'm pretty sure the detectives will have no interest in that and an overwhelming interest in the rest.

I shrug. "Family scrapbooks, my passport. Those sorts of things."

"Can we take a look inside?" He smiles, a friendly smile.

I return the gesture. So much cordiality bouncing around. "Not without a warrant."

The woman clears her throat. "Can we get to the questions?"

Oh yes, the questions. This should be interesting. I pull out a chair from the table and sit.

The woman follows suit; the man fidgets in a familiar way. "Got a bathroom?"

I point, my eyes following his steps, purposeful and direct.

I listen to the door close and thank God I never killed anyone in the bathroom. I hear the drizzle of urine and move my eyes to the woman. EyelinerCop's eyes are suspicious, they crawl over my face as if they can dig the truth from my skin. I relax against the seat's back and wait.

I should be nervous but I only feel excitement.

❖

"Where were you last night, Ms. Madden?"

An unexpected question. I bring my eyes up from the water bottle and into the woman's eyes, wonder if all criminal investigations start with that question or if last night is of particular consequence. Think of my wake on the concrete floor, my crawl to the bed. "I was here. In my apartment."

The woman's eyes dart, from left to right, like a Pong paddle. "All night?"

"Yes."

"Can anyone verify that?"

When she speaks, her eyebrows pinch together in a sharp V of distrust. I watch their narrow exclamations and wonder what they have on me. Anything? Is this a fishing expedition or a sharpening of the nails that will seal my coffin?

"Umm...yes. My neighbor. Simon." I try to push into last night's vault of recollection, try to move earlier than my pounding headache, but find nothing. Strange. Then again, I was locked in. How much trouble could I have possibly caused?

"Simon was with you?" From the bathroom, the door opens and TheOtherOne walks out.

I feel the upward curl of my lip. "No. But he locked me into the apartment. From nine till sometime this morning."

That surprises them. I feel the shift of air, the rigid tilt of the woman as she fights against turning her head to the man. Ha. My alibi is unbreakable. He pulls out a chair, sits, and speaks. "I don't understand."

I sigh, an action that buys me a moment to deliberate the wisdom of information sharing. "Simon lives a few doors down. He locks my door at night. So he can verify that he locked me inside last night, and I was here all night until he unlocked me."

"Your door locks from the outside?" EyelinerCop finds this very interesting. I watch the tip of her pen, the increased tremor of it as it scratches against the page of her notebook.

"Yes." I lift my eyes from the pen. "What evidence do you have against me?"

Her mouth widens into a grin, a stretch of raw lips that looks painful. I don't like that grin, that tell that I just stepped into a pile of shit. "Why, Ms. Madden, what an interesting question. An innocent person would be more interested in finding out what crime was committed."

"Who said I was an innocent person?"

CHAPTER 12

Present

"WHO SAID I was an innocent person?"

The response slipped out, snarky and unnecessary. I'd wanted to shut the cop up, to wipe that smug grin off her face. The question was much more passive than what I wanted to do. To spring across the table and claw at her neck, pulling and ripping the delicate cords of her throat. Yank at her belt and palm her service revolver. Celebrate the gun's weight in my hand in the moment before I pointed the gun at her temple and pulled the trigger, her head exploding in one beautiful blood-splattering second. Take that, bulletproof vest. Compared to that scenario, my egotistic response was tame. Tame and stupid. The pair of detectives all but high-fived each other with their eye contact. I settled back in my chair and waited. Counted to ten and swore to behave.

The woman composes herself and speaks. "What are you guilty of, Ms. Madden?"

I wonder why she is in charge of this interaction. If it is her rank or if it is because they thought I'd associate with a woman more. Thought I would buddy up and confess away, all because a penis didn't hang between her legs. I tap my fingers against the arm of the chair. "I'd like you both to leave now. Unless you have something to charge me with."

They have to have *something*. Surely they didn't show up at my apartment on a whim. I must have slipped up somewhere, forgotten something in my past crimes. Left a gaping hole big enough for them to stick an arrest warrant through.

TheOtherOne speaks. "Let's get back to the neighbor. You said he locks you inside? Why would you let him do that?"

This is wrong, bad. I shouldn't be here, shouldn't be talking to them. I asked them to leave; doesn't that mean they have to? I take a sip of my water and look away from the man, make accidental eye contact with the woman. She leans forward and points, her finger one long arrow of invasion. "What happened to your nose, Ms. Madden?"

Oh, right. I had forgotten. "My nose?" I reach up and touch it. Feel the caked blood, the split across my bridge. I push on the joint and suddenly realize how much it throbs. The Vicodin for my headache must have taken off the sting. It's been five or six hours. I close my eyes and try to remember how many pills I have. Calculate the time it would take for the doc to send me more.

"It looks broken." She looks concerned, but she's not. Her voice sounds giddy; she'd probably reach out and grip my nose herself if she could.

It looks broken. It feels broken. I push on the tip and get light-headed. Pull my hand away before I faint. I stare at a strand of the woman's hair that has escaped her ponytail. Focus on it until the spots clear from my vision.

"Ms. Madden?" the man prods.

"What?"

"What happened to your nose?"

Good question. I look away from the strand of hair and into the man's eyes. "I'm not sure."

"You forgot?"

All of the caution signs in my head are lining up for battle. Why am I talking to them? Why are they here? Why am I offering information when I'm not getting any? I stand up and watch for a reaction. A reach for a paper, for evidence to wave in my face, but they do nothing, just stay in place and watch me. "I'd like to be alone."

I walk to the door and wait, the pair slow as they stand, step, then pass through the open door. I am almost free, about to shut it, when the woman's hand settles on my arm, a firm and hard grip that tightens against the sleeve of my Marilyn Monroe sweatshirt. I turn, raising my brows at her in question.

"Why did you kill him?" the cop whispers, her eyes glued on me.

I don't answer her. I hold her eye contact while I reach down and pull back on her index finger until she releases my arm with a pained wince. Then I drop my hand, step back, and shut the door, the slam of the steel against the frame loud and unfamiliar.

I didn't not answer to be smart or mysterious. The main reason I didn't answer was because I wasn't sure how to answer. I wasn't sure which death she was asking about. To be honest, I am starting to lose track.

CHAPTER 13

Present

"SHE'S GUILTY." DETECTIVE Brenda Boles speaks quietly in the close confines of the elevator, the pair of detectives watching the panel warily as it wheezes down. "No doubt. Did you see her face before she let us in? The way she stared at my gun?"

"I saw it. But a lot of women are scared of guns. It's got to be intimidating to let two armed strangers into your apartment." Detective David Reuber chews his gum and leans against the side of the elevator.

"Oh, please." She snorts. "Intimidated? That girl wasn't intimidated. She was cornered. And guilty. I'd bet my pension on it."

"We got nothing. A body who knew her. Nothing else. You know that."

"Yet. We've got nothing *yet*. We will. And next time we're on this damn elevator, it'll be to arrest her. You know she's good for this, David."

"I don't know..." He shakes his head. "She doesn't fit any profile."

"Skinny white chicks can't be killers? You already forgotten Jodi Arias?"

He shrugs, gesturing her forward when the elevator doors open. "Maybe. I'm just saying. Don't close the suspect list yet."

"I'm not closing anything yet. But she's topping it."

"It's your case. You bark, I follow."

She laughs, and they exit the building, stepping into the afternoon sun, her question held until they are both settled into the squad car. "You find anything in the bathroom?"

"Oh, right." He reaches in his pocket and pulls out his phone. Flips through to the camera roll and holds it out.

She snatches the phone, zooming in. "Meds?"

"They're in her name. But the bottle's three years old and full. A Dr. Derek Vanderbilt in Dallas prescribed them to her."

Clozapine. She looks up at David. "Isn't clozapine an antipsychotic?"

"If you want to tell the judge that, then yes. But between me and you, my sister takes it for anxiety. I think they use it for all sorts of things. One pill will mellow my sister out. Two will put her on her ass."

"And the bottle was full?"

"Yep." He buckles his belt. "You gonna call the doctor?"

She passes the phone back to him. "You better believe it. Let's head in and do it now." In the moment before pulling off, she glances up, to the sixth floor. There, in the dark window, Deanna Madden stares down at her.

CHAPTER 14

Present

WHEN I SHUT the door behind the cops, I walk to the center of my apartment. Look right, then left. Close my eyes and try to put my finger on the nagging thread that has bothered me since I woke. Something is off. Something more than cops showing up at my door and random broken noses appearing from nowhere. I walk to the bathroom and take a second look at my reflection. On this round, I notice the dark lines under my eyes. They'll be black soon. My barely functional makeup skills won't be able to cover up two black eyes and a broken nose. So I won't, for the next few days, be able to cam. Damn.

I run a soft finger over the break in my nose. When I told them I didn't know what happened to my nose, it wasn't the entire truth. I don't know exactly what happened, the events from last night a blur. But my weak, pathetic memory does have one clear picture, one of *Jeremy*, his face pinched. Worried. Scared.

It doesn't make any sense, but I think *he* broke my nose. Why? I don't know. I called him earlier this morning and he didn't answer. I pull out my cell and call him again. Listen to the dull tones of unanswered rings, each one feeling like a step downward into hell. Then, the unfamiliar words of his voice mail. Hmmm. One unanswered call is nothing, two—a problem. His not answering my calls says something. I feel a flicker of fear, pulling from a spot of insecurity. I did something and he's mad. I glance at the mirror. I did something and he broke my nose. I must have lost control. Maybe over that stupid family dinner.

I step out of the bathroom and to the window, the afternoon light flooding in. Oh, right. The window. That's what it is, the other nagging thread that is off on the equation of my apartment's normality. The window that, for four years, has tormented me and tested my level of control. The window, my one peek into the world that exists outside 6E. I have painted it shut five or six times, scraped it open a similar number of times. Six months ago, I got bold. Started running around town like I had options. Started opening the window and sitting on its sill, listening to the city and smelling its air. The window had been the crack in my world that had condemned it to hell, and after I had single-handedly endangered everyone I cared about, I closed it a final time. Stopped going outside, resumed my life of reclusedom, and covered the window with cardboard. Eliminated its pull the best way I knew. Now, I run my toe along the floor below the sill and remember the pile of cardboard pieces I discovered this morning, during the microwave of my tasteless oatmeal. I look at my fingers and am surprised I didn't break a nail last night. I must have lost control and torn it all off in my maddening desire to be free. The hundred bits of ripped cardboard evidence had been there, under the sill, pieces I had swept up and put in the trash after I'd eaten. Now, I pop open the trash can's lid and look down at them. Wonder, as I did while cleaning up the mess earlier, why I can't remember tearing them. Wonder why half of yesterday is a fog, the latter half is gone completely. Maybe it was the knock on my head. Dr. Pat said it could have unpredictable consequences.

"Where were you last night, Ms. Madden?"

I was locked in. I couldn't have done anything, and there are no bodies sharing this space with me.

Of all times for me to lose my mind, this is a really bad one. The flicker of fear grows into something more.

CHAPTER 15

Past

"I HAD A break." I lay on my bed and stared at the ceiling, the fan's slow spin breaking up my peripheral view. My fan blades were filthy, a black carpet of dust along their edges. I should have Jeremy clean those. Bring a ladder over. Pull off his shirt to improve the view. All it would take is to run a wet paper towel over the top of each blade. It wouldn't take long. Fifteen minutes, tops.

Dr. Derek didn't respond. He rarely does, the habit enhancing the moments when he does speak. I hate the habit, but love the result, each word a coveted gift, though I typically hate what each says.

"Jeremy wanted me to meet his family. His family. Then he complained about us not being normal. It was too much."

"Which part was the hardest? His mention of his family or normality?"

I swallowed. Considered. "I don't know. It was like an avalanche, having all of it at once. I was jealous...of him having a family. And of him being normal. But I also felt inadequate. And...God...I don't know. Frustrated."

"I'm sure he is frustrated too."

"That doesn't make me feel any better." It actually made me feel worse. One of the best things about my relationship with Jeremy was that he made me feel like I, like we, were great—just as we were. He didn't make me feel like a circus freak. Until that conversation. Until those three sentences that stabbed a knife into our relationship and ripped out its heart.

"It'd be nice for you to meet my family."

"For us to be normal."

"Is that too much to ask?"

"What would you do, Deanna, if he broke up with you?"

"What?" I hadn't even considered the possibility.

"How would you handle it if Jeremy broke up with you? Ended your relationship?"

"I'm familiar with the concept," I said tartly.

"And?"

"And what?"

"And what would you do?"

"It's a stupid question. Jeremy isn't going to break up with me." He won't. He loves me. He tells me that all of the time so it must be true.

"But you'd be fine if he did," Derek said gently. "I need you to mentally come to terms with that."

"That's like asking a child to mentally prepare for her mother's death. It's a stupid exercise."

"Most relationships end, Deanna. It's a fact of life, especially at your age."

"Not this relationship." I am the stronger party, I am the unfeeling one. He is the one who is in love, the one who pursued, the one who has stayed. He will never leave me. He can't. Literally, he is unable to. I know it. Imagining anything else is a stupid, stupid exercise, especially right now, when I should be focused on other things. Like considering whether or not to break up with *him*. That's what we should be talking about.

"We can talk about it at a later time. Tell me what happened."

"He's not breaking up with me." Dr. Derek needed to understand. This conversation didn't need to continue "at a later time."

"Okay, Deanna."

"Don't talk to me like that!" I snarled, propping myself up on the bed. "I'm not a child. I'm perfectly capable of reading people, including your condescending tone."

He sighed. There are times when I love his sigh. Love the caress of humanity it gives him. He is not perfect, he gets frustrated, he cares enough to sigh; I affect him enough to make him take a moment and breathe. Once, I stopped his breath. I described a sexual act and he stopped breathing, the line going so quiet I thought he'd broken the connection. He followed that with a sigh that was almost a groan, a painful release of breath that brushed lips down my neck and unzipped my dress. In that one sound, my fantasies around this man multiplied tenfold. That night, with every client, I fucked Derek. I imagined him on the other end, arched my back under his gaze, whispered his name through my moans. I came for him twenty different ways that night. Never again has he sighed that way. Never again has he asked about what I physically do with Jeremy, hasn't opened that door for another moment. Never again has he given me that peek. Now, I only have the occasional sigh. I fall back on the bed and savor, for one long moment, the sigh.

"Please tell me what happened."

"The white room didn't work. And I needed...I mean, when he said all that, I got angry. Angry and I started to lose control."

"Did you curl?"

"No. I—" I didn't know what to say. I'd practiced it ten times in the shower since the moment, tried to figure out how to present it in the manner that was the least psychotic.

He waited. Of course he did.

"I fell off the chair onto the floor. The tile. It knocked me out. Very briefly." There. Words spoken. Concept communicated.

"You knocked yourself out." He spoke slowly.

"Yes. Briefly. I was only out for a couple of seconds." Thirty or sixty, tops. Maybe a few minutes. I'd come to with Jeremy above me, his face tight and worried. There hadn't been any discussion of family or dinners or being normal after that.

"And you were fine after that?"

"Yes. It kind of reset me."

"You can't go around knocking yourself out whenever you lose control, Deanna."

I didn't say anything. Instead, I ran my hand over the top of my head. Lifted slightly off the mattress and felt at the tender spot at the back of my head.

"Have you been to a doctor? Head injuries can have a number of complications."

I snorted. "Says the man who doesn't want me to leave the apartment."

"I thought you had a doctor on call. Something of that sort."

"I do." I dropped my hand and rolled over slightly. Pulled a blanket over me to fight off a chill. "I guess I can call him."

"You should. And don't do that again, Deanna."

"It's better than me hurting him."

"Hurting yourself is a path you don't need to go down. Can you hold off on seeing him for a little while? Have some extra sessions with me?"

Hold off on seeing Jeremy? I bit my bottom lip and considered the possibility. A horrible prescription for him to give me. "I don't know."

"One day at least. Let's talk tomorrow at three."

"Short this month?" I joked. "Trying to increase your hours?"

He didn't respond.

"Fine," I finally said. "Three."

"Talk to you then."

He hung up first. After a long while, I locked my phone and tossed it aside.

Then I looked up Dr. Pat.

CHAPTER 16

Past

SUCCESS, IN MY life, has been a balancing act. If one end of the seesaw got too heavy, I hit the ground. Game over. Or, as has happened in the past, I killed someone. My balancing act used to solely exist within the walls of 6E. I spent three solid years in these walls, not leaving once. Then, a year ago, I left the apartment. I told myself it was a one-time thing and believed the lie. But that step, that experience? It was a drug, one that itched through my veins and stretched my blood vessels, my body hungry for another fix as soon as I locked myself back up. So I took more hits in the form of evening jaunts to the convenience store across the street. Inhaled deep, bought a car, and put a few hundred miles on her. Visited a few stores. Killed someone else. After that death, I withdrew completely. I shut the door and vowed to not step back out. In the last nine months, I've occasionally cheated. Twice I went for a drive in FtypeBaby. I got wild and visited a dentist three months ago. Caught up with a few years of dental neglect and four cavities. Took the gas the doctor offered and managed to not hurt anyone. Other than that, I have behaved. Haven't hurt anyone, though I've fantasized a thousand scenarios of screams.

My life as a recluse had been set up and coordinated very carefully over the last four years. Dr. Pat was a piece to that puzzle. He provided me the drugs I use to pay Simon. He also, in rare moments of ailments, stood in as my doctor. Dr. Derek wanted me to see a doctor, so Dr. Pat is whom I texted.

I need your services.

It took almost an hour to get a response, a record in the four years of our working relationship.

When?

Whenever you're free.

Will I need visual?

No. I don't think so.

He called me ten minutes later, his voice muffled, with a bit of an echo. Most likely in the bathroom, leaning against the wall as he took care of his dirty little secret's medical needs. Our conversation was quick and efficient. I described my injury, he asked a series of educated questions, I answered truthfully. We determined, in the course of four minutes and twenty-two seconds, that I was fine, but needed to watch out for a handful of symptoms, the appearance of which should prompt a visit to the ER. Then I thanked him, we set up a time for payment, and the call ended. An eavesdropper would never have known the truth. That the happily married father of three liked to ride dildos while I watched.

CHAPTER 17

Past

"HEY, BEAUTIFUL."

I relaxed against the pillows and pushed aside the keyboard. "Hey, Mike."

"Long time, babe."

"I know." I didn't say more, even though there were a hundred things I could have said.

My boyfriend doesn't like you.

We've fought over these chats.

He resents you for his house.

He thinks I enjoy our cybersex.

I do enjoy our cybersex and maybe that's a problem.

Tonight though, I needed Mike. I needed Mike in a way that none of my other clients would do. I needed the comfortable grip of a man who knew my buttons. I needed to hear someone breathe my name and to know that they found me attractive. The real me, not Jessica Reilly. The me that did evil and lied and lived a life of solitude. Mike knew me, and when he moaned my name, it was real and pure and fulfilling.

What will you do if Jeremy breaks up with you?

Damn Dr. Derek. His words haunted me, they stalked the empty corners of my day, and I wanted nothing but an escape.

"What do you want, baby?"

I grinned into the camera and curved into my pillow. "Aren't I supposed to be the one asking you that? You are paying me for a reason."

"Fine." His voice deepened, a trace of masculine authority entering it. "Take off that shirt. I need to see your perfect body."

I dragged the shirt up and over my breasts.

"Further. All the way off." He growled into the mic. I arched my back off the mattress and worked my shoulders out of the material. "Perfect. Lie back down, baby. Lie back down and close your eyes." I did as I was told, my eyes closing as I sank into the pillows. "Tell me, Deanna."

I wet my lips. "I want you."

"Keep those eyes closed. Keep them closed and picture me right now. I have my cock in my hand and it is so fucking hard for you. It aches it's so hard. What do you want to do with it?"

I kept my eyes closed and pictured him, sitting back in his chair. Saw his pants unbuttoned and his legs spread slightly. Pictured his cock standing straight up, his hand tightly wrapped around it, the head swollen and ready. I ran my hand down my stomach and slid it under my thong.

"No." His voice was gruff. "Over your panties. I want you to tease yourself and imagine it's my tongue."

"What would you do?" I asked, my fingers quick to obey, quick to slide over the satin and tease at the outside of my clit.

"Good, Deanna. I can't even watch you without needing you." He groaned the words and I imagined the pump of his cock, the squeeze of his hand, the jerk of his touch as his hips bucked underneath the action. "I want to worship you with my mouth. Go over your panties and suck you into my mouth. Tease your clit with my tongue before I pull aside your thong and bury my face in you. Taste your cum on my mouth. Feel you tremble under my hands. I—" His voice breaks and my eyes open, wanting to see, wanting more. God, if he was before me…

"Touch yourself," he demanded hoarsely. "I want to see it."

…I'd come apart if he touched me. If he leaned in and whispered these words. If he groaned against my pussy and jacked off his cock. I'd grip his hair in my fingers and ride his face shamelessly. I'd cry his name and buck my hips and wrap my legs around his head and come on his mouth, my body shaking, my legs squeezing, my voice cracking. I—

When I came, he growled my name over and over, his voice breaking, his harsh moan at the end telling me the moment he followed suit, the soft whisper of his hands, cool breath blown against my hot skin, his mouth kissing beads of sweat off my chest.

And, in the moment before he signed off, I felt the remorseful pull of guilt.

"Thank you, baby." He whispered the words, his voice slack and sleepy.

"Anytime, Mike." I dropped my head back and closed my eyes. Stretched out my limbs and wondered how long it'd be before I could move.

"I missed you." His voice was quiet and lazy, but the emotion was there, pushing, reminding. Reminding me that, like it had been for a long time, there was something there. Something between us.

"I missed you too." I said the words softly and wished, for the hundredth time, that he'd show me his cam. Let me see his eyes and know what lay there. If it was just lust, or if... Maybe it was better he didn't. Maybe it was better for us if there was this layer of disconnect. Maybe he was about to turn off his computer and walk into MysteryBarbie's room. Curl into bed with her and forget his online slut. I reached out a hand and clicked the mouse. Ended the session.

Twenty-six minutes. $181.74 earned. Because it was, despite the *I miss yous* and joint orgasms, a business transaction. Just like I keep reminding Jeremy. That's all.

CHAPTER 18

Present

"MRS. MCCLINTOCK, WHY were you behind the Quik Mart at that time of night?"

"The Dumpsters are emptied on Monday mornings. I like to glance through them, see if anyone's thrown out anything good. You wouldn't believe the perfectly good stuff that people throw out, even in this neighborhood."

"Ever found anything like this before? In or near the Dumpster?"

"A body? No. I've never found a body before."

"Anything else? That stands out as odd?"

"Could I have a glass of water? I'm feeling a little light-headed."

CHAPTER 19

Past

JEREMY KNOCKED AND waited. Pressed a hand to the wall and leaned forward slightly, stretching out his back. He should wear the brace. Too many heavy boxes lifted improperly. One day he'd be hunched over like the oldies on the loading dock. He rolled his neck and glanced at his watch. Tilted a head toward the door and tried to hear something. Considered just opening it. He knocked again.

Deanna's voice came through, sweet and quiet. Such a contrast to reality. "Just leave it."

His hand stopped an inch from the handle and he looked up, into the dead peephole. "What?"

"I'm in a session. Just leave the box like we used to do."

Used to do. Right. In the first three years, back when he had never seen her. Knew only her voice and her cryptic insistence that he leave all packages and walk away. They'd left that stage a year ago. "What are you talking about? Open the door." He wanted to reach out. Turn the knob and push it in. It'd be unlocked. He was a hundred times stronger than she was. But he resisted. Tried to respect the request, even if he didn't understand it. "Are you okay?" Maybe someone was there. Maybe she was being held captive, against her will. Someone, right now, might be holding a knife to her throat. He should try the door. He stretched his shoulders back and clenched his fists, every muscle prepping for a possible confrontation.

"I'm fine. Just leave the fucking box." She didn't sound scared. She sounded irritated. Then again, the woman didn't have the sense to be scared, her inner compass too fucked up for her own good.

He looked down at the box, a small one from a beauty store. "I'm not leaving until I see you."

An irritated huff that somehow passed through the steel door. A string of curses that tumbled louder when the door snatched open, the girl who owned his heart, standing before him in a T-shirt and hot-orange boyshorts. "Happy?" she demanded.

His eyes danced over her, then shot left, to her pink bed, brilliantly lit by ten thousand watts of professional lighting, a pile of sex toys front and center on its bedspread. To the kitchen, the table empty, counters clean. The door to the bathroom open, shower curtain pulled, green tile showing. The right side of the room, where stacks of novels framed a box spring and mattress, a messy pile of sheets and pillows. Further right, the sea of cardboard boxes encroaching, almost pushing to the door frame. No one else. Just her, the loft apartment empty. "What's wrong?" he asked.

Her eyes rolled upward and she leaned forward, yanking the package out of his hands and tossing it in the general direction of her bed. "Nothing. I'm working. I'll call you later."

She pushed the door closed and his hand shot out, stopping it. "Kiss me."

Her eyes narrowed. "No."

"Tell me what the fuck is wrong," he growled. "Is this about dinner with my family?"

"Move your hand before I chop it off." Her upper lip curled into a snarl.

He lifted it and stared her down, her eyes darting away from his in the moment before she slammed it. Then, to his absolute shock, there was the click of a lock.

A *lock*. He wasn't even aware she had a lock on that side of the door. She prided herself on keeping it open during the day, had some fanatical obsession with it. Yet here, now... she didn't let him in and locked the door. Locked him out. Wouldn't kiss him. He stared at the peephole and wondered if she was looking through it. Wondered, with a pain in his heart, if this was the beginning of the end. Was it his invitation to dinner? He knew he shouldn't have asked. Damn Lily for pressing it. Damn him for bending under the pressure. Damn—

"She's a fucking peach."

He kept his eyes on the peephole, fought an inner war with himself before turning to the voice. Of course. The blonde. What was her name? He searched his mind and came up blank.

"I gotta say, I think you can do better." She sauntered forward, her hands pushing into the front pockets of her jeans, the motion pushing them farther down on her hips, the edge of yellow lace giving a hint at her panties.

He said nothing, just pulled his eyes from her impressively tight abs.

"The strong silent type?" she asked, stopping before him, a hand leaving her pocket to brush through her hair, her back arching from the motion. He noticed her breasts. She grinned and he wanted to leave. Didn't want another moment of this. Wanted to be inside Deanna's fucking apartment and sliding his palms over her ass. Taking her mouth as he pushed her against the wall and pulled her against his body. Wanted to beg against her ear for five fucking minutes inside her, his cock pushing against his brown pants, her hand freeing him, gripping him, guiding him inside her. The catch of her gasp when he pushed inside, the hot grip of her body when she took him in, the widening of her eyes, dig of her nails, moan of her voice when she came.

Instead he was stuck with this woman, who was stepping closer, her hand reaching out to trace over the badge of his sleeve. "UPS, huh? So...if I order something, you'll handle the package?" She raised her eyebrows suggestively.

He said nothing and glanced toward Deanna's door. Wondered if his girlfriend was catching this. If she cared. If she was about to open up the door and yank him inside. His cock awoke at that thought, at the reminder of what the last interaction with this woman had led Deanna to do. Wondered what it would take to push her buttons back to that point. He let his eyes return to the blonde, whose hand slid lower and wrapped around his bicep. "Wow," she gushed. "You're so strong." He reached across and gently wrapped his hand around her small wrist, pulling gently, her grip releasing at the contact. He glanced at the door and willed it to open. Welcomed whatever punishment his beautiful brunette wanted to dish out.

"Don't worry about her," she whispered. "Simon says the freak never comes out."

"She's not a freak." He dropped his hand from hers and met her eyes, which widened slightly at his tone.

"I'm sorry. It's just... he said she—"

"Simon should mind his own business," he said darkly.

Her eyes fell downward, as did her hand, the returning push to her pockets drawing her pants a little farther down. Her panties were sheer lace. High on the sides. She didn't, from this angle, appear to have tan lines. His cock refused to soften from his earlier fantasy; it pushed stubbornly. He needed to turn around and leave. Fuck provoking Deanna. "I'm sorry," she repeated, softer this time, a whisper of submission.

I'm sorry. Had Deanna *ever* apologized to him? Ever? Maybe at the hospital. Maybe. She wasn't the apologizing sort, not like this woman, who was now meekly glancing up, through thick lashes. *Meekly.* It activated a sudden, unnecessary, caveman urge to protect her. "It's okay," he said quickly, stepping back before he reached out. "I've got to run. Other deliveries."

"Sure." She stepped back, mirroring his move, the space between them stretching farther. "I'll see you around."

"Chelsea, right?" Her name came to him like manna, and her mouth curved at the name, a smile spreading over her face.

"Yeah."

"See you later."

When she waved good-bye, her breasts shook a little from the motion. He turned quickly and walked toward the elevator. Fought the urge not to run.

He'd turned into a pussy.

CHAPTER 20

Past

I SAW IT all. That slut with her paws all over Jeremy. When I shut the door in his face, I put my hands on the door, twin cracks of phalanges on either side of the peephole, my forehead resting above it. I breathed hard when she came in stage left. Stepped away and shook my hands to relax my arms. Yanked open the safe, pulled out the closest switchblade and flipped it in my hands just to refamiliarize myself with its weight. Snapped the blade out and then in as I leaned against the door and gritted my teeth. Watched him reach out his hand and *touch* her. Turned his head and looked at me. I stepped back, spun around. Dropped the knife before I used it. Raised hands to my head and gripped my hair. Backed up until my heel hit the door and I sank against it. Turned my good ear to the steel.

"Chelsea, right?"

"Yeah."

"See you later."

Chelsea, right? See you later. He had reached out and *touched* her. *Smiled* at her. Had glanced toward the peephole like he was motherfucking *goading* me.

I will kill him.

Slowly. Seductively. Painfully.

I will kill him.

CHAPTER 21

Past

JEREMY CALLED DEANNA from the truck, the cold metal of his cell against his ear, the shake of the truck roaring to life. His GPS chirped at the same time that her voice mail came on, the cheery tone absolutely false to the girl six stories above him. He pulled out abruptly, the squeal of tires promptly accompanied by a horn, his side mirror giving him a clear view of the Ford Focus that he'd almost hit. He let out an aggravated sigh and spoke tersely into the phone.

"Deanna. What the fuck was that? Call me. I don't know if this is about dinner at my sister's or what but...just call me." He hung up the phone and swore, tossing it into the open glove box, the cell hitting just short and bouncing down into the floorboard. He ground his teeth and took a right, accelerating onto the freeway. He didn't need this. She was always a loose cannon, but one that had come with clear rules. Habits. Habits that involved him having, as one of the few strengths in their relationship, free access to her apartment. Never, not since they officially dove into this whirlwind of a relationship, had she done that. Shut him out. Locked the door. Well...once she had.

"If you love me, you need to let me go right now. Trust in me, in us, and go home."

And he'd trusted her that day. Had been the good submissive boyfriend that he was and had gone home. A colossal mistake, one that had almost killed him. But their relationship had changed since then. Strengthened. They'd grown closer. Shared more. Their lives had intertwined tighter, the strands of their connection thicker. Unbreakable. A week ago he'd have said they were unbreakable. Now, they felt like china. Delicate, breakable china.

It had been the invite to dinner. Had to have been. He'd pushed her. He didn't ever push her. Didn't like to rock the boat. Enjoyed her smile too much. So why had he pushed? Part of it had been his sister. Her questions. Her points. Her pushing to light all of the things that he liked to bury and ignore. She'd been right, his sister. She always was. And it had been her silent questions, her silent pokes, that he had heard the loudest.

He'd been out of the apartment with Deanna. They'd gone on dates, and it was fine. So why was she still locked up? Why still live the life of a recluse? Why could she go to Outback with him but not to his sister's house?

And then there was the other issue, the nagging thought he'd been pushing around for the last few months. The thought that had been growing roots every time he broke her rules and logged onto the camsite. Eavesdropped on her in free chat and watched her work. When she was on camera, she was someone else. She smiled differently. Laughed more. Cracked jokes. Danced. On camera she played the role so well that he forgot the truth. Believed that she was a nineteen-year-old college student who went to keg parties on the weekends. And every time he watched her work, his hypothesis grew.

Maybe her self-imposed exile was just an excuse. To stay online. To keep her job. To excuse her behavior and stuff it behind the "it's my only option" shield. As far as he knew, she had never acted on her so-called urges. Maybe she'd imagined the whole thing. Was an overly dramatic individual who liked the attention and drama of locking herself away. Had grown addicted to her job and decided to keep the status quo. Play with naïve him while still enjoying all the perks of her prior life.

Maybe he was the fool in all this and she was laughing at him right now. Up in her Mulholland Oaks tower, surrounded by the lights and the cash and her hundreds of admirers.

Or maybe he was just trying to convince himself that his beautiful girl wasn't really insane.

CHAPTER 22

Past

"I WILL KILL him, I swear to God I will."

"Deanna, you don't mean that." Dr. Derek's voice was, like always, balm. Too bad he was trying to apply it to sandpaper.

"You've worried about me killing for four years, why are you so calm now?!" I shrieked the words, the switchblade still in my hand, the blade handle cool and comforting in my grip. I paused beside my bed and stabbed at a pillow, the puncture quick and smooth. I stopped and held up the blade, impressed. Damn. Well worth the six-hundred-dollar price tag.

"Believe it or not, this emotion is a good thing, Deanna."

He needed to stop saying my name. It's like there was a page in his psychology textbook that he was stuck on, in the Say the Client's Name chapter. "Stop saying my name."

"Jealousy is a perfectly normal human emotion. It's good that you care for another person enough to be jealous. It's a reminder of the world outside your apartment."

"I don't need to be reminded of the world outside my apartment. I'm in no danger of forgetting it." Forgetting? It's my obsession, second to my thoughts of death. Third to my new thoughts of jealousy.

"The negative is how you are turning your anger into violence. That's what we want to avoid."

Obviously. I stabbed the pillow again. A puff of air resulted, blowing the ends of my hair slightly. If only pillows bled.

CHAPTER 23

Present

JessReilly19: Mike

JessReilly19: u there?

HackOffMyCock: hey bb

JessReilly19: is this chat secure?

HackOffMyCock: not really

HackOffMyCock: let's cam instead

HackOffMyCock: there's something about schoolgirl plaid that helps too

JessReilly19: don't be an ass. Seriously, is it secure?

HackOffMyCock: yeah. What's up 007?

JessReilly19: cops showed up today

HackOffMyCock: about what?

JessReilly19: I'm not sure. They didn't say.

HackOffMyCock: you didn't ask?

HackOffMyCock: hello?

HackOffMyCock: u there?

JessReilly19: sorry. Someone called. Anyone come by to see you?

HackOffMyCock: nope.

JessReilly19: let me know if they do.

HackOffMyCock: u know it. U need me to do anything?

JessReilly19: no. Thx

HackOffMyCock: chat this week?

JessReilly19: yeah.

HackOffMyCock: your enthusiasm is a little out of control. Rein that shit in.

JessReilly19: :) *dancing excitedly* *hanging up my I Love Mike poster*

JessReilly19: better?

HackOffMyCock: better. *unzips pants*

JessReilly19: lol. Stop.

HackOffMyCock: *frowns in a sexy manner*

JessReilly19: *raises her middle finger*

HackOffMyCock: *gets hard*

JessReilly19: OMG STOP or else I'll start charging you.

HackOffMyCock: *making it rain with Benjamins*

JessReilly19: BYE

HackOffMyCock: BYE *tucking gigantic cock back into pants*

---CHAT ENDED: JessReilly19 has left room

CHAPTER 24

Present

DETECTIVE BRENDA BOLES sits at her desk, a crowded space with forgotten paperwork, each case more important than the last, her weakness time management. Hidden behind the stacks, three coffee cups, handmade gifts from her kids, their touch in the formed clay, the brightly painted surfaces, the names painstakingly dug into the sides. One for each child: Matthew, Sage, and Bricen. At one time, she'd attempted to drink from them. Now they collect pens, scissors, and rulers. She glances at one and notices the thin layer of dust across its surface. Rubs a finger across the top of it as the call connects, the dull ring humming in her ear. She closes her eyes and lets out a long breath. Rolls her neck. So much left to do today. No chance of leaving soon, not with cases like this on her desk. A freakin' jigsaw puzzle, each new pry into Deanna Madden's life bringing up more questions. Hopefully this call will yield some answers.

"Hello?"

At the man's voice, she pries an eye open. "Dr. Vanderbilt?"

"Yes. May I help you?"

"This is Detective Brenda Boles from the Tulsa Police Department. Is this a good time?"

"It is. How can I help you?" The man's voice is deep and calm, the type a tired mother of three would love to crawl into and confess all her woes.

"I have some questions about one of your patients. Deanna Madden?"

Complete silence. She pushes the phone against her ear. "Dr. Vanderbilt? Are you there?"

"I thought you were calling from the Tulsa City Police Department."

"Yes. I'm a detective. Brenda Boles."

"May I ask what your interest is in Deanna?"

Deanna. Interesting. "She's a suspect in an investigation we are conducting."

"In Tulsa?"

God, this guy, for his incredible voice, is denser than dirt. "Yes."

"But Deanna lives in Utah."

"I just left her apartment. I can assure you that she lives in Tulsa."

There is another long moment of silence before he speaks again. "I see. I must have been confused. What is your question?"

"We found clozapine in her apartment, which you prescribed to her."

"Yes. She's had that prescription for several years."

"What is it supposed to treat?" She spins in her chair, tapping her pen on the arm of the chair.

"I'm bound by doctor/patient confidentiality, Detective

Boles, a fact that I am sure you are aware of." She raises her eyebrows at the tone, which has taken a hard turn.

"I'm just trying to get to the truth, Dr. Vanderbilt."

"Please call me Derek. May I ask what you are investigating?"

She spins a paperclip and debates what to share. "No, you may not." He won't share his goods, she won't share hers.

"Have you arrested Deanna?"

"Not yet. But it's not for lack of trying, Derek." The name comes out incredibly awkward, like the first time she introduced herself by her married name. She shouldn't have said it, should have stuck to Dr. Vanderbilt. Shouldn't be trying to picture the man with the sexy voice. That's what she gets for ... God, how long has it been? A month without sex? Her marriage will crumble if this keeps up. Other than sex and children, there isn't much they have in common. She draws a line on the piece of paper before her and tries to remember where this conversation had been going.

The man on the other end coughs. "Will she need a psych evaluation?"

David's frame appears on the far side of the room, his head turning left as he speaks to another badge and she stands, the phone captured in the crook of her shoulder, waving to catch his attention. "Oh, I think she'll need a lot of things. I'd keep your phone on."

"I'm sorry I couldn't be more helpful, Brenda."

"Me too."

She hangs up the phone and rolls her neck, grimacing through a smile as David approaches.

"Get the doc?"

"Sure did. He clammed up, wouldn't give anything. But an interesting side note, he was under the impression that she lived in Utah. So maybe we can call over, do some digging, see if she lived or raised any hell there."

"I'll do it. Anything else?"

"If I had to guess, they have a personal connection. A friendship...maybe something more."

"That's interesting, given that this girl seems to have a shortage of friends."

"Interesting and problematic. Last thing we need is a doctor who'll protect her."

"You think he will?"

She taps her fingers against the arm of the chair, a slow rhythm that only serves to deepen her agitation. "Not necessarily. My mind's jumping ahead a bit." She watches him toss his coffee into the trash. "You heading out?"

"Got to run downtown. There's a lead on the Downover case I'm going to follow up on. Then I'll be back."

"Call me on your way back. Depending on the time, I may get you to pick me up something to eat."

"Thought Sage had that recital tonight."

"She does. But there's no way I'll make it. Not with all this." She gestures to the pile on her desk. Matt will take pictures, video her solo with his phone. She'll get sporadic texts throughout the night, enough to make her feel included, but not so much to reach the point of guilt. They "understand." A horrible word that ranks right up there next to "I'm not mad at you, I'm disappointed." They never should have had another child. The added guilt has only pushed her deeper into the hole of work-related depression. She should be at home. She should be a mother to her children. She should cook dinner and know about their classes, and help with homework, and not be wearing her ass out chasing down psychotic prom queens like Deanna Madden.

She smiles when David waves good-bye. Opens up her right-side drawer and pulls out her headphones. Plugs them in and hits the Play button on her phone. Inhales a deep breath and flips open the folder, shaking out the images, the initial strands of music starting as she flips over the first photo and looks down at Jeremy Pacer's battered and broken face.

CHAPTER 25

Present

I USED TO worship this window; it was my altar to the outside world. Now, with its cardboard barrier gone, I can still feel its pull. I stand before it, the window fully raised, the fresh flow of outside air blowing over my skin and carrying with it the scents of life. Of garbage, fried food, car exhaust. I close my eyes and drink them in, a smile on my face. I need to lock it. Paint it shut again. Cardboard it up again, or just paint the glass. I'll do it soon. But not yet.

From behind me, I hear the chime of my phone, Derek's ringtone. I frown, my eyes still closed. It's not Wednesday at three o'clock. Why is he calling me? I move forward and snag the phone, returning to the window and holding it to my ear. "Hey."

"Deanna, I just got a call from the Tulsa Police Department."

Shit. I feel the twist of guilt that I used to get right before my father would ground me. I swallow. "And?"

"What did you do?"

I look out the window, the night falling over the skyline, the resulting effect one that hid imperfections and painted the scene in one of rosy Instagram perfection. "Do they have any-thing on me?"

"Answer the question, Deanna."

I hang up the phone and bend over, resting my hands on the sill and hanging my head out the window. The wind blew as if in response, blowing my hair in gentle brushes against my face.

"*What did you do?*" Such an accusatory tone, completely devoid of trust or positive expectation.

But it was a great question. What *did* I do? And why can't I remember it? I pull out my phone and call Jeremy again. This time, there is no ring, his voice mail picking straight up. I hang up and feel sick.

CHAPTER 26

Past

IT TOOK TWO days for me to get over myself and forgive Jeremy. Unfortunately for me, he was in the right. And I didn't wear humility very well. At all.

He had every right to ask me questions.

Every right to invite me to his sister's.

Every right to want a normal girlfriend.

Every right to not be locked out of my apartment.

Every right for an explanation when I refused him entry.

I, on the other hand... didn't have many points in my favor. I'd been wrong in how I handled it. How I handled him. I needed to share more, speak more. I needed to open up a bit and let him further in. I needed to be able to have a conversation with him without slamming my head into the tile and giving myself a concussion.

"How would you handle it if Jeremy broke up with you? Ended your relationship?"

It'd been a stupid question on Dr. Derek's part, but it was a question that hadn't left my mind since. How *would* I handle it? My first instinct was to shrug off the question. Like I did

with Derek. It isn't going to happen so it doesn't matter. But...
what if?

What if he broke up with me? Would I go back to my life?
Keep the door shut? Restrict my human contact to the digital
variety? How much of my sanity lay in my ability to touch someone? Be held? Be kissed and caressed and loved? Jeremy was my
bodyguard, the person who could escort me out into the world
and whom I knew would keep me from hurting someone. He
was my security blanket, the person without whom I could
have never stepped out into that hall. He, literally, handed me
the keys to freedom that first day. And he'd held my hand ever
since.

What if he left? Would I survive? Would my madness stay
in check? What about my heart? How would I react? Would I
retreat into a sniffling ball of patheticness? Or would I lash out,
angry and vindictive and red with rage?

A hundred different combinations of reactions. No wonder
Derek had pushed the horrific question upon me.

A knock sounded, hard and firm. I rose from the bed and
walked to the door. Opened it and raised my chin. Looked into
Jeremy's eyes.

"I'm sorry."

CHAPTER 27

Past

A WOMAN APOLOGIZING is a rare thing. Deanna apologizing is a rarity that had only happened once before. Jeremy blinked and tried to form a response, her delivery hanging between them from his outstretched hand.

"For...?" It wasn't a test. In that unexpected moment he couldn't think of what she was apologizing for. It didn't help that all coherent mind processes stopped when she stood before him in panties and a sheer tank top.

"For being a bitch. For not letting you in. For shutting you out. For not explaining." She lifted a shoulder and dropped it, a half shrug, as if it was an obvious answer. Which, now that she'd verbalized it, it kind of was.

"Oh." He lifted his free hand and scratched at the back of his neck. Let the hand containing the package drop to his side. "So...I can come in?"

"Of course." She stepped back and gestured him in. When he stepped inside, he noticed her tennis shoes, kicked off and lying next to her bed.

CHAPTER 28

Past

YES, I WENT for a run. Whatever. It didn't mean anything. It was the middle of the day, I was having a mini–panic attack after a short conversation with Dr. Derek, and I laced up my tennis shoes and ran.

Well...ran/walked. Like those 5kers who can't make it the full 3.1 miles so they plod down to a walk, their fists still enthusiastic in their swings through the air, ponytails bobbing, their heads jerking right to blab to whatever poor soul suffers along next to them.

My run was a little different than that. I started out strong, my tennis shoes smacking the pavement fluidly, my arms loose and in rhythm, my breath even and clear. Then I hit the fourth block and my exhales became a little ragged. Sixth block I had to shake out my arms. Tenth I cut left in preparation for my return home. Twelfth I began to wheeze. Fourteenth I stumbled to a halt and bent over, gripping my knees for strength.

It was so stupid. The entire thing. The "brilliant" idea I'd had to go and blow off steam. Because I'd done it in high school, when pissed at my parents or wound up over a test. Because back then, when everything in my life was rosy and perfect, I'd pounded pavement, chalking up three or four miles in one flawless, sweat-glistened athletic event, my heart pounding as I sprinted the final stretch home, my abs tight, endorphins high, grin triumphant. That was then.

My new reality, the one wheezing to a slow death against a fire hydrant, only sent me deeper down stress road.

I straightened, my heart pounding, everything coming into focus, the blaring sun beating down. The hard rattle of an approaching car. The woman, ten feet over, sitting on a step and bitching into a cell phone.

I suddenly realized a variety of things.

I was outside the apartment.

I was unarmed.

I was free.

I had walked slowly home, one tired foot before the other, listening to everything, absorbing it all. And I wasn't sure, by the time I pushed a sluggish hand on my building's front door, if the beating in my chest was from exertion or exhilaration.

"So, you went out?" The question came from behind me, an edge in Jeremy's voice, and I turned, stalled, unwilling to put all of *that* into words. I had just *apologized*. And I wasn't particularly used to apologizing. It felt weird. Icky. Ridiculously unnecessary. But half of me, the part that got panicky at the thought of Life Without Jeremy, insisted on it. That half of me was a nervous, weak little thing. I wanted to cut open her throat and watch her die. But instead, I'd just let her out, let her apologize. And Jeremy had seemed to respond well. He'd stepped inside. I'd seen the light enter his eyes. The hint of a dimple in his cheek. And when he'd followed me in, I'd given myself a little pat on the back, was already squashing the weak, apologetic half of me back down, into some dark piece of myself where she'd hopefully starve to death and die. Was busy doing all of those things when he asked the question. A simple enough question. One a thousand people probably used every hour, but it came out hard. Accusatory. And when I turned, he stood in place, his hands on his hips, eyes down, on my tennis shoes. The inside soles were probably still warm, the outside glistening from the puddle I hadn't quite skirted.

"Yeah." I folded my arms across my chest. *For a run* I almost said. But that felt like an excuse, an explanation, and I have enough of that with Derek. I didn't owe Jeremy that. Didn't need to ask permission from him.

"So... why can't you go to my sister's?" He looked up. "I mean, you're obviously doing everything else."

When the fury came, it was hot and red. I lunged without thinking, my palms hard on his chest, catching him off guard, and he stumbled back, his eyes meeting mine, leftover irritation turning wary as he raised his hands and scowled at me. "Deanna...," he warned.

"Get out." I growled the words, my hands in fists, and wanted to tilt back my chin and scream at the heavens. He stood before me, the kitchen too far, the butter knives in it useless anyway. The safe behind him, behind a stack of boxes that would take minutes to wade through. Nothing useful. Everything planned for moments of weakness like this.

"No." He said the word with force, and I took a deep breath

in, flexed my hands and regripped them. "We need to talk, Deanna, you can't just go fuckin' crazy on me whenev—"

"Get OOOUUUUTTT!" I closed my eyes and screamed the final word, my entire body shaking, the blissful black of the moment one I didn't want to let go of. Not seeing his face. Not hearing his voice. Not hearing words like *crazy* or *talk* or *no*. I didn't need this shit. I didn't need a fucking parent pushing me, wanting things, asking for explanations. I needed my four walls. My prison. My solitude. My online world where I was fuckin' prom queen and perfect. The world where my word was God, and they were all parishioners. The world where there was no black; there was only the pink of my bedding and the green of my cash. There was no blood, there was no dark, only 10,000 watts of warm light. The world where Mike understood me and everyone else worshiped me. The world that I could turn on and off. The world that wasn't right here and now, confronting me and pushing my buttons and refusing to leave. I opened my mouth to scream again, my eyes still shut, my world still black, when the force of the door shook the floor, the whoosh of air giving me one blissful breeze of finality.

When I opened my eyes, I was alone.

CHAPTER 29

Past

WHEN JEREMY SLAMMED the door, the force of impact shook the whole floor. Why did she have such a heavy door? To keep her scrawny ass in? What a joke. Especially when she then proceeded to drive around. Walk outside. Do whatever she freakin' pleased, except the one thing that he asked of her. One family dinner. So easy. Ridiculous.

He took a minute, pressing his palms against the filthy wallpaper and dropping his head, inhaling deeply. Rolled his neck to the side. Contemplated and discarded the notion of going back in. Pushing her further. Demanding an answer for once. He deserved that. After all that he'd—they'd—been through ... one answer needed to be given. Hell. A hundred answers needed to be given. He should sit down and write a list. When he groaned, lifting his head up and turning, the girl was there. She, the blonde, was a freakin' cancer. A cancer leaning against the wall, arms crossed, a friendly smile on her face.

"You okay? I think half the picture frames just fell off the walls."

"I don't think anyone in this building has pictures hung."

She laughed, pushing off the wall. "You headed downstairs?"

"Yeah." He dropped his hand from the wall.

"Me too. Come on, you can escort me. Unless, of course, you only talk to crazies." She tilted her head toward Deanna's apartment and laughed. She was in a soft blue sweatshirt today, one that covered her stomach and hid her curves. One that, paired with jeans, made her look more innocent. Less predatory. Yet he felt more vulnerable.

"She's not crazy." Part of his mind instantly argued with the words.

She clucked her tongue and tucked her hand under his bicep, squeezing the muscle there. "Easy, tiger. I'll lay off if it gets you worked up." She pulled gently on his arm, and he took a reluctant start down the hall. "Meant to tell you the other day. I love the uniform. Very sexy." She gave his arm another squeeze, and he forced himself to relax the muscle.

"You do anything other than stalk the hall?"

She laughed and they came to a stop before the elevator, her finger reaching out and jabbing at the down arrow. "I just moved to town for a new job. I'm just crashing at Simon's till I find a place. Not sure which part of town to look in." She looked up at him. "Where do you live?"

He coughed, gesturing her forward when the doors opened. "In Bethany Park."

"Ooh…fancy," she cooed. "Unfortunately I think that's out of a cop's price range."

I'm not a cop. He started to say it, then realized that she was talking about herself. He turned his head. "You're a cop?" It shouldn't have put a pain in his stomach. It shouldn't have made his palms sweat, his heartbeat increase. He had never, from the day he'd been born, broken a law. Committed a crime. Done anything to warrant a thickening in his chest. But it was there. Just like when a police car pulled up behind him. Just like when he got a letter from the IRS.

She grinned at the question. "The nerdy kind. Forensics. So . . . don't bother killing anyone." She leaned into his personal space, and he smelled the faint scent of lavender as she whispered. "'Cause I'll catch ya."

CHAPTER 30

Past

FETISHES ARE MY bread and butter. The freakier a kink, the more the afflicted feels the need to hide it, to explore it in the anonymity of the Internet as opposed to an actual face-to-face experience with someone who might reject them. And that's where my alter ego, JessReilly19, comes in. I, like the thousands of camgirls online, breathe digital life into their kinks and let them blossom.

I understand my clients' shame. Their fear of rejection. I get the glee of discovery that can only be fully celebrated in private, without judgment peeking around the corner with a giant YOU ARE A FREAK sign. My fetish isn't sexual, but it still is that, a fetish: a course of action to which one has an excessive and irrational commitment. My course of action is killing. My commitment is excessive and irrational. So I don't judge my clients. I don't judge the things that bring them pleasure. It's not my place to be the hypocrite.

A day after my blowup with Jeremy, the current client of the hour was Justin488, who jerked off to his next-door neighbor, an elderly woman who liked to prune her roses and take naps in her front porch rocking chair. Justin, from the sound of his voice in my ear, the hiccups of his orgasm, seemed to be in his twenties. A boy who took no issue with my young appearance, but who told me, at the end of the chat, that I gave "good old woman." Awesome. Maybe this job does have some longevity.

I thanked him for the chat and hung up my cell. Logged back into free chat and watched twenty greetings fill the screen.

Freeloader22: hey sexy

BigDick4You99: hey

---ShaunUofM enters room

FinDomFreak44: hey Jessica. Up for some FinDom?

"Hey, guys. Sure, Fin. Open up that wallet and get ready to pay up." I grinned and rolled onto my stomach. Ignored my cell when it buzzed beside me.

AlaskaPaul: hey Jess

I smiled, surprised. "Hey, Paul. Surprised to see you here."

AlaskaPaul: got off early. Private?

"Sure. Hit me up on my site."

I logged out of the camsite and onto my personal site, where 95 percent of Paul's $6.99 per minute would go into my bank account, versus the pathetic cut I got on the corporately controlled camsite. Paul sat, where he always did, in one of my private rooms, and I started the chat, the pull on his credit card beginning.

A minute later, my cell rang.

"Hey, babe." I closed my laptop and stood, walking to the lights and turning them off, the room instantly cooler. I headed to the thermostat to turn the air conditioner off.

"Hey. How's your day going?" Paul sounded, as always, happy. He's always happy. I've chatted with him at least twice a week for over two years, and I've never heard him be anything other than cheerful. On a normal individual, in an ordinary situation, it'd be downright annoying. Like that cheery coworker that you secretly wish would trip and fall into a muddy puddle. But with Paul, it's endearing. Even more endearing since I was earning four hundred dollars an hour to chat with his cheerful self.

"It's good. Slow. It feels weird, talking to you this early." Given Paul's Alaskan time zone, I typically talk to him late in the morning, when he's headed to work, or late at night, when he's on his way home from the pipelines.

"Yeah. A blizzard's coming in. We all headed in early to hunker down. I got the fire on now. Me and Oscar are warm and happy."

I smiled at the thought of his husky, stretched out before the fire. In my mind it's on a fur rug, in a cozy house filled with books and the smell of cinnamon. In real life he's probably in a doublewide, this chat pushing his credit card debt a couple hundred bucks higher. I took the moment to bag up the kitchen trash. Propped the phone on my shoulder as I yanked the ties tight and carried it to the door, leaning it against the wall. I'll stick it in the hall tonight and Simon will get it. Carry it down to the Dumpster when he locks me in. "How long will the blizzard last?"

"They're saying six or seven hours. Nothing too bad. But it ruins the orgy I had planned."

I laughed, snagging the closest cardboard box and dragging it to the table. Heavy. Used a pen to break the plastic tape and rip it off. "Damn blizzard. How dare it."

"Exactly. What are you up to tonight?"

"Working till ten. Then I'm going out with my roommate." My lie comes out easily. They all do.

"Where?"

I pulled the cardboard box open. Bottled water. A hundred Fijis. I opened the fridge and began stocking it. "There's a house party she was invited to. It's a theme party. Toga, but we're gonna be rebels and dress cute."

He chuckled. "Wild thing."

"Oh, you know it. Not to mention, it's too damn cold for togas. The party organizers should be ashamed of themselves." Six six-packs fit on one shelf of my fridge. I stopped stocking and shut the lid. Grabbed a Sharpie and labeled the side of the box. Then I slid it back, letting it join the sea of others, this time on the bottom of the "Food" tower of boxes. My madness was nothing if not organized. I lifted over the next unclaimed box and broke it open. Did a mini-celebration when I saw the tampons. Just in time. And, with 480 applicators of different absorbencies enclosed, I should be covered for the next year, easy.

I counted out a dozen tampons and headed for the bathroom, tossing them into the basket under the sink. "You ever get toga parties in Alaska?" Paul didn't go to college. He grew up in Oregon and was recruited out of high school for the pipeline. Stood out as a big kid. Moved to Alaska three months after graduation. That was fourteen years ago.

Another laugh. "No. But promise me, if you do decide to

yield to peer pressure and dress in a toga, that you'll take a picture for me."

I smiled. "Promise. But I can guarantee you that I won't."

"Oh...never say never. You might get a few drinks in you and end up stealing some poor guy's sheets."

I folded the tampon box back into place and labeled it. "You know I don't drink."

You know I don't drink. One truth. I think, looking back, that it was the only one I offered during that fifty-four-minute conversation.

Don't tell Dr. Derek, but I've become much more comfortable with lying than I've ever been with telling the truth.

CHAPTER 31

Past

I WAS SEVENTEEN when I saw my first dead body. It was Summer, my sister, her head slumped over and stuck to our kitchen table, blood staining her blond strands. Maybe, had I been older, it wouldn't have affected me so strongly. Maybe, had my eyes not moved to the right, to the lifeless form of my brother, it would have all ended differently. Maybe, had I stepped back and left the scene, I would have ended up normal.

"You gonna check out or not?" The snap of the voice jolted me out of my daze, my eyes stuck on the magazine shining out at me from beside the register, the blonde on the front bearing a slight resemblance to Summer. A not-as-cute Summer. I reached in my back pocket and pulled out my debit card. Swiped it through the reader without responding. Felt the moment the guy next in line shifted impatiently.

This was a horrible idea. I blame Paul. He'd started crunching on an apple halfway through our phone call, and I'd had the sudden urge for fruit. I could just picture a crisp green apple. Then I'd wanted grapes. And watermelon. I hadn't had watermelon since Before. Before Summer's dead head on that table. Before the night that had destroyed everything. A few years ago, I'd have just suffered. Ate a few extra TV dinners and ignored the cravings. But now, with Jeremy in my life, I'd gotten used to demanding. Texting him and asking for ice cream, or Olive Garden breadsticks and Alfredo, or whatever freakish thing my stomach was suddenly aware it was deprived of.

But I couldn't exactly scream Jeremy out of my apartment, then ask him to run to the grocery store for a snack. Even relationship-impaired me knew that. Plus, his obsession over his sister's dinner seemed to cause any outing of mine to be cause for debate. So it was out of principle that I put the tennis shoes—the same ones that started our damn fight—*back* on, grabbed my keys, and jogged down to my car.

Dr. Derek will flip out when I tell him, his controlled exhales audible through the phone receiver. He'll be upset at me. Yell in the only way that he does: calm, controlled sentences laced with sexual intent, his hand unbuckling and drawing out his black leather belt, his eyes darkening as he orders me to bend over and pull up my skirt. At least that's how I picture it. And maybe the threat of a Dr. Derek lecture had been another catalyst for my grocery run. It was apples and oranges for God's sake. I could handle it. Of course, I had said that before to disastrous results. I waited for the receipt and vowed to not leave the apartment again. Not for at least two weeks.

Two weeks. It seemed an eternity, but a year ago, it would have been nothing. Fourteen days out of a thousand.

Yes. I'd carry my eight apples, two pears, three oranges, and two mangoes into my apartment and then stop. Stay. Return to the plan that works. Me: inside. Everyone else: outside. With Jeremy the lone exception.

I took a final, wistful breath of grocery store freedom, and pocketed the receipt. "Thanks." I smiled at the cashier.

"Have a nice day and come back soon."

"I will." Not. I will not. I will behave.

CHAPTER 32

Past

THE PHONE RANG and I reached for it blindly, my hand thumping along the bed until I felt it.

"What," I mumbled into the receiver, the word muffled by a down pillow wrapped in a thousand-thread-count pillowcase.

"Hey, baby."

"Mike."

"You don't sound happy to hear from me."

"What time is it?"

"It's ten fifteen. You should have been online an hour ago. Get your ass up."

I rolled over. Ten fifteen? That was weird. I never slept past eight. I lifted the phone from my ear and checked the display. Damn. He was right.

"What?" I repeated, my limbs loose and relaxed, going right back to sleep a serious consideration depending on the rate at which I could wrap up this call.

"Just wanted to let you know the final deposit just hit your Cayman account. You are officially paid back in full."

"With interest?" I rolled back onto my stomach.

"My finger was the interest. I just wanted to give you the good news so that you could gush your thanks verbally."

"Thanks."

"Your gushing sucks."

"Your timing sucks. Let me go back to sleep."

"Come on . . . you should be up and working. This isn't like you. What's wrong?"

Sometimes I would have preferred he didn't have such a finger on my temperature. "I'm tired. Sleepy. You're annoying me. I'd hang up on you and turn off my phone if I thought there was any way of avoiding you."

He laughed. "No. It's something else. Talk to me. Normally I'd have at least got a halfhearted slap on the back for replenishing your accounts."

I said nothing. Closed my eyes and tried to sink further into the bed.

"Is it Jeremy?"

I didn't respond.

"What, you guys get in a fight?"

I frowned. "Try not to sound so excited at the possibility."

"That's not excitement, it's shock. About time the idiot wised up and ran away from you."

"He didn't 'run away.'" I spit out the words. "And I'll have you know I'm an excellent girlfriend."

"In what way?" There was a flirtatious challenge in the words. "Please, you beautiful vixen. Tell me exactly what you do to him. Let me turn green with envy."

I evaded the easy bait. "I didn't have to buy him a house. There's not a line in the girlfriend manual that says if you blow up his house that you have to replace it. So there. That counts for something. I am an awesome girlfriend."

"Did you listen to what you just said?" He laughed. "The blowing up of his house cancels out any replacement. WAY cancels it out. Try again, princess."

"I'm really done talking." And I was. The phone call had only gone downhill after his update of money.

"Aww…don't be like that. I'm sorry, babe. I'll behave. Hey, you know I love you regardless. You can come over here and chop me to bits anytime. Just be naked when you do it."

I couldn't help myself. I smiled despite every urge to frown. "I'm going back to sleep." I managed the words without any trace of humor, my smile hidden by the manufactured grouch in my tone.

"I know you're smiling."

"I'm not," I growled.

"Whatever. Get up. Get sexy and treat yourself to lunch with this Cayman windfall. Just don't take the delivery boy. It'll ruin all my good feelings over crossing this off my list."

"Bye, Mike." I should have hung up, but I waited, a smile on my lips, my hand raised, the phone smushed to my ear.

"Bye, baby."

I hung up.

CHAPTER 33

Present

"WE GOT THE report back on Pacer."

"And?"

"He was stabbed five times. The majority in the chest area, but you've seen that from the photos."

"What happened first, the ass kicking or stab wounds?" Brenda looks over at David, her pen slowing in its journey across the form.

"They don't know. Can't tell."

"Can't tell?" She snorts. "That's bullshit."

"Then go to med school and march your ass down there and correct them."

"I'd rather go to Firehouse. You up for a Hook and Ladder sub?"

"Thought you were going no-carb."

"That was last week. You coming?"

He straightens to his feet. "Only to keep you company."

"Whatever, Trivette."

"Trivette?"

"Yeah. You know, the black guy from *Walker, Texas Ranger*. I thought it could be a nickname."

"No."

"No?"

"No."

CHAPTER 34

Present

WHEN THE RAPS hit my door, I lean quickly forward. Finally. A chance to confront Jeremy and find out what all of this not-answering-his-phone bullshit is about. I end the session and walk to the door. Swing it open and smile. Stop smiling. "Who the fuck are you?"

The guy stares at me, slack jawed, a cardboard box hanging limply from his hand. It's not entirely his fault. With my assumption that it was Jeremy, the timing right, the knock quick and familiar, I didn't bother to get dressed, to put something on over my fishnet top and panties. I groan. "Just a second." I shut the door and grab the closest shirt, yank it on, and jerk the door back open.

The man, a thirtyish redhead with an overly healthy amount of freckles, appears to have composed himself. He holds out the package and manages to look sheepish. "Deanna Madden?"

"Yes. Who the fuck are you?"

"I'm Gary." He points to his name tag and I snatch the box, tossing it in the general direction of the others.

"Where's Jeremy?" A stupid question I hate to ask. I should know this, I should know my boyfriend isn't working, should know in intimate detail the reason for him to not be present, before me, right now. I touch, without thinking, the bridge of my swollen nose. Damn my dramatic chair crash earlier. Damn its effect on my brain and this inconvenient memory lapse.

"He's out sick." The guy fidgets uncomfortably.

"Sick?" Jeremy's not sick. Didn't so much as sniffle this weekend. I hold up a finger. "Wait here."

"Ma'am, I don't really have time…" I ignore him, my fingers quick across my cell screen before I hold it to my ear, praying this time I will be wrong, this time it will ring and he will answer. I listen to silence, then Jeremy's voice mail. Hang up with a frown.

"Have you talked to him?" I snap my fingers in his face, bringing his eyes up from my bare legs.

"Uh. No. I work the south side normally. Just covering today. I need you to sign for the box." He holds out the pad, and I take it. Scribble my name and pass it back. "And, uh. You had a pickup scheduled?"

Oh yes. The pickup had half been an excuse to force an interaction with Jeremy, half been necessary for self-preservation. I step back and point. "It's the one on the table. It's heavy."

"Got it." GoodLittleGary sets his pad on top of the box and squats slightly, sliding the box into his arms, then lifting with his legs in proper save-your-back fashion. He turns back to the door and misses my entire cam setup. I smile politely and he returns the gesture awkwardly.

I hold the door open behind him and look left, toward Simon and Chelsea's, and wonder at what point in time Chelsea stopped stalking the hallway. Maybe she finally moved out. One good thing in a day full of bad.

CHAPTER 35

Present

"MR. EVANS, PLEASE sign this. It states that everything you will tell us from this moment forth will be part of your statement. After we finish our questions, you may be asked to write down a summary of our discussion. Do you understand you are being recorded?"

"Am I under arrest?"

"No, this is more of a witness statement. Do you understand that you are being recorded?"

"Yes."

"Good. What is your full name and date of birth?"

"Simon Reynolds Evans. May 14, 1989."

"Address?"

"It's the Mulholland Oaks Apartments...I don't know the street number. It's on Glenvale."

"What is your apartment number there?"

"6G. It's on the sixth floor."

"And when did you meet Deanna Madden?"

"Deanna? Uh...years ago. Right after I moved in."

"When did you meet Jeremy Pacer?"

"Around the same time."

"And what was your impression of their relationship?"

"He was the delivery guy. They didn't have a relationship. I mean, back then. Now...I don't know if they're just fucking or what, but he's there a lot. Sorry, am I allowed to say *fucking*?"

"Yes. Ms. Madden gave a statement that says you lock her in at night."

A long pause. "That a question?"

"*Do* you lock her into her apartment at night?"

"Well...only 'cause she asks me to. That's not illegal, right?"

"Why do you lock her in?"

"She says she sleepwalks. So I normally lock her door at night, unlock it in the morning. It's called being neighborly."

"Did you lock her door on the night of August 19?"

"When was that?"

"Night before last. Sunday night."

"No."

"No? Why not?"

"She told me not to."

"So you did *not* lock her door on Sunday night."

"Nope."

"It was unlocked all night, she was free to come and go as she pleased?"

"Yeah."

"Last question, Mr. Evans. Does Deanna strike you as a violent individual?"

"Violent? Out of everyone in our building, she's the person who scares me the most."

CHAPTER 36

Present

JessReilly19: something's up with Jeremy

HackOffMyCock: in what way?

JessReilly19: he's not answering my calls or texts. His phone is going straight to voicemail

HackOffMyCock: for how long?

JessReilly19: two days. Plus he isn't delivering my packages. Some new guy showed up.

HackOffMyCock: I'm sure that went well.

JessReilly19: well, you know me

HackOffMyCock: give me 20 mins, let me see if I can track him down

JessReilly19: thx babe

HackOffMyCock: anything for you

HackOffMyCock: u there?

JessReilly19: yep

HackOffMyCock: when did you say the cops came by?

JessReilly19: Monday

HackOffMyCock: well...his truck's at his house. It hasn't moved in days. And the last place his cell pinged was near your place.

JessReilly19: meaning what?

HackOffMyCock: who the fuck knows? It's weird. When's the last time you talked to him?

JessReilly19: Sunday night. I think we got in a fight.

HackOffMyCock: a normal girl guy fight? Or...

JessReilly19: Maybe Or...I don't know. Everything is really strange right now.

HackOffMyCock: think the cops are talking to you about Jeremy?

JessReilly19: I hadn't even considered that. But now... I don't know. You think something happened to him?

HackOffMyCock: maybe

JessReilly19: well that's definitive. Thx

HackOffMyCock: its hard for me to know anything from Massachusetts.

JessReilly19: I have 2 go. Need to think.

HackOffMyCock: ok

JessReilly19: bye

---CHAT ENDED: JessReilly19 has left

CHAPTER 37

Present

"MS. EVANS, I understand that you work for the department in Forensics, is that correct?"

"It is. I started three weeks ago."

"Did you work the Jeremy Pacer scene?"

"Yes. I was called to the scene when the body was discovered. My notes are in the file."

"But you also know Jeremy Pacer?"

"Yes. We met about the time I started with the department."

"And you've also met Deanna Madden?"

"Yes. The same day I met Jeremy."

"And what was your impression of Deanna?"

"Hostile. Unfriendly. She and Jeremy seemed to have...a very strange relationship."

"Please elaborate."

"A lot of fighting. Mostly her screaming, him trying to calm her. She seemed to fly off the handle over every little thing. And it seemed to be the norm. I mean, he wasn't surprised by it, best I could tell."

"And what was your impression of Jeremy Pacer?"

"A nice guy. Kind of the strong silent type. I'm pretty surprised..."

"Surprised by what?"

"Well...that she could do that much damage to him. She's so tiny. He...there was just so much blood."

"But you do think she's guilty?"

"Oh, absolutely. I'd bet my life on it. There's...well, you've met her. Almost an evil about her."

CHAPTER 38

Present

MY APARTMENT'S FLOORS are concrete, painted over thirty-some years ago with white latex paint. In some places, the paint peels. In others, it's worn through, a dirty tan shade beneath. I kneel on the floor and scrub, a green Scotch-Brite pad in each yellow-gloved hand, protection that extends up to my elbows. The concrete is hard, my knees damp against my jeans, and I work my way from one side of the apartment to the other.

Scrub.

Scrub.

Scrub.

Scrub.

I stop every three or four feet to pour down more bleach and to wipe up behind me.

Scrub.

Scrub.

Scrub.

Scrub.

Scrub.

I open the window and stick my head out. Sunday night's rip of cardboard making today's to-do list one step shorter. Inhale to clear my lungs. Look down a hundred feet, at the crumpled mess of dirt, grass, and trash, and get dizzy. Pull in a breath and my head, walk back, and get back on my knees. If I wasn't hiding evidence, I'd turn on my webcam and do this naked. Get a few thousand bucks richer in the six hours this is taking.

Scrub.

Scrub.

Scrub.

Scrub.

Scrub.

And this is only step one. Step two will involve powder, then solution. Step three will involve another round of bleach. The floors, then the walls, then the windows. Somewhere in the corner of my mind, Lil Jon gets crunk.

"Move in with me."

I looked up from the magazine, my elbows on the bed, belly flat, feet kicked up to the ceiling. "I can't." Not that I hadn't thought about it. I had. Thought, envisioned, fantasized. It'd be great. We'd do laundry together, have impromptu sex, make late-night brownies, and pick out throw pillows. Then I'd kill him, and the fantasy would be over.

"Come on . . . it's got two bedrooms. You could have a separate one if you wanted."

"And leave all this?" I tossed a sloppy hand out, sweeping it around in a gesture that encompassed all of the grandeur of the Mulholland Oaks apartment building.

He laughed, putting a knee next to me on the bed and sitting down, his hand rolling me over onto my back, then lifting me up and toward him until my head rested in his lap. "Yes. Leave all this. The new house is gorgeous...but it's lonely. It needs you."

I made a face. "I saw the pics. The new house needs nothing. You're a big boy. Fill it with masculinity and fishing pictures."

He tucked a strand of hair behind my ear and stared down at me. "Please?"

I sighed, looking up and meeting his eyes. God, those eyes haunted me. They were golden retriever eyes, the kind that begged while putting all of their trust in you. "I can't. You know that. I like it here. This...this is my safe place."

"I want to be your safe place."

"You're not. You're...you're the door to everything that isn't safe. And it's okay. It's what I love about you, but it's also what scares me."

"Just say it again." His thumb was soft when it brushed across my mouth.

"I love you."

He smiled. "Think about it."

I smiled. "Okay."

But I never would have moved. I knew that. He had to, deep inside, know it too.

Scrub.

Scrub.

Scrub.

Scrub.

Scrub.

I got up and moved the table, dragging it over to my cam bedroom. Then I went back and got each of the chairs.

"I don't need that." I watched him carry in each of the chairs, my brows raised. I don't have room for chairs. I know every foot of this place and use it all. Chairs and a table are something I'll have to navigate around. I'll trip. Bruise myself.

"Yes you do. Everyone needs a table."

"I've done perfectly fine without one for three years. Haven't missed one once. I could have ordered this myself, you know." I was beginning to get irritated, especially as he carried in the large box, a toolbox balanced on top. "Is this going to take long? I've got appointments in an hour."

"It'll take twenty minutes, tops. Just stop bitching. If you hate them in a week, I'll carry the set out."

"And put it where?" I grumbled, flopping onto the floor and watching him. His eyes smiled when they looked at me, and I could hear the point his mind was making, but I liked sitting on the floor. Eating on the floor. This floor was the blueprint to my life.

I scooted back to the wall and leaned against it, watching him work. He moved with easy efficiency, ignoring the folded directions, his hands quick as he put pieces together and used a drill. When he bore down on the wood, his muscles clenched beneath the fabric of his uniform. When he concentrated, his forehead pinched, mouth firmed, eyes narrowed. It was surprisingly arousing, watching him work, some inner cavewoman instinct stirring in me. I see man. He works well. I want man. When he lifted the table up and flipped it over, the round piece settling on the floor evenly and without a wobble, I hoisted myself to my feet. Stood beside him and surveyed his work. "I guess you're pretty proud of yourself, huh?"

He looked over, his eyes darkening as they dropped to my face, his hands falling from his hips. "Not yet." He bent, his hands settling on my hips, and spun me up and onto the table, my knees opening, his body pushing in, his hands sliding to and gripping my ass, pulling me to the edge of the table. "But I'm about to be."

Scrub.

Scrub.

Scrub.

Scrub.

Scrub.

CHAPTER 39

Present

"MR. MALCOVE, PLEASE tell us about Jeremy's girlfriend."

"Deanna? Not much to tell."

"Because?"

"Because we never met her. It's pretty strange. You see, the five of us all hang out together, all the time. And the girls are always part of that. Some of my girl's best friends are the other guys' girls. That's just how it is, when you've been friends as long as we have. But this chick...she was different from the beginning. Jeremy never said much about her, and has avoided bringing her by, for anything."

"Did you ask him about it?"

"Did we ask him about it? Man...yes. *Hell* yes. All the time. It's our main thing to pick at him about. Thought he had a quadriplegic or bug-eyed girl, or some other crazy shit he was keeping from us. But then he showed us her pictures and, well...we shut up after that. He wants to keep that smokin' hottie to himself, then whatever. I mean, he's probably worried she'll get tempted. I was prom king, you know that? Senior year,

Altoma High School. 2003. I can send you a copy of the year-book page if you want it."

"We don't want it."

"Well, I can. If you change your mind. Just let me know. Anyway, Jeremy's our pretty boy and all, but sometimes the girls like a man that's a little rougher. Like me. Maybe that's why he hasn't ever brought her around. Or maybe... maybe she ain't real after all. I mean, shit, have you seen her pictures? Girl could be one of those Victoria's Secret models, seriously."

"Did they fight a lot?"

"Fight? Man, I don't know. Like I said, he's all tight-lipped about that girl. But I know he's whipped. *Seriously* whipped. When she calls, he jumps. And he doesn't give two shits what we think about it. That's... I've known that kid twelve years and this is the only time he's ever been like this over a girl."

"Thank you for your time. We'll call you with any further questions."

"What's this about, anyway? J in some kind trouble with the girl?"

"Would that surprise you?"

"J's clean. Always has been. He wouldn't get involved with anything shady."

"What if she asked him to?"

"I don't know. I don't think so. He's whipped, but he isn't stupid."

"Again, thank you for your time."

"Wait—you never said what was up."

"We're not at liberty to discuss this with you, Mr. Malcove."

"Well that's some bullshit. I had to leave work for this."

"I'm sorry for the inconvenience. I'm sure you'll find out more soon. If you are, after all, good friends."

"Who do I talk to about validating my parking?"

CHAPTER 40

Present

WE SHOULD MOVE for a warrant." Brenda pushes an energy bar into her mouth and balls up the foil, stuffing it into a pocket of the car door.

"Too early. We won't get it."

"Mort will. If we get him late in the afternoon. Nap time. Brosky said she approached him then, and he all but gave her his firstborn grandchild just to get rid of her." The words tumble out through granola, a speck of matter flying out and landing on the center console.

"For God's sake, Brenda." He glares at the piece of food. She lets it sit there. "You really think this girl's got it in her?"

"I can't believe you don't. You're letting her pretty face turn you stupid."

"And you've been wanting a female killer since you lost the Howard case. You gonna clean that off?" He shifts in his seat, his feet stretching out, hand reaching for the glove compartment for a wet wipe. This is why she drives. No one can maintain his level of cleanliness and stay sane. Or married. The man has two ex-wives to prove it.

She swallows the last bit of granola down with a swig of bottled water. "I still say that bitch did it. You men don't understand the depths of our psyche. Hell, I come close to killing you about three times a day." She smiles at him and rescrews the lid to her water, flicking at the piece of food and watching it bound toward the floorboard. Beside her, David lets out an irritated sigh, a wet wipe finally in hand. Pansy.

"You talk to Chelsea Evans yet?" He glances over as he asks the question.

"Yeah, questioned her yesterday. It's in the file. Why?"

"Had a voice mail from her this morning, wanting an update." He balls up the dirty wipe.

She shrugs. "She's a rookie. Doesn't know the ropes yet. I'd bet you it was her first time ever being questioned. She probably just wants to make sure we got everything."

"Well, you call her back. Last thing I need is a newbie crushing on me."

She laughs in response. "That newbie might be the key that cracks Deanna Madden wide open."

"We got bigger shit to deal with than this chick. You know that, right?"

"Talk to me about that at Jeremy Pacer's funeral, when we still don't have an arrest."

He looks out the window, across the street and to the apartment building, a prostitute on the front steps raising a middle finger in greeting. "Hopefully it won't come to that."

"That's your job, optimist. I'll stick to reality. And the reality is, this girl's guilty." Putting the car into drive, she glances over. "You done sitting here? I'm starving."

CHAPTER 41

Present

RUN THIS BY me one more time. What you have on the girl." Judge Thomas Mort sits back, the chair creaking, his eyes falling on the desk clock. The clock is dead. Its arms haven't moved in years, the dust layer dulling the brass top. The pen, stuck in its side, also dead. He should throw it out. No one would notice; his grandchildren never visit anyway. He closes his eyes, linking his fingers on his chest and dropping his head back. He'd seen the pose in a movie once, Robert Duvall assuming the position, and it had looked intelligent, like a deep meditative thought on whatever fate was being decided. The pose has the added benefit of hiding whenever said decision making led to a short nap, a frequent reprieve when one deals, as he does, with so many heavy topics each day. Why did these clowns insist on coming in the afternoon, right after his lunch? This is the third pop-in this week.

Somewhere from the right, the female detective speaks. "She's the girlfriend, for one."

"Which means nothing," he barks, his eyes still closed. "That's *why* you investigate her, not a motive for any crime."

Hell, if love and sex are suspicious, he'd be arrested a hundred times over.

"Well she's a girlfriend he seemed to hide from everyone. Maybe she got sick of it. Didn't want to be put in the corner any more."

Those lines of stupidity come from the left, from the man, and it's a dumb enough statement to crack an eye open for. He arches a brow in response before letting his head fall back to the headrest. "Tell me you didn't come here and waste my time over circumstantial theories my eight-year-old grandson could poke holes in. You guys know the drill. Stop massaging my balls and get on with it."

"Deanna Madden has a familial history of psychosis. Her mother murdered her father, along with her two younger siblings."

"She ever, herself, demonstrate any violence?"

"Hints of it, sir. Chelsea Evans, a new hire in the department, lives a few doors down from her. Madden attacked her once, in jealousy over Jeremy Pacer."

"Define attack."

"Shoved her onto the floor and climbed on top of her. Evans says she tried to strangle her."

Now he opens his eyes, sits up enough to see the woman's face. "She put that on the record?"

"Yes, sir." The woman flips a few pages in the file and slides it forward. He pulls his reading glasses onto his nose and skims the passage, then looks up.

"Is this it?"

The male detective leans forward. "Also, the proximity of

where the body was found to where Madden lives. It's less than three blocks away. Pacer's house is up in Bethany Park . . . so the crime scene is most likely Madden's apartment. Give us the warrant, and we can make a big move either toward or away from this girl. If we're wrong and she's innocent?" He spreads his hands out. "Then we're out of her hair. No more bothering her."

The judge flips through the file, glimpses of the girl's face, direct and unsmiling, peeking through the passing pages. He turns pages forward, then back, then forward. Finally, he snaps the file shut and tosses it across the desk.

"Limited search. Luminol up the place, poke around a bit, then get out of her hair. I don't want a lawsuit coming out of this, you hear?"

"Thanks, Judge." They stand as one and the woman leans over, pushing a form forward.

He scrawls his name across the bottom, then looks up. Nods somberly and waits for them to leave. Wonders if he'll have time for a nap before his next interruption.

CHAPTER 42

Past

MY APARTMENT WAS pitch dark when someone knocked on my door. When I opened my eyes, I didn't move. I was on my back, one leg kicked free of the covers, the other toasty warm. The right side of my face was sticky and I lifted a hand, wiping at the drool at the corner of my mouth. I rolled onto my side and slid a hand under the pillow.

Knock knock knock.

I sat straight up, my heart beating, a pause passing before I scrambled from the covers, my ankle tangling, my body pitching forward, and I rolled off the bed, trying to find my bearings and wondering what time it was. So dark in the apartment. I moved to the door and grabbed the handle, pushing to my tiptoes and looking through the peephole.

Simon had a hand on the door, his weight on it, his chin lifted up, eyes on the peephole. Something caught his attention and he turned his head, said something too soft for me to hear. He made a fist and pounded on the door, and I waited. Thought. Waded through the final layers of sleep.

"Simon." I called his name during the fourth set of knocks.

"Deanna?"

"Stop fucking knocking."

"Okay." Simon. Such a polite little waker.

"What time is it?"

"Uh... four something."

"What do you need?" I squatted down and eyed the door frame's crack. The dead bolt was in place. At least he'd done something right. My psychosis twitched. Damn him for sticking to the rules.

"I have to go to Oklahoma City. I won't be back till late tomorrow night. So... uh... you know today, the..."

"You can't lock me in?"

He looked confused for a moment, then shook his head. "Oh. No. I mean... yes I can't lock you in tonight but today is the first. So... uh..."

Oh. Right. This wasn't about concern over my lock-in. This was about his drugs, the day he waited for all month. The trip must be important; the kid scheduled his bowel movements around getting his pills. "The delivery. You want me to hold it?" I could have Jeremy give me the package from Dr. Pat. I could hold it for Simon. No biggie. Let him stop by when he gets home tomorrow night. Could even invite him in. Tie him down and feed every last pill down his throat. Pop some popcorn and watch the excitement. I traced a finger over a dried drip of paint on the door. Scraped my nail over it and watched it drop to the floor. I've neglected this door. I used to spend a lot more time here, a piece of me pressed against its cool metal, a

TV dinner or laptop on my knees, loneliness my best friend. I almost miss the simplicity of that time. Back then I had no expectations of anything else. No aspirations, no fantasies other than those that involved death. I just existed, worked, breathed, behaved. I was content. And others were safe.

"Just tell the UPS guy to give them to my sister."

"No." I'm not having that bitch sit in my hall all day and wait for Jeremy. Not gonna happen. I'm not gonna be able to work all day knowing she's out there, hearing her giggle. The day before, she sat in the hall on her cell and carried on a twenty-seven-minute conversation. I know that because I timed the damn thing. And I had better things to do with my time than listen to her on the phone. She didn't even discuss anything relevant. It was the stupidest, most pointless conversation I had ever eavesdropped on, the bulk of the chatter around a *House of Cards* plotline. After they'd exhausted that topic, and touched on a new OPI polish color (Over the Maroon and Back) and bitched about Delta's new policy on carry-ons, she finally hung up. Heaven forbid the woman has more friends. More conversations to conduct. More unintelligent chatter that might occur should she have to wait on Jeremy. At least Simon is quiet when he waits. He just leans or sits and plays Bejeweled. Occasionally he'll groan, or cheer, or pop his gum. Sometimes he paces, an entirely silent activity. But Blondie... She'll be loud and annoying in her waiting, I have no freakin' doubt about that.

"Come on...*please*. I never ask you for anything."

I frown and turn over the sentence. "You ask me for things

all the time." More pills, more pills, more pills. It's a freakin' mantra out of his mouth. Though, to his credit, I never say yes. Does it count as a question if the answer is always no? I think it does. He slammed a hand against the peephole and I flinched, then cursed myself for the weakness. "Back the fuck up, Simon," I snarled.

He lifted his head and stared at me. "Just give it to my sister. That's all I'm asking."

"Jeremy can give it to me, you can pick it up from me. I'm not going anywhere, I'll be here. You'll get it at the same time as before."

"But you'll be locked in."

"Not if you're not here to lock me in." That stopped him and I could see the mental struggle, his stagger as he tried to work through the pieces in his mind. I tried not to be excited, tried to stop my mind as it went to the dark, to all of the possibilities that a night of freedom might mean. *How late?* I wanted to scream. *How late will you be back? Will I have a second night of freedom? Or will you return at the disappointingly early hour of ten?* I could feel my breath quicken, the gentle tremor of my fingers.

"I have to lock you in." He said the words so quietly I almost missed them, his head down, the words not direct. "You've always said, it doesn't matter what you say to me at night, I have to lock you in."

Damn him. The man fucks up his entire life a hundred different ways a day yet somehow, through the haze of whatever cocktail he's currently on, remembers the cardinal rule, the one that I've spent three years pounding into his brain. I watched him step back, his hand falling off the door. "Please give them to my sister."

Then, ignoring the scream from my mouth, he turned and headed toward the elevator. I jerked at the knob but it didn't move.

CHAPTER 43

Past

THE MORNING AFTER Simon's late-night visit, I slept in. Screaming for forty-five minutes at an empty hall is, apparently, my cocktail for a good night's sleep. I don't know what it says about my neighbors that no one once pounded on the walls or screamed at me to shut up. I guess the soundproofing really does work. Either that, or they've gotten used to a litany of ridiculous noises from my apartment.

I finally fell asleep curled against the door, wrapped in a comforter, my neck at an odd angle that I'd spend the next twelve hours paying for. I assumed, when I did finally drift off, that the unlocking of my door in the morning would wake me. It didn't. Mainly because it didn't happen.

When my mind did crawl from sleep, I blinked in the lit room, then rolled my neck, wincing at the ache. I stretched out my legs and pushed slowly up, the comforter falling off me. Plodding over to my phone, I checked the time. Ten fifteen. Late again. I glanced down, approved the cami and matching panties, and grabbed a bottled water from the fridge. Drank half, rinsing out my mouth, spit, then finished off the bottle.

Took a leisurely tour of my cam setup, flipping switches, turning on my laptop, cameras, and lights, then flopped on the bed and logged in. Smiled lazily into the camera.

"Morning, boys."

The morning crowd is always a pleasure. A mix of foreign souls up late, work-from-home dads, and at-their-desk addicts. I greeted the regulars, had a dozen ten-minute flings, and took a break just after noon, a thousand bucks richer.

I was sitting at the round table, a bowl of Jenny Craig oatmeal half-eaten, when I noticed the door. I paused, carefully setting down the spoon and standing, taking a few slow steps in its direction, my journey still too fast to accept reality. When I reached the door, I slid to my knees and stared at the crack, at the gold glint of the dead bolt, still flipped. I closed my eyes and went back through my early morning conversation with Simon. Tried to place where, in that conversation, we'd discussed his unlocking me this morning. Tried to remember if I had told him not to unlock me. Came up blank on all counts.

I have to go to Oklahoma City. I won't be back till late tomorrow night.

Had he meant right then? That he was leaving right *then*? He had walked away from his place, toward the elevator. Hadn't returned, at least not in the forty-five minutes I'd spent screaming for him. It was Saturday morning, meaning...he'd be back Sunday night? I glanced toward the window, at the small hole in the cardboard. Remembered pressing against the cardboard, my nails scratching against its surface, poking and picking until the hole had emerged. Remembered pressing my eye to the hole, searching for his car on the street below. Remembered alternating between running from the peephole to the window, anxious for a glance of him, a continuation of our conversation. Now, in the morning's normality, I see my craziness. The complete lack of sense in my actions. What was I so panicked about? What had I hoped to accomplish by screaming? I couldn't exactly, while swallowing the forgotten scoop of oatmeal, recall what the huge deal had been. He'd wanted me to give his pill delivery to his sister. That had been the gist of the entire interaction. Not a huge request. But...I'd said no. Can't really remember why. Spite, probably. And he'd walked away. Which left us...where? And why in holy hell hadn't he unlocked my door? Or had her do it? I felt a rise of panic at the thought that I was locked in, a push of claustrophobia. What if something happens? What if there is an emergency? A hundred things that could happen at any given night yet right then they seemed terrifyingly possible. I breathed in, then out, in, then out, and carefully walked back to my seat at the table.

I won't be back till late tomorrow night. At one, my bowl was washed, teeth were brushed and flossed, the door was still locked. I should have been back online; my clients would wonder. But I couldn't. I sat, I stared, I contemplated.

The main question was whether Chelsea had the key. That was what it all boiled down to. Either Chelsea had the key, or I was locked in until Simon returned. And if Chelsea had the key, why hadn't she unlocked the door? The bitch. Goes to show that, in four years of undisturbed precedent, she'd be the one to fuck it up.

I moved my waiting game to the door. Leaned against it, my eye to the peephole. Considered calling Jeremy, but I didn't really know what to say. I hated, more than anything, hearing "I told you so." And that's what he'd do. He'd bitch and moan about how, for a year, he'd been telling me that this was a horrible idea. How I shouldn't put my livelihood in a druggie's hands. How I should give him a copy of the key in case of emergencies. How he should lock me in instead of Simon, if I insisted on the ridiculous precaution to begin with.

But I didn't want Jeremy locking me in. For one, because it'd set the wrong tone to our relationship, one where I was no longer the dominant but instead the submissive, him literally holding the key to my freedom. Fuck that. The second piece to that puzzle is what happens when I struggle. When I claw at the door and beg for release, the breaking of my soul when the darkness drags it under and suffocates its life. I didn't want him to see me like that. I didn't want his cell to ring at three a.m. with a psychotic, bloodthirsty girlfriend on the other end. I didn't want that image to stick, grow roots, and overtake anything good that we'd built. And it would. His becoming my keeper would be the first rock in an avalanche of disaster.

I heard a door shut and pressed my eye closer to the peephole. Saw the blonde wander down the hall and stop in front of my door. Stared into her face when she lifted up her hand and knocked.

CHAPTER 44

Past

SHE HAD PRETTY eyes. Go figure. Simon's sister, with her painted nails stretched out for my boyfriend, had pretty eyes.

Well, so do I. So there. I narrowed my pretty eyes and wondered what to do. A person knocks, you answer. This girl knocks....Answering seemed too passive, too subservient. I wished I could yank open the door and tackle her.

She knocked a second time. Leaned forward and licked her lips. Opened her mouth and spoke loudly, as if I wasn't *right* there, as if she needed to call out through an apartment's worth of space. "I know you're in there."

Of course she knows I'm here. What a dumb waste of five words.

"It's Chelsea, Simon's sister?" This girl should really just not speak at all. She didn't seem to understand the point of meaningful communication.

"What?" I couldn't help myself. The response fell out of me, half fueled by my desire to end the entire interaction.

"Has Jeremy come by yet?"

An incredibly rude question. Her casual use of his name, like she had ownership of it. The complete lack of mention of my door being locked, her idiot brother the cause.

"Yes."

"He has?" She glanced at her watch, then up at my door. "Shit. I thought he came in the afternoon."

"It varies. He came about an hour or so ago." There are times when I am really and truly brilliant. I'd like to think, at that moment, that this was one of those times. This lie... it was going to be my crowning achievement of the week. I almost rubbed my hands in glee. Instead, I cooled my jets long enough to assume an irritated tone. "I couldn't open the *fuckin'* door, so he left." The curse was the punctuation of my sentence, the underlined exclamation that said *you messed up* in gigantic capital letters. I would have patted myself on the back if it didn't interrupt my view.

"Are you joking?" She turned her head, putting her ear closer to the door. Her ears were pierced up the sides, four baby rings in the one closest to the peephole. If I slid a pencil through them and ripped, her scream would be delicious.

"I'd love to be joking but I'm not. And thanks to whatever idiot didn't unlock me this morning, I missed a package a hell of a lot more important than Simon's drugs." Redirection. The glitter that distracts an ugly lie.

She swore and I smiled. A moment of success before I realized I was still locked in the apartment. "Do you have the key?" A painful question to put out, one that put me on my figurative knees before her.

She chewed on her fingernail and that told me all I needed to know. I slammed a palm on the door. "Open the door."

"I'm not supposed to open the door until I have the package."

"Aren't you a cop? What are you doing picking up drugs for your brother, anyway?"

She looked up. "They aren't drugs."

I laughed, hating the peephole for a brief moment. In its skewed view, I couldn't tell if she actually believed the crap spewing from her mouth. "You know they're drugs."

"My brother has a lot of problems." She looked down the hall. "It doesn't make me love him any less."

Problems? Join the freakin' club. "Enablers don't love. They ruin." I know this. I enable myself every day, and look at me. A mess of indecision and barely controlled hell.

"Well." She ran the wet fingernail down the front of my door, and I hated the action.

"Well." I repeated. "Where's the key?"

She glanced to her right, toward Simon's apartment. "In the apartment."

"Get it." I should have added a *please* but I'm not good at pleases and thank-yous. Especially not for this chick.

She didn't like it. I saw it in the narrow of her eyes, the step back she took. I closed my eyes and tried to relax my vocal cords. Tried to sound pleasant when my mouth opened and words came out. "Please. Do you mind getting the key? I'm going a little stir-crazy in here."

She stepped closer, like a kid to an aquarium tank. She, the grubby toddler, I the lazy shark who stared through the glass and dreamed about eating everyone in sight. "Why do you lock yourself in, anyway? Simon says its because you sleepwalk."

Why ask a question that you already have the answer to? I swallowed that question and tried to continue the ridiculous pleasantries. "I do. This isn't really the neighborhood to wander around in in the middle of the night."

She laughed, tucking her hands in her back pockets. *Good lord, please tell me this woman isn't wanting a friend.* "You're right about that. This place is a shithole." She winced. "No offense."

"None taken." I fought the urge to ask for the key again, society's prerequisite for idle chitchat not quite fulfilled. "How long are you staying?"

"Not sure. I'm looking for a place now."

"Do you mind getting the key? I've got to get to the pharmacy." I shouldn't have said the pharmacy. That would remind her of the drugs. I should have said the grocery store...or the post office...or wherever normal individuals head on Saturday afternoons.

She tilted her head, pulling down on the front of her shirt, the move deepening the V of her cleavage. *Hooker.* "Sleepwalking isn't that big a deal. I mean, people do it all the time. There's got to be something else you can do."

"You're right. My mistake. I'll stop this arrangement with Simon and let him get his drugs somewhere else. I'll be sure to tell him you suggested the change. Thank you for clearing up my night issues; this conversation has been so helpful. Now, since he's *not* locking me up anymore, I won't need to pay him with pills. Unlock my fuckin' door or else I'll call the cops and tell them you're keeping me against my will." I tried to be friendly. I really did. But the woman had it coming. Refusing to unlock my door. Making stupid suggestions about things that she knew nothing about.

Hooker didn't like my response. She stepped back, her face hardening.

Then I heard the elevator.

CHAPTER 45

Past

JEREMY RODE THE elevator with two packages, both with Deanna's name on them, only one that would go to her. He shook the smaller of the two, the rattle inside causing his frown to deepen. Two floors before he'd have to deal with that punk. He rolled his head back, the pop in his neck doing little to alleviate his stress. Deanna needed a new system; there had to be another option. Hell, he'd offered ten times to do it. Better him than Simon. Just the kid's name gave him the creeps.

When the doors opened, the first thing he noticed was Chelsea. He hated that he already knew her by name. Hated worse the small lift that hit his step, the surge of testosterone that quickened his heart. Sexual attraction, that's all it was. Nothing that compared to Deanna. Nothing that tugged on his heart the way her smile did. It was only a man's ingrained reaction to a female, pure human nature. He didn't see Simon, and smiled for that reason. Only that reason.

Closer, he saw her scowl, her eyes drop to his parcels, heard the low hum of her voice as she said something toward Deanna's door.

"What's going on?" He stopped a step away, pulling his arm out of reach when she reached out, an aggressive move, his body turning to keep her at bay.

"Don't give it to her." The growl came from Deanna's door, and was laced with venom. He turned his head, surprised. Deanna wasn't exactly the kind to hide behind a door.

"Is that the package for Simon?" Chelsea stood on his other side, her hand still reaching for the parcel, a finger pointing toward it accusatorially. "I thought you said he already came." That comment she directed in Deanna's direction, and he went from confused to completely lost.

"I lied." Satisfaction in Deanna's tone.

"I'm not unlocking you unless he gives me the package."

Whoa. What? Jeremy turned his focus on the blonde. "She's locked in?" He stepped forward, and her face blanched a little in response.

"Simon told me not to unlock her. That she had a rule about being unlocked—"

"Liar!" The scream through the door was so livid that Chelsea jumped.

"Jeez," she huffed. "I'll go get the key. No need to get your panties in a wad." She looked at Jeremy, holding up her index finger. "Don't move. I'll be right back." She stepped backward, holding eye contact with him.

"Hurry," he spit out. When she shouldered open the door to the apartment, he turned his head to Deanna's door. "What the hell did I just walk into?"

"I'd have convinced her to unlock the door." Deanna's voice had dropped ten octaves in anger. "But this works too."

"You shoulda called a locksmith. Or me."

"I don't have anything else to do today. It's been mildly entertaining. But yes, a locksmith was my backup plan."

He leaned a shoulder on her door. "This reminds me of old times."

She laughed, her muffled voice closer, and he imagined her leaning against the frame. "Our courtship? Miss it?"

"I'd say yes, but the sex is too good." He grinned and heard her laugh. Yes, having her in person was ten times better than from afar.

"Good point."

Three doors down, Chelsea reappeared, a key chain in hand. Her face stony, she came to a stop, dangling the keys out, waiting for Jeremy to step out of the way. He stayed in place and held out his hand for them.

"Let's trade." She nodded for the package.

He tilted a head toward Deanna. "The boss says no."

She laughed softly. "And…you always do what she says."

He smiled. "Pretty much."

She smiled back, and he regretted the connection as soon as it happened, their eyes meeting as she dropped the keys into his open hand. "I'd let you take control."

"Good. Gag her for me, Jeremy." Deanna called out, a muffled thud following the angry jiggle of the knob.

He laughed despite himself, flipping the key ring over and inserting the lone key into the lock. It turned easily, the dead bolt loud in its motion, and the door flew open, a hundred and twenty pounds of fury acting on the other side. There was a blur of pink and black, Deanna's hair streaming behind her as she launched herself onto Chelsea.

"Shit," Jeremy cursed, tossing the package of pills inside the apartment and going after her, his girlfriend's weight now on top of the blonde, Chelsea kicking and screaming underneath Deanna's concentrated effort to, from all outward appearances, strangle her to death.

CHAPTER 46

Past

IT'D BEEN OVER six months since I had last had my hands around a throat. Since I had felt the bend of tendons and the puff of breath. I didn't have the hand strength to squeeze a throat to death; it takes a good minute of concentrated effort, but GOD it felt good. I straddled her waist, wrapped my hands around her throat, and whispered every curse I'd held in to her face as it darkened underneath my grip.

Jeremy broke the moment, his hand tight on my arm, his fist rough when it gripped my ponytail and ripped backward, hard enough to bring tears to my eyes and a yelp from my throat. "Jesus, Deanna. She's a cop." *She's a cop.* I knew that, somewhere in my mind. Had forgotten it once, twice, a few times since Jeremy had first told me. But I heard it that time and stumbled back, into his arms, the heat of his touch grounding me, the strength of his chest against my shoulder blades comforting, the black dots in my vision fading as I found my bearings. My breath was too loud, panting like a rabid dog, my hands shaking as I grabbed at the wall and stood to my feet. I pointed at the girl, watching her feet find carpet, her hand at her neck, wincing as she touched her throat, her eyes cutting across the thin space at me with a look that could kill. Ha. Right back at you, sweetie. "Stay away from me," I spat.

"You crazy bitch," she swore, the curse diminished by her fit of coughing that followed. "I'll have you arrested for that."

Jeremy stepped between us, his hands up. "You provoked her, Chelsea. I'm pretty sure imprisoning someone against their will is a crime."

"Not to mention bartering with illegal narcotics," I called out from behind him.

"You're just as guilty of that as I am," she said.

"I'm not a cop."

"Both of you, go back to your apartments." When my man spoke, it had bite. Bite that turned me on. I flashed him a grin and he glared at me. Reaching forward, I grabbed at his belt, hooking two fingers underneath the top of his pants, and kicked open the door, pulling him in with me. He didn't resist, pushing the packages inside before stepping into my apartment, his palm swinging at the door and slamming it shut.

❖

When Jeremy turned to face me, he was mad. I saw it in the lines of his forehead, the rigidity of his shoulders, the strength of his stance. He was mad, which was inconvenient, because I was horny. Dr. Derek would find issue with that, with the correlation between a violent outburst and soaked panties. But it wasn't my hands around her throat that had made me horny, it'd been the force in Jeremy's tone, the aggression in his vowels, the order. *Both of you, back to your apartments.* On the plus side, a woman being aroused by her man's dominance is entirely sane, so maybe this was an item I could share with Dr. Derek. Omitting the strangulation incident, of course. Dr. Derek doesn't seem to respond well to slips.

"Jesus, Deanna." He stepped forward and I stayed in place. When he gripped my arms, the squeeze hurt, the intensity of his grip painful. I looked up into his face, the pinch of his features saying as much as the fear in his eyes. "You can't do—you can't fly off the handle like that."

"She locked me in. She wouldn't unlock the door."

"No, Simon locked you in. Like he always does. *You* created that. That's your doing. She should have unlocked you, yes. But you are the catalyst for this situation. Own that."

I tried to step back and he held tight, the second time that day I was in a place I didn't want to be. I looked down at his right hand and he released me. Stepped back and ran his hands through his hair. Spun away from me, and that hurt more than anything. This wasn't *my* fault. This was *her* fault. I was just defending my freedom, asserting my opinion, giving her what she deserved.

"She's a cop, Deanna." He spoke toward the pile of boxes, his head down, back tight, shoulders hunched.

"I know that."

"Do you? 'Cause I don't know a hell of a lot about your secrets, but I'm pretty sure that the one thing you don't want is a cop getting pissed at you."

I turned away, walking to the fridge and grabbing a water. Didn't offer him one while I twisted open the top. There, take that. My shun via poor manners went completely unnoticed, and a small part of me mourned.

"I don't have anything to hide." My lie came out white and confident and beautiful. If it were on paper, I'd have had it framed.

He didn't even laugh, just shook his head. Pulled out his keypad and scrawled my signature on it. "I've got to go."

"Just like that?" I set the water bottle down.

"Yeah. I can't... I just can't deal with this today."

I just can't deal with this today. I just can't deal with you today. That's what he was really saying, in between his pauses and tight muscles, in between his eye contact with her and his curses at me. I watched him walk out and said nothing to stop him.

It was a quiet moment when the door clicked shut behind him. Too quiet for the magnitude that it was.

CHAPTER 47

Past

IT TURNS OUT that worries over my relationship are stronger than thoughts of death. I was free, my door unlocked, Chelsea licking her wounds in some dirty corner of Simon's apartment, and all I could think of was Jeremy.

"I can't...I just can't deal with this today."

He can't deal with this. And then he left. It had been eleven hours since I stood at my window and watched his truck pull off. In eleven hours I hadn't thought about killing once. Not even Simon, the very thought of whom made my blood boil. All I could think of was what I'd put in jeopardy. I ignored the late hour and picked up my cell. Called the person I knew would answer, and who would ground me.

He was asleep. I heard evidence in the rasp of his hello, the soft clear of his throat, his second hello, which sounded more professional than the first. The first spoke of messy sheets, a dark room, a bare torso, cock semihard in his boxer briefs.

"Hey, Doc."

"What's wrong?"

"Nothing." I wet my lips. "Everything."

"You red?"

I laughed. "No. For once, I'm not red." I was black and blue from years of emotional beatings. Gray as dust from solitude.

He sighed. Not one of exasperation or relief, but the gentle exhale one makes when they relax back in bed, their head settling into the pillow, their eyes closing. "Tell me."

I told him everything. About the lockout. The fight through my door. Jeremy's arrival. My break.

"Did you really want to hurt her? Or were you just expressing anger?"

I slid my back down the wall until my butt hit the floor. Considered the question. "Are you asking if I was in control?"

"People lose their tempers all of the time, Deanna. Normal people. I lose my temper. Most people's don't turn physical, but a lashing out is normal. I'm asking you if that's what this was."

I closed my eyes and tried to return to that moment, to that place. To what I felt when that door finally broke open and I had the freedom to move. How Jeremy wasn't even a consideration, his audience to my actions inconsequential. I had stormed, I had grabbed, I had screamed and wrapped my hands around her neck and wanted to kill her.

But would I have stopped? In an empty setting, in the middle of the day, with no one there to pull me off, no night urges to combat…would I have stopped before her skin lost its heat?

I think…I think I would have, which is…surprising to say the least. Especially considering how much I really hate that bitch. I'd never really asked myself that question before. Not that I'd had my hands wrapped around too many throats. It wasn't my ideal way to kill, took a lot of hand strength and endurance. We're talking about consistently squeezing a cord of struggling muscles for a good minute or two. It's difficult. A knife was so much easier. And fun.

"Yes." I interrupted my mind's fall down its slippery path. "I think it was just anger. I don't think I would have killed her."

"That's a great exercise to work through, Deanna. We can control anger and reactions."

"Well, honestly, I don't care if I did kill her. I was calling you about Jeremy."

He chuckled, a long, low sound. "Oh...Deanna. We have so much work to do."

I like midnight Derek. He lectures less and uses his bedroom voice more.

"What's the issue with Jeremy?"

"He pulled me off of her, pushed me inside. Was *mad* at me about it."

"It's a lot for someone to swallow."

"Yeah but..." I dropped my head against the wall and looked up. Noticed a healthy collection of cobwebs on the overhead light. "He seemed frustrated. Said he couldn't deal with it."

"I've told you to be up front with him. To explain your disorder."

"I have. Mostly. I've told him about my urges. He kind of pushes them to the side." And I didn't chase the issue and shove it down his throat. If Jeremy didn't want to believe I was a psychopath, that was fine with me. I didn't need to roll a dead body in front of him. I kind of liked the starry-eyed way that Jeremy looked at me. And, when I wasn't shoving him out the door so that I could be locked in, we felt like a normal couple, with a normal relationship, and I felt like a normal girl. I liked that.

"Was this the first time he saw your violent side?" I heard the trap in his question. Derek thought I hid violent activity from him. I'll just set that sentence to the side and let it be.

"Sorta. I mean, you know what happened when we met." When I jumped naked off my bed and tried to kill him with my bare hands and later, his box cutter.

"You have to see this hole in your relationship. You have one hiccup and he's running away."

"It's kind of a big hiccup," I pointed out. "It's not like I was late to dinner."

"It's you. If he's in love with you, he needs to be in love with all of you, not just your good side."

My good side. Do I have a good side? That's a long discussion I needed to have with myself someday. Though a current toss-up of that subject would delay the processing of what Derek just said. And the excellent point that he just made. I leaned forward and examined the dark blue polish on my toes.

"Deanna?" Of course he wanted a response.

"What are you doing right now?" I sat back, away from my polished toes, and closed my eyes.

"I'm in bed."

"What do you look like?"

"That's not really an appropriate question."

"I've looked for you online. No pictures. That's weird. Most people have pictures." A confession I never thought I'd voice, but it hovered in the air between us.

"That's the pot calling the kettle black."

I opened my eyes. "You've googled me?"

"In a purely professional sense."

I looked left, to the mountain of technology that was my cam production. "I'm not big on pictures."

"Well...neither am I."

"You can send me a pic. I won't tell anyone."

"Let's talk about something else."

"You alone right now?" The question jutted out from my lips and hung there, a step in a direction he never lets me take. I closed my eyes and begged him to answer it.

"Yes." Short and sweet, without the elaboration I would have preferred, but I'd take it.

"Me too."

"What did Jeremy—"

I spoke quickly, before the sentence grew a point. "Please don't ask me about Jeremy. I don't want to talk about him anymore."

"Whether you talk about it or not, you need to think about it. What's healthiest for you is a strong relationship, built on an honest framework." His voice grew strength when it was on topic.

He and I, by that thought process, could never be in a relationship. I'd buried enough lies between us to dam a river. I wondered what a relationship with Derek would be like. If it'd be a hundred different analyzations or a perfectly executed coordination of emotions. I wondered if it'd be heaven or hell.

"Think I should call him?"

"Yes. Always yes. Communication is what is most important."

"Okay." I looked back down at my toes. "Thanks for answering."

"You know I'm billing you for this, right? I'm on after-hours rates now. Double."

I smiled. "Yeah, yeah. Send me the bill."

"Good night, Deanna." I loved the way he said my name.

"Night, Doc." I hung up the phone and looked at the display. Eight minutes thirty-two seconds. My average cam session lasted longer. I wondered if my clients end our chats feeling as conflicted as I did right then. I opened my phone log and scrolled down to Jeremy's name. *Communication is what's most important.* I locked the display and pushed myself to my feet. Headed to the closest dresser for something to wear. Grabbed FtypeBaby's keys off the hook on the way.

CHAPTER 48

Present

IN THE STATE of Oklahoma, there are a variety of conditions that must be met before a warrant is issued. I researched the conditions, did my due diligence, and then waited, my butt on the floor, back against the door, a paperback in hand. On the second day, the second paperback, I hear the elevator, hear the steps, hear the voices. Voices that don't belong to any of the fifteen residents of this floor. I press my good ear to the door and listen, try to gain a sliver of insider knowledge in the moment before they knock. When I open the door, there is a moment of standoff.

"I'm not sure that you understand, Ms. Madden. You have to let us in." TheOtherOne. This guy again.

I fold my arms across my chest. "I understand that this is the second time you've bothered me in three days." *Is it Jeremy?* I want to scream the question but bite my tongue.

"We have a warrant, Ms. Madden, to search your apartment and your vehicle." I envision dirty hands across FtypeBaby and want to snarl.

"Searching for what?" I snatch the page from his hand.

"Please step aside, ma'am." Oh, there she is. The pit bull in cheap Dockers. EyelinerCop. I watch her stroll around the man and step forward, into my space, close enough that I can pretty much guarantee you her lunch involved meatballs and onions.

I step aside. I step aside and watch them walk in. Wonder, as the man nods and passes me, how much evidence they'll find.

How many loose ends I've missed.

CHAPTER 49

Present

IT'S HOT IN the house, summer officially here, the sunshine taunting Mike through the windows. Maybe he should open the doors. Let in the breeze. Move to the backyard and sit in the sun. Take off his shirt and actually get a tan. Thinking about it, he pulls his shirt over his head. Grabs at an abandoned bottle of water and finishes it off. Moves to the closet and tosses the shirt in the hamper. Grabs a fresh one, and vows not to sweat through this one. It was finally time for the AC. He flips the switch on the thermostat and prays that it works. Hears the slam of Jamie's car door and wheels to the living room. Two p.m. The woman is nothing if not regular.

The front door latch switches and the door flies open, one Toms-encased foot the catalyst, a swift kick in its center causing it to slam into the wall. "You expecting a box?" Jamie's pile of red curls pops through the front door, quickly replaced by her ass, the shimmy of her body working a large cardboard box through the front entryway.

"Not particularly." This is interesting. Mike hadn't gotten a package in ages, his last one a "care package" from Mom and

Dad, an inappropriate gift for a man his age. But this isn't a care package; that much is immediately obvious. It's large, the cardboard heavy duty, a full roll of tape securing it. He moves closer, his head tilting to get a better look, his name printed in clear block font on the front, the return address blank.

"No return address," she says ominously, her head jutting out alongside his. "Maybe it's a bomb."

He shoots her a sidelong look. "That's optimistic."

"I'm just saying. Let me run across the street before you open it."

"Grab me a knife to open this with before you run for your life."

She flounces off and he hefts the box onto his lap. Shaking it, he listens to a muffled shift of contents. It's not the worst way to go. One bomb. Poof. An end to a lifetime of wanting a woman he'll never have. How painful is love if you embrace death as an escape from it?

A minute later, a pair of red scissors are thrust before him. "Here. Your knives suck. I couldn't find a sharp one."

"Thanks." He turns the box on his lap and opens the scissors, glancing up at her. "You gonna cross the street or die with me?"

She rolls her eyes. "Go ahead. But note this moment in time as the day I was brave."

"The day you were nosy," he corrects.

"Open the damn thing."

It is pretty exciting, the thousand different possibilities of what this box can hold. The unknown sender, all of the tape, the narrow chance that he is risking his life just by opening it. Sliding the sharp edge of the scissors across the top of the box, he slices through the line of flaps. Undoes the sides, taking his time and prolonging the expectation. He'll have plenty of time to be disappointed by the contents. Best to ride this high as long as he could. He sets aside the scissors and pulls back the first flap. Braces for an explosion but the air is quiet.

Behind him, Jamie lets out a noisy exhale. "Dodged that bullet."

"Shh," he hushes, and flips back the second flap. Slides his hands inside and lifts out a large box, the size of a tool chest, the black wooden lid ornate and carefully carved.

"What's that?" she whispers loudly and he turns his head to glare at her.

"Sorry." She holds up both of her hands, then makes the zipping motion across her mouth.

He refocuses on the box, running his hand carefully over the top. Pushes his fingertips into the carved design, over the gold hinges. Picks his fingernail over the lock on the front. Tests the hinge and finds it doesn't move.

"It's locked." Captain Obvious behind him huffs, as if it is her present that is unopenable. He sucks his lower lip into his mouth and fights to not snap. Sets the wooden box on the table and reaches back into the box for the card, a yellow envelope that has slipped down into the packing peanuts. The front of the card is blank; he flips it over and works at the seal. Twists away from Jamie and opens it.

You never got this.

The message is written on a blank white card, the edges crisp and expensive, the oddest message he's ever gotten, via card or any other method. He flips the card over, another

message on the back, along with a small key taped to the card.
I'll want these back.

You never got this.

I'll want these back.

Whoever sent the package needs to work on their tenses.
He peels the key away from the card, his excitement growing.
Grabs the box from the coffee table and fits the key into the
lock. Holds his breath as it turns. Beside him, Jamie leans forward, her cinnamon breath fanning the air between them, the
energy in the air high with expectation as he lifts the lid.

There is a long moment as they stare inside.

"Well," she finally says. "Guess your knife problem is solved."

He looks down, into the box, his eyes dragging along the
neat row of knives, each in their own place, a strip of felt holding them down, the green suede doing nothing to undermine
the sharp glint of silver. At least twenty, lined up like soldiers,
each primed and ready for action. His mind flips to an image
of Deanna, astride a stranger, the flash of a knife in her hand.

At least he knows who the package is from.

cops showed up today

The girl works fast. He closes the lid and wonders how many
of the blades are stained with blood.

CHAPTER 50

Present

I THINK, AFTER debating the reasons for most of my life, that I understand why some individuals smoke. It's the same reason that we instinctively reach for our cell phones during a lull in brain thought. It's the need to do something with our hands, our mouths, our bodies, something to distract us from that which is life.

I have never smoked, yet right now, I want a cigarette. I lean against the wall and watch three bodies search my space. The room gets darker when the front door opens and Chelsea Fucking Evans waltzes in, wearing a black vest with Crime Scene Investigation on the back. I bite back an objection and wonder if she's blabbed to EyelinerCop our tussle in the hall. I'm sure she has. Chelsea seems to like to talk. I feel her eyes on me and stare straight ahead, find EyelinerCop and track her movements. That woman I like. There's no rhyme or reason why; she seems to hate me with every vein in her body, and maybe that's why I like her. She doesn't hide her feelings, lets her venom show, has practically lifted her middle finger in my direction with her body language and words. I respect that, want that. Should I meet her in a dark alley at night, it would be my pleasure to fight her to the death. Chelsea doesn't deserve that, doesn't deserve to stand in my apartment, doesn't deserve to touch my stuff. Chelsea deserves to starve to death chained to a stake in the middle of the Ozarks.

Speaking of deaths, the man...he'll die quietly. Will probably grasp his chest and say something poetic in his final moments. I spend the next ten minutes of their search trying to figure out who he reminds me of and I think it's Denzel Washington. But a softer, sweeter Denzel...like that guy who played the president in *24*. TheOtherOne would make a good president, seems fair and honest, two good qualities to have when tossing my apartment.

The other guy in the mix is someone I've never seen before. He shook my hand when he came in, introduced himself as Mark. Hasn't looked in my direction since, but blushed bright red as he went through my camming bedroom. The woman finally pulled him out, said she'd tackle that, and sent him to the bathroom. He's probably going through my tampon wrappers in the trash now. How embarrassing. Thank God I flushed the applicators, but still. Would super absorbency wrappers be lined up in a photo at my trial? *Deanna Madden, members of the jury, obviously likes blood.* I stifle a smile and look to my feet. I can smell the bleach. I hope they can't. They haven't reached for the luminol yet, but I can see it on their cart, alongside evidence baggies and Tupperware containers holding who knows what. Thank God Chelsea walked in empty-handed. I don't trust her with a cartful of things, don't trust that the vest she's wearing isn't packed with incriminating evidence she plans to plant. I switch my gaze to her, watching her shift through my fridge, and think of Jeremy. It's now Tuesday and my hope for our relationship is draining fast. I didn't sleep last night, my mind ticking through the hundreds of possibilities for his silence, his absence from work, his phone going straight to voice mail. None of the possibilities are good, and the knot in my stomach has reached ulcer proportions. After these assholes leave, I will go to his house. See if he answers, sick with a dead cell phone battery—that is my most hopeful scenario right now.

I slide down the wall and sit, kicking out my feet. Watch the foursome closely and try to keep track of what is going into the evidence bags. They've taken both of my cells, my cam line and my personal one. Packed up all three of my laptops, taping them shut and wrapping them in bubble paper. Without them, without my phones...I feel lost. Floating. How will I survive in here without a line to the outside world? When EyelinerCop reaches for FtypeBaby's keys, I almost sob. They can't take my car, surely they wouldn't do that. Aren't there laws? Restrictions? They've barely asked me anything, and nothing I've said would incriminate me in my crimes. What do they have? I clamp my hands over my head and try to muffle the shouts of my thoughts. Try not to think about these invaders in my space, Chelsea touching my things, Jeremy's disappearance. A hundred stresses on an already frail ecosystem. I almost miss the movement of the female detective, her step into the center of the room, her slow stop, facing away from me. But I hear her, through my hand headphones, through the screams of my mind. I hear her call the man, and I lift my head in time to see him join her in the center of the room.

They are looking at my window. I stare at them, confused, and watch them step toward it, the man, at one point, crouching then standing, the woman pointing as if that accomplishes something. I strain to hear their words but can't, their low mumble facing away from me. The woman turns suddenly and catches me watching. Stares at me, and I raise my shoulders, stare back as if to say *So what?* I mean, seriously. *It's a fucking window.* She turns back, tilts her head toward the man, then steps forward and tugs on the frame. Tugs harder.

I smile. It's a bitch to get that thing open. For one, it's a tall window, the builders overcompensating for the fact that it's the only one this apartment gets. For another, it's got four years of me being wishy-washy, bits of dried paint all along its tracks. She finally gets it open, then she and the man kneel before it. Smart move. You look out of that bitch standing and you're one awkward skip away from falling. Though, how awesome would it be if they fell? If this whole situation disappeared in one easy moment, with the added bonus of me getting to hear screams, the crunch of bones, maybe a few agonizing last shrieks. EyelinerCop would cooperate. Give me a few bloodcurdling ones. TheOtherOne... Like I said earlier, he'd be a massive disappointment. They'd fall, MarkyMark and Chelsea would come rushing over, and I'd plant a big foot in their backs. I could kick that high, definitely. Or, should my flexibility not cooperate, I could be unimaginative and just push. Hold on to the window frame and watch them fall. Enjoy the landing, then go and get my cell phone back. Computers back. Whatever they took out of my bathroom back.

Unfortunately, their secure post on their knees puts my fantasy securely in that realm: a fantasy. I let out a long sigh and lament my limited hearing.

Did they think I snuck out? Simon locked me in, so I took the window as an escape? This isn't a fire-escape-stairwell-type building. This is a you-step-out-that-window-you-die-type building. I'm not scaling the side of that thing with a catsuit on. The woman glances back at me a second time and I shoot her my best "you're a dumbass" look. She doesn't look affected. I'll give you this, the woman has balls. May be stupid when it comes to window escapades, but she has balls. She breaks eye contact, dials a number on her phone, and lifts it to her ear, her stare returning to me. I break eye contact and attempt to read her lips. Fail horribly.

She hangs up the phone and they heft to their feet. "Mark's gonna dust the window," the woman says, reaching for my keys, Chelsea following closely, like she plans on coming along. "We're going to head downstairs, knock out the search of your car."

My car. I dig my nails into the top of my thigh. Try to smile and nod, like the thought of their paws on my baby doesn't make me want to rip out their throats. They step closer and I push to standing, unwilling to let them dominate the space. They open the door and he steps through, holding the door open. "You coming?"

I hesitate, torn between protecting my space from Marky-

Mark or defending FtypeBaby's honor. It's a long thought process, one that, around the forty-five-second mark, elicits an irritated huff from the woman. Finally, I reach for my shoes. "I'm coming."

Stepping outside. For them, it's nothing. For me, like always, it is a test.

CHAPTER 51

Present

MIKE SITS IN the living room and stares at the box. His house is silent, Jamie sent home, a goodbye laced with tension and irritation. They'd had plans. A new *Family Guy* episode to watch, lasagna to eat, weed to smoke. All gone the moment he opened that box.

Cops visiting Deanna. And now, a box of liability delivered to his house. What if cops show up here next? Ask questions, produce a warrant? How many years of jail time sit in this box? How many deaths crow at him from those blades?

He sits, adjusting his hips out of habit when he gets sore, and stares at the box. Stares at it as night falls outside and the room darkens. Finally, he leans forward, pulling the box into his lap, and moves to the dining room. Hefts it onto the table and wheels around, raising his chair until he has a better view into it. Pulls back the flaps and reaches his hand inside.

She had smiled into the camera, her eyes focused on the lens, giving her full attention. That, in itself, was rare. Most of the girls had their phones out, music on, hands flicking through their hair as they stared at their image on-screen. But she had just smiled, then blushed, pulling down on the front of her shirt. JessRiley19, her screen name said. "Hours Cammed" was sitting at the ridiculously low number of three. Her first day, and he had been there to witness it. To click on her name and take her private. She'd been so nervous. Her hands shook when she'd pulled on the straps of her shirt. He'd told her to keep it on and she blushed. He'd told her to never do anything she didn't feel comfortable doing and she smiled. He'd felt like her guardian angel and had vowed to himself that no one would ever hurt her, would never take advantage of her, would never make her cry. He'd had no idea, his fingers quick on his keyboard that day, what she was capable of.

She'd taken his advice to heart. Back then, her first few weeks online, she had been a prude, in the sense of camgirl standards. Had mostly flirted, done soft play, lots of tease work. But she'd grown sexually, had found her confidence, her footing. Found out what she liked and didn't. Got a voice and used it. And there, from his seat, he'd watched it all, saw her blossom into the Internet superstar that she is today.

Their relationship had taken a business turn three months in, when he could no longer sit quietly by and see her personal information so easily accessible. He reached out, set her up a website and secured her domain. Moved her hosting into a private server. Set up mail forwarding and ghost cell phones. Buried Deanna Madden so deep behind the JessReilly19 alias that no one would ever connect the two names. Sat back, patted himself on the back, and slept well at night, knowing that his sweet little cam princess was protected.

Then, Statesboro happened. Annie happened. And he saw a

different side of his vixen. He'd protected her, hidden her, covered for her, dug, researched, and enabled her. Broke a hundred laws and endangered himself. And he'd thought it was over; then it began again. Worse this time. Much, much worse. They'd barely made it through together. And he'd learned exactly how dark her pink persona really was. How much she was capable of. And God, if he didn't love her. For the dark, for the light. For the innocence that still existed behind her insanity. For her fight, through it all, to be good.

He pulls out the large wooden box, setting it on the table before him and reaching for the note. Opens it up and runs his fingers over the paper, her handwriting. The first time he's seen her handwriting. It is messy and awkward, as if she is out of practice in writing it. Beautiful in its imperfection, as all of her is. He closes the note and lines the card up with the box. Cracks open the box and folds back the lid. Sits back and stares at the lineup. Counts the knives, considers the guns, and rereads the note from Deanna. Closes his eyes and wonders if, one last time, he'll protect her.

A stupid question. He'll protect her to his death. He's failed once. He never will again.

CHAPTER 52

Present

THERE IS SOMETHING creepy about having this girl behind you. And that is the thing that was pushing this whole movement. The crawl across her skin when she was with this girl. Detective Brenda Boles knew killers. And now, walking down the hall, with the soft squish of the girl behind her, she knew.

They get on the elevator, a group of four, the girl moving to the far side of the car and pushing herself against the wall, as if they are toxic and she needs space. She had wondered if the girl would come outside, could see the mental ping-pong game that had gone on behind those intelligent eyes when she'd posed the question. Simon and Chelsea Evans had both stated that the girl didn't like to leave the apartment. The girl herself had said she "didn't get out much." And no one in Jeremy's world has ever met her. Yet...she has a car. And, from the DMV records, not just any one, but one worth being driven. The elevator stops, on the bottom floor, and she steps back. Gestures for Deanna Madden to go ahead, which the girl reluctantly does. Brenda smiles to herself and steps off behind her, David rounding the corner in the lead and pushing on the exit door. It'll be interesting to see David's reaction to the car. She hasn't shared what she found on the DMV, saved up this tidbit just to spice up the warrant search, should it get boring.

"Which one's yours?" David stops outside the building, a chain-link fence to their right, enclosing, in halfhearted fashion, the square piece of concrete that is the parking lot. Before them, a menagerie of cars, from rusted Toyotas to tricked-out Caddies, to... through the sea of crap, a midnight-blue Jaguar F-Type convertible. Deanna raises her arm slowly, pointing, the look on her face that of a five-year-old who is forced to share her toy. "The blue one," she mumbles.

David looks. Pauses. His head whips to Brenda, and his eyebrows raise, Chelsea shifting behind her on the concrete. She's done the math. Three years of his salary sits before them, two cars over, a fat cat in the middle of starvation. How, in the seven months since her purchase, this car hadn't gotten jacked was beyond her. Hell, her Galant had been robbed twice. Maybe that was the issue. This thing was too hot for the boys to touch and her Galant... well... wasn't. Or maybe the little girl with the big eyes had earned her spot in this neighborhood.

David and Chelsea walk forward; she stays in place. Cars aren't really her thing. The girl beside her, that is.

"Is he going to find anything in there?"

The girl turns her head and considers her. Then shrugs, smiles. "Depends on what he's looking for."

Brenda looks forward, the trunk quietly opening, David moving around its back. Well. *That* was a new response.

"You know he'll die." The words are a test, a pull at one of her seams to see the reaction. David will kill her, doing this out of the station, without Miranda rights read.

The girl turns her head and meets Brenda's eyes. Looks, for the second time in the last fifteen minutes, off. Confused. And...for the second time, Brenda herself feels off-kilter. She watches the close of the girl's lips, the movement of her throat when she swallows, the hesitation that is pushed through. Finally, her lips open and an unexpected word comes out.

"Who?"

❖

Best I am aware, everyone I have killed is in the ground. Gone. No chance of them popping up their heads and having tea. There is no wondering *if* they'll die, it's done. I was there for the final wheeze of their lungs, for the falter of life in their eyes. I stand in the parking lot of the Mulholland Oaks complex and, for the first time, wonder if this is all a mistake. Could it be that this *isn't* about me? Isn't about my victims?

When Brenda responds, the name floating through the air like a bad scent, I inhale it. Cough on its poison. Reach out and grab for solidity, something to hold me up. Her arm comes out, I ignore it. Reach, stumble, reach, stand. I am standing, I can do this. I look over at her face and smile. I don't know why I'm smiling, but I'm smiling as widely as I can and the smile is keeping me sane, keeping the scream in my stomach where it belongs, and I don't know what to do because the name she just spoke isn't right, can't be right, it's not Marcus or Ralph or Momma, it is pure and beautiful and will live to be a thousand.

No, Jeremy Pacer will not die and I will cut out your vocal cords and wear them as a necklace so you never ever have to worry about misspeaking and saying those words again. No, Jeremy Pacer will not die, because he is far away and someplace safe and I know this because he is mad at me because of something I did and mad people don't die, they get drunk with their friends and bitch about their girlfriends and kiss strangers like Chelsea. No, Jeremy Pacer will not die, because I love him and I've never loved anyone except for Momma and Daddy and Trent and Summer and they are all dead and life is not that cruel. No, Jeremy Pacer will not die, because he broke my nose a few nights ago and I don't know why and I ripped the cardboard off the window and woke up on the floor and have been haunted by police and *ohmygodwhathaveIdone.*

CHAPTER 53

Present

I DIDN'T KNOW about the other officer, a cop outside the complex. I didn't know but through my stumbles, and silence, and moment of hell, I hear his shout. I hear the shout and turn my head and see the black uniform on the black cop standing on the black pavement. He shouts Brenda's name and cups his hand to his mouth and I strain in my shoes for his words because they will be different and a distraction and I need a distraction right now. And my sneakers bite into the pavement and my knees bend when he speaks.

We've

The word leaves his mouth in slow motion and I can hear it clearly, my legs pushing off.

got

I need to be there, he has found something, I can see it in his stance, in the cry of his mouth. I will rip the item from his hand and prove EyelinerLiar *wrong* and everything will be okay.

blood

The wrong word, a bad word, a word my madness loves but I hate, especially right now, especially with Brenda's *Jeremy*

Pacer lie so fresh off her stupid lips. My right foot leaves the ground and I will sprint toward him and he will be wrong and maybe I'll never stop running until the entire world is on fire and everyone but him and I are dead.

When Brenda's arm closes around mine, it is hard and strong and cruel. I am jerked back and the man comes from nowhere and no one is watching FtypeBaby and *where are her keys* and then my hands are behind my back and I feel cold metal and everything stops when the man wastes his time and opens his mouth.

"Deanna Madden, you are under arrest for the attempted murder of Jeremy Pacer. You have the right to remain silent. Anything you say can or will be used against you in a court of law..."

I find my sight and it collides with Brenda. She stares at me and I see confusion and am, for a moment, comforted. Then, I lose control and scream.

I can only keep crazy confined for so long.

PART 2

They say that if you love something, you should let it go. I should have let Jeremy go. Let his life slip from my fingers and onto its own path. I should have opened my mouth and spoken the truth, bared my soul, confessed my sins. Watched his eyes widen and his feet step back. He would have left; he would have let go. Despite the words of love that fall so often from his mouth, he would have run. Any smart man would have. But I didn't. He was the one clean thing in my life, so I held him close. Seduced him further, let him love. I was too selfish not to. It's my fault, in a hundred different ways, what happened to him.

CHAPTER 54

Past

I BOUGHT JEREMY'S house and closed on it without ever setting foot on the property. Strange to be here now, past midnight, the lights inside all off. The front porch is dark, unable to show off the polished wood floors, the decorative fans that the MLS listing had bragged over. I reached forward and rang the bell.

I waited, curling my toes against the plastic foam of my flip-flops, hearing the chime ring and fade, ring and fade. Saw the light when it went on in a back room, most likely the master, saw the dark outline as it walked down the hall, the shoulders wide and strong, the waist corded and tight, pajama pants low on hips that have pumped against me. I crossed my arms against the night's chill and waved a hand at him through the front door's glass. Wished I could see his face, see whether it broke into a smile or scowled. I expected him to reach for the switch, to flood the front porch with light, but he did neither, just unlocked the front door and swung it open. Stepped out and wrapped a hand around my waist. Dragged me inside and into his chest. Wrapped his arms around me and inhaled a deep breath into my hair. Lifted me up against his chest and carried me four steps back. Set me down long enough to move his hands to my waist and lift, boosting me up into the air and then down onto the island, his hands settling down on the granite on either side of my legs, his mouth coming down on my mouth and kissing me hard and greedy, long deep pulls, the room silent, the only sounds in the space ours. He leaned forward, my knees parting, legs wrapping around his waist, my flip-flops hitting the floor, the left and then the right. I felt the trail of his hands, first at my ass, sliding up and under my T-shirt, skimming off the fabric, our kiss breaking as my shirt was pulled off, his big hands balling up the cotton and tossing it to the side. He leaned forward, his hands brushing at items behind me, and I flinched at the crack of glass as something hit the floor. "Shh…" he said, though I hadn't said anything. Then he leaned me back, his hands guiding me onto the hard island counter, his lips soft as they trailed down my neck, and my breasts, sucking one through the cotton of my bra, then down the centerline of my stomach.

I closed my eyes and dug my fingers in his hair. Lifted my butt when he looped fingers underneath my shorts and pulled them and my panties off. Gasped when he lowered his mouth to my skin, his hot breath fanning the area first, his mouth so warm and wet and gentle when it settled, right in between my open legs. His hands slid up my stomach, each finger a pleasure center, the trail and tease and bite holding me in place and controlling my arousal, the squeeze of my breasts in tune with the chorus of his mouth. I arched my back against his touch, pushed on his head with my hands, and whimpered his name as he moved lower, taking a deeper taste of me before returning to my clit. "Please," I whispered, holding his head in place, my legs shuddering as my body seized and my orgasm took flight.

He growled when I screamed, and held me down when I curled up. His tongue was perfect, flicking across the bud of my pleasure, and not stopping, not when I thrashed against him, not when I cursed his perfection and dug my nails into his scalp. He carried me to my death, then gently swept me up to heaven, stretching the experience further than I've ever had it, my limbs trembling underneath him by the time he slid his hands underneath me and carried my limp body to his bed.

Jeremy was different that night. Harder. He ordered rather than asked. Took rather than pleaded. I turned my body over to him and he used it every way he wanted. I loved it, but I recognized it for what it was. Submittal. Punishment. A plea with him to keep me as I was, broken.

❖

I lay in between olive sheets and wondered if he picked these out. They were nice. Nicer than I would have expected. The last time I lay in a man's bed was back in college—those nine months back in the day—my nine months of normal. Away from my grandparents' house and the whispers of high school kids. Away from newspaper clippings, police reports, and gravestones. I had plucked a community college at random, electronically submitted a half-ass application, wrote an entrance essay about female empowerment, and gotten accepted. Worn colorful tanks and Ray-Bans and chugged beers in crowded apartments. Almost killed three different times, one near miss occurring in a bed just like this one. Only that bed had smelled like Froot Loops and beer, and Jeremy's smells like dryer sheets and soap. That bed had cheap navy sheets that scratched my legs, versus Jeremy's, which slid smoothly. I rolled over and nuzzled the line of his backbone. Inhaled his scent and marveled at the heat that rose off his skin, even in sleep.

I felt disconnected in his space. Like my tethers had been cut and I was floating, pinwheeling my arms yet not moving in the right direction. There was no lock on his bedroom door. It wasn't even shut, the thin crack outlined and capitalized in black. I could see the darkness creeping through that crack, stealing into and filling the space. How could he sleep with it open? I rolled right, away from his body, and put my bare feet on the floor. Pushed to standing and walked over to it, the floor quiet and cool. Long and thin ceramic tiles, they looked like gray driftwood. The Realtor had raved about them, promising durability and style. The grout in between their planks was black. The color scheme and tile combination would hide bloodstains well. I twisted the knob of the door and pushed it shut, the door settling quietly into place, no slam, no loud noises. Well made. Good for me, I'd purchased a well-built house. I turned to move back. We hadn't discussed me spending the night. It had just happened. We'd practically broken the bed making up, then collapsed on it, his arm dragging me into his chest, his kiss soft against my head, his voice sleepy when he said, "Stay."

So I'd stayed. Wrapped a leg around his hip and curved into his body. Listened to his breath settle into sleep. I'd closed my eyes and hoped for sleep. Said my prayers and sent a few messages upward to Summer and Trent. Lied a little in the update I sent to my father. I didn't pray to my mother. There are nights I do, nights I don't. I thought about my grandparents, how it had been too long since I called them to check in. In college, I did it monthly. Now...it's mostly limited to holidays and birthdays. Honestly, I think they dread my calls almost as much as I do. I thought until I ran out of things to think about.

I moved to the window and tweaked the blinds. Stared through narrow slits at FtypeBaby, who sat like a coiled cat on the curb, a devil in suburbia. I saw a shadow move and hoped for a car thief, someone looking in her windows, a crowbar in hand. *It's not murder if it's justified.* I closed the blinds and turned back to the bed. Looked at the man lying there and wondered how vulnerable he made me. How deep in I really was. Wondered if the tug on my heart was love for him or desire for the life he represented, one of freedom and normality.

"What's healthiest for you is a strong relationship, built on an honest framework."

I knew that Derek was right, that Jeremy needed to love all of me, including the dark corners. But J didn't know those corners. I've flooded our relationship with enough sexy sparkles and deception to distract him. It's easy to distract a man who doesn't want to look in the first place. Our relationship worked because we both had the same goal, to avoid the inevitable. But what was the inevitable? Was it for Jeremy to leave me because of the secrets he finds out? Or was it for me to snap and kill us both in a moment of breakage?

CHAPTER 55

Past

WHEN I WOKE up in Jeremy's bed, I cried. I shouldn't have cried. When a person wakes up to the smell of bacon, to the sound of a spatula scraping against a skillet, it shouldn't produce tears.

"Deanna." *Two tiny hands pushed at my hip and I rolled onto my stomach.*

"Go away."

"Get up!" *Trent's voice, when properly worked up, had an expectant air of authority that closely mimicked my father.*

"No. It's Saturday."

"Mom says to get up. 'Reakfast is ready."

I lifted my head long enough to smell bacon. Weighed the temptation and lowered my head back to the pillow. "Tell her I'm skipping breakfast." *My pillow was wet from drool, and I twisted my head to the other side.*

"Hi." *The whisper was directly in front of me, a huff of breath hitting my cheek, and I opened my eyes. Summer's eyes widened when she smiled, her tiny hot pink nails biting into my bedspread*

*as she rested her chin on the bed, our faces inches apart. On her
head, for some unknown reason, sat a crown.*

"Hi, pumpkin." I closed my eyes. "Tell Trent to leave me alone."

*"TRREEEEENNNT!" she hollered louder than any little
girl on earth. "'Eeanna says to GO AWAY!"*

*The little boy's hands pushed on my legs again, the sheet drag-
ging away from me as he got hold of it. I grabbed at the material
and kicked out with my feet. "Stop it, Trent! Go downstairs!" I
turned to Summer and waved my hand at her. "You too! Both of
you—out!"*

*"Deanna!" I heard my mother yell from downstairs. "Come
down to breakfast. It's past ten!"*

*"Please let me sleep in!" I called back, ignoring the dramatic
stomp of Summer, her blond curls flying, her parting look one of
indignation.*

"I'm not warming this back up for you!"

*I plopped back down. Like anyone wanted warmed-up eggs
and bacon. "I'll be fine!" I called out, pulling the spread over
my head and closing my eyes. From downstairs, something was
called up, but I missed it.*

That afternoon, I'd left for my grandparents'. That night,
everyone died. I missed the last breakfast we'd ever had had
together as a family. I opened my eyes in Jeremy's house,
smelled the familiar scent, and was flooded with a hundred
memories I'd hoped to never find again. I curled into his pillow,
rolled my lips between my teeth, and tried to contain myself,
the break of emotions pushing through, shaking my body, my
eyes burning wet at the corners. It was fucking bacon. Not a

family video of the five of us. Not the sound of Summer's giggle or Trent's shout. It was Jeremy, probably attempting to be sweet and cook his insane girlfriend some breakfast. I needed to be normal right now. I needed to be bright and grateful and sexy. I needed to be the girl who wrapped her arms around his waist and squeezed his ass. Who crunched on bacon and perched on his counter. I could be that girl; I could play that girl. I closed my eyes and pretended the cameras were rolling, hot lights on. I pretended I was in my pink bedroom, with a hundred clients before me. I pretended I was Jessica Reilly and rolled out of bed.

"Please tell me that's bacon!" I called out the words and checked out my reflection. Wiped a smudge of mascara under my eyes and blinked rapidly. Put a skip in my step and rounded the corner, skidding across the floor and meeting his eyes, a smile easy and natural when I saw him there, shirtless, in blue boxer briefs, the love on his face when he smiled at me warming every corner of Jess Reilly's soul.

I stepped closer and he reached for me, holding the spatula out of the way as he hugged me, the pop and sizzle of the pan behind us. When he dipped his head I lifted my chin, and smiled against his kiss when he pulled me closer. Hard. My man was hard while scrambling eggs. I giggled and pushed him away.

"Not yet." I rounded the corner and pulled up a stool. "I'm starving. Food, then sex."

He winced and pulled a plate from the cabinet. "Well then...in that case, let me feed you."

I smiled, I ate every bite. I knelt on his new couch and

moaned his name as he took me from behind. But I never forgot about the bacon. And I never washed my family from my mind. Not that morning, not that day, not even now.

I could play the part.

I could walk the walk.

I just didn't know how to make it stick.

❖

After bacon and eggs and sex, we washed the dishes, Jeremy's hands in the suds, mine on a towel. Our elbows bumped, his wet hand occasionally brushed mine, and there was a moment when he pressed against me and put a gentle kiss against the back of my neck. Once the dishes were washed, we moved to the couch, his arm looped around my shoulder, my head resting on his chest. And I realized, my bare feet digging under a throw blanket, that it was the first time we'd ever been on a couch together. We watched *Andy Griffith* episodes, then a show called *Beachfront Bargains*, and discussed vacation destinations we'd try and houses we'd buy. Pretended, while he ran his fingers through my hair, that we had a chance at that future. Then, in the third episode, he lifted me up and slid behind me. Lying down, he held me against his body, his breath warm on the back of my neck. I closed my eyes, wrapped in his arms, and didn't think about the clients who were waiting for me, missed appointments ticking by. I enjoyed the moment, in his house, in his arms. I enjoyed the moment and drifted off to sleep.

Four hours later, the sky newly dark, streetlights flickering on, we pulled FtypeBaby into my complex. When we stepped off the elevator, his fingers were looped through mine, the swing of our hands in tune with our steps down the hall. I moved my thumb slightly and it brushed against his knuckles. He glanced down, at our hands, then at my face, and smiled. "I love you."

My next step cut off his path, my free hand moving up and pushing at his chest, his resistance weak, his back hitting the wall at the same time as my lips met his. I released his hand and grabbed at his shirt, gripping the blue fabric and pulling it out of place, his mouth responsive against mine, pushing back, the palm of one hand sliding down my back and into my jeans, squeezing the top of my ass as he leaned against me and deepened the kiss. When I pulled off, he smiled at me from under the brim of his baseball cap.

"I love you too." I grabbed his hand and pulled, his back lifting from the wall as he followed me. I couldn't help myself, not when he said those words I so desperately craved. And yeah, a part of me wished that the hall rat saw us. Saw the connection that she had no chance of breaking.

I kept his hand in mine those final steps. As I twisted the knob and shouldered the door open. As I stepped inside, I pulled him toward the bed, one imminent goal in mind.

I didn't know. I didn't know that it would be our last moment.

CHAPTER 56

Present

THE POLICE CAR smells, the handcuffs put my wrists at an uncomfortable position, digging into my spine, and I can't evade the glare of the afternoon sun. None of it matters. I close my eyes against the sun and rest my head back, the hell in my head drifting down into a muted chaos. I climb the mountain of thoughts in my head and try to find the top. A lie. Brenda had lied. *Deanna Madden, you are under arrest for the attempted murder of Jeremy Pacer.* No. Never. *Attempted murder. He is not dead.* One good current in a sea of bad.

Seconds pass in the silence of the car. I turn my head and shift in the seat. Rotate and crane until I can see the huddle of cops, Chelsea on its flank. The car I sit in is on Glenvale Street, the front of Mulholland Oaks stretched out in all of its depressing squalor along the side of the car. *We've got blood.* The man had yelled from the front of the building, from the place around the corner of where they now stand, looking behind the pitiful bushes that lie in front of the brick, in the thin alley of nothing where bums like to sleep and cigarette butts and beer bottles collect like leaves in a neglected gutter. *We've got blood.* There?

I think of the cop, her point, focus, examination of my window. The slow turn and stare she had given me. *We've got blood.* Oh. The tumblers of my mind finally line up, the pieces turning into place, the door to awareness opening. I lift my eyes from the group, traveling slowly up the building, my stomach dropping as my eyes rise. *They think he jumped. They think he fell. They think he was…pushed?* A cop turns away from the group, ziplock bag in hand. Evidence. I lean closer, my breath fogging the glass, my eyes burning as I try to focus, try to see… a flash of metal, a bit of yellowwwwww…no no no no no no noooooo…my Spyderco Pacific. A bright yellow handle, short sharp blade. Online reviews swore it was one of the sharpest knives on the market, with an added bonus of being rust-free. I hadn't expected a true rust-free product, my mind pushing that aside with the exuberant joy of its razor-sharp edge. It's one of my favorite knives and it's in an evidence bag. *We've got blood.* I had to unlock the safe in preparation for the cops. I had to unlock the safe to pack up its contents and ship them to Mike. I had, at some point in the night that Jeremy broke my nose, locked the safe. The Spyderco Pacific, at some point in that night, had ended up outside my apartment. Covered, best I could tell from my awkward place three parking spots up, in blood. I turn away from the window and drop my head against the seat. *My window. My knife. We've got blood. Deanna Madden, you are under arrest for the attempted murder of Jeremy Pacer. Attempted. He is not dead. Attempted. He is still alive.*

The doors open and shut with quick efficiency, the two detectives getting in. I wait for the car to start, for the pull away from the curb. Sit on my question for three blocks, then speak.

"Where is he?" A question I've been asking myself for two days and I may have finally found someone with the answer. The car turns left and my body rolls right, my right sneaker pushing out and finding the floor to brace myself. I was locked in all night. Before, I thought that proved my innocence. Now, with him lying underneath my window, everything in my world is unsteady. I need to remember, I need to find my footing, but I'm worried that there is nothing solid and good for me to stand on.

"Hillcrest South."

I swallow. "And he's alive?" *You know he'll die.* That's what she had muttered to me on their first visit.

"He's in a coma."

A coma. My heart falls another story. "From what?"

"I'm sorry?" the woman turns her head and her profile is ugly.

"What caused his coma?" I roll my lips and inhale a deep breath. My nose screams in pain.

"A six-story fall from your window, along with six stab wounds."

The fall I survive, the stab wounds pry open my chest and ravage my soul. My Spyderco. Stab wounds. I run my whole life and end up slamming into my enemy head-on. Anything but stab wounds. My Spyderco, covered in blood.

The bitch reads my mind. "You like knives, Deanna?"

They'll find the order; I paid with a credit card. Even worse, my prints are all over that baby. I look out the window. "My mother did."

"But you don't?"

"I avoid them." *When I can.*

"Interesting choice of words."

I turn my head and see her watching me in the rearview mirror. "I'd like to speak to his doctor."

"Why?"

"Because I don't believe anything that comes out of your mouth."

She laughs and pushes on the brake, the car jerking to a stop at a red light. "That's funny, Deanna. I feel the exact same way about you."

A car pulls up next to us and I turn my head, a boy in the backseat leaning forward, his breath fogging the glass, his eyes widening when they meet mine, a criminal in the backseat of a police cruiser. "I've never lied to you, Brenda."

"Maybe because I haven't asked the hard questions."

The car pulls forward, and I lose sight of the boy.

CHAPTER 57

Present

SOMETHING IS WRONG. Brenda felt it before, felt deep in her gut that the girl was guilty, the girl was evil. But now...having her in cuffs, in the back of the car...something is off. She turns into the precinct's parking lot and glances at David. He winks at her and rubs his hand on the knee of his pants. He always loves a collar. She parks and turns the key, looking up and into the rearview mirror, at the side profile of the girl.

I've never lied to you, Brenda.

She is too old and too smart to be jerked around. Huffing out an irritated breath, she shoves the door open and kicks a black-toed boot outside. Time to get this bitch behind bars.

CHAPTER 58

Present

I THINK, AS I walk down the white hall, following the detectives, a stranger's hand pushing on my back, willing me forward, about my mother. Had a dozen tiny details been different, she'd have walked down a hall similar to this. She'd have pushed out with her wrists, and realized the futility of movement. She'd have heard her shoes slap against dirty floors and recognized her end. She'd have been alive and imprisoned instead of dead.

I am not my mother. But like her, I belong here. I inhale air that smells of cigarettes and cheap labor and wonder if this is the end of my story.

We turn left, a foursome of silence, and Brenda stops at a door, twists the knob, and pushes it open with her foot. "Sit down in here. I'll bring in a phone, we'll knock out some questioning, and then move you to general pop. You'll have an arraignment in a few days to determine bail options."

A few days. A hand pushes gently between my shoulder blades, and I step forward. Cross into a gray room with a black floor and sit carefully on a folding chair that creaks. They shut the door and I hear the turn of a lock.

Locked in. Some people would feel claustrophobic. For me, it's freeing.

❖

I spend the long minutes in the room deciding whom, once my one phone call privilege is allowed, to contact. I decide upon Jeremy's sister, the only member of Jeremy's family I am really aware of, and someone who, given the circumstances, probably knows the most about his health condition. I also decide that, given our complete lack of proper introduction prior to now, I should have gone to her damn dinner. Go figure.

When Brenda walks into the room, a phone in one hand, both of my cells in her other, I sit straighter. Put my feet on the ground and try to scoot the chair forward. Start to reach forward toward the phone and stop myself. Search for patience and find none. I hold one fist in my other hand and watch her sit down in the seat across from me.

"Here's the deal. You can't touch your cell, but if you need some numbers out of it, just let me know and I'll pull them for you." She pushes the phone forward, pulling a line from the wall and plugging it in.

"Numbers?" I look up. "I thought I get one phone call."

"That's Hollywood. In the real world, as long as you're not a pain in the ass, you can make a reasonable number of calls to get your affairs in order. You also only get privacy when you speak to your attorney, so keep that in mind when making your calls."

A reasonable number of calls. I look at the bare table

between us and try to think. One phone call was easier to navigate. "Okay. Do you have a phone number for Jeremy's sister? Her name is Lily."

"No."

Very helpful. "May I have a phone book?"

That got me somewhere, her head dropping, hands moving, the screech of a drawer and then, the deposit of a large book, its spine worn, cover showing its age: four years old. I pull it to me and flip through, finding the number for Hillcrest Hospital South and dialing it slowly. Underneath my hand, the receiver feels dirty.

It takes twelve minutes and two calls to get to someone who knows who Jeremy Pacer is. When I ask about his condition, I am asked to leave a message; I glance at Brenda and she shakes her head. I ask to speak to any visitors in Jeremy's room and am patched through, the ringing of the phone terrifyingly bleak.

On the ninth ring, a woman picks up. "Hello?"

I swallow. "Is this Lily?"

"Yes." Short. Concise. I close my eyes and choose my words carefully.

"My name is Deanna, I am Jeremy's girlfriend." I am, not *was*. Am. Forever and always. I pause and she says nothing. I glance at Brenda and wish I had asked more questions in the car. "Can you tell me how he is?"

"It's nice of you to call, Deanna. It would have been even nicer for you to visit. He's been here for three days."

Three days. *When I come to, the apartment is dark and I am on the floor.* I swallow. "I didn't know—no one told me."

Silence. She whispers something to someone else, and the

words are muffled. Then, she is back. "I don't have much to tell you, Deanna. He has a subdural hematoma, a buildup of blood in the brain. At the moment, he's comatose. The doctors are going to reduce his meds over the next few days, see if they can pull him out of it. He's not"—she sighed—"not in great shape."

"But he'll live?" I wrap my finger around the cord of the phone, then release it.

"I—the doctors say it's too early to know for sure. They've told me that the brain is fickle. He could wake up tomorrow and be fine for the rest of his life, or he could have a sudden rebleed and go comatose again. Or he may never wake up."

Or he may never wake up. I try to think of something else to say but come up blank. When I hang up, it is to her breathing.

I push back the receiver and look up to Brenda. She raises her eyebrows. "Who next?"

I shrug. Try to speak but can't form a word. *The doctors say it's too early to know for sure.* Try again. "I'm done." The words rasp out of me, like a gate that hasn't been opened in some time.

She frowns. "You sure? No lawyer? No house sitter? No boss or bail bondsman?"

I shake my head. "I'm sure."

A short, lonely sentence. She yanks at the cord, gathers the phone in the crook of her left arm, and heads for the door. "I'll be back."

I listen to the door slam behind her and close my eyes. Questioning, she had mentioned, would come next. Then, general pop. It will be a very long night.

CHAPTER 59

Present

MY DEFINITION OF time doesn't match Brenda's. "I'll be back," in my world, refers to fifteen minutes, a half hour. Maybe forty-five minutes if I take an extra-long bathroom break, or get distracted on Pinterest. But I have now been in this tiny room for, according to the clock on the wall, three hours. I shift in the seat, lifting my right butt cheek, then my left, off of the hard plastic, my muscles cramping from the unforgiving chair. I lean forward and lay my head on the table. Close my eyes. Roll my wrists and wiggle my fingers.

He's in a coma. The doctors are hoping to pull him out of it in the next few days. He's not in great shape.

I've tried not to think about Jeremy for the last three hours. I've thought of nothing but him during that time.

The doctors say it's too early to know for sure.

The last time Jeremy was in the hospital, it was from my actions. And I thought he was dead. And I cried when he lived. And now, he's back. It hasn't even been a year.

A six-story fall from your window, along with six stab wounds. They will question me next. But I have questions too.

Questions I am terrified of, but also need answers to. Stab wounds. I wouldn't have. Not with Jeremy.

I fumble with them briefly, then flip the blade out and straddle his body, bringing both hands together above my head. Bringing my hands down together, in one quick motion, the sharp point descends toward his neck.

I squeeze my palms together behind my back. That was before. Way before. I am not her anymore. I am more in control. I have been around him a hundred times. I have bought a car. Grocery shopped. Walked around humans and came back with clean hands. I wouldn't have hurt him. Not six times. He is stronger than me, he can control me; he's done so many times before.

A blur of his face, concerned, his grip on my skin, a tightening of his features, the hard jerk of his elbow across my face, and a blinding sea of red pain.

I push my face into the table and wince at the pain that courses from my nose. Why can I not remember?

The knob jiggles and then the door swings open and both detectives fill the doorway. I take a deep breath.

◈

She sits, he stands. I slouch back in my seat and stare at the floor. Think better of it and lift my head. "May I ask a few questions?"

The woman stops some complicated process of shuffling papers and looks up. "Not right now. After our questioning, you'll have the opportunity to ask questions. That's assuming your questions relate to the nature of the crime, and not to your rights or your judicial process. Those questions should be answered by an attorney."

I nod, she nods, and we're one big nodding family. I look at the man but he doesn't participate. "Are you waiving your right to an attorney?" the woman asks.

"For now."

She sets down the final piece of paper and looks at me. She has a fresh pimple, on the right side of her chin, and I perversely wonder if the stress of this entire investigation is what put it there. Probably not. My attempted murder charge is most likely small potatoes in her world of crime. I feel, for one ridiculous moment, criminally inadequate. She probably wants to wrap this baby shit up and go tackle a real danger to society. She lets out a breath and it sounds like a sigh. "Everything you say in this room is being recorded and can be used in a trial. Should you decide you'd like an attorney, we will stop questioning you until the moment upon which an attorney is secured. Do you understand?"

"I'd like to go ahead and get this over with."

"As would we. This will go a lot quicker if you are honest with us." She looks at me and I wonder what she doesn't understand about getting this over with. After a long, wasteful moment, she continues.

"Where were you Sunday night?"

"At home."

"Were you alone?"

I hesitate. "Yes."

A blur of his face, concerned, his grip on my skin, a tightening of his features, the hard jerk of his elbow across my face, and a blinding sea of red pain.

I bite my lip. "I think so."

"Explain."

"Jeremy had come over…earlier. I mean, I spent that day with Jeremy and he dropped me off at my house that night."

Brenda had pulled a pen out and held it to the paper, scribbling down words as I spoke. She stops, the pen tip pausing. A red pen. Those notes would be hell to read later, like lines of blood. "Did he come into your apartment?"

"I love you too." I grabbed his hand and pulled, his back lifting from the wall as he followed me.

"Yes." The crack in the wall of my memories crumbles, and a fresh wave pushes through. Nothing new, information I've known. Information I've hid from. Information that runs without brakes down a path that falls off a cliff.

"What time was that?"

I blink and twist my lips, considering the question. "I'm not really sure. Before nine. Probably seven or eight. I remember thinking we'd have time…before Simon locked me in…"

"Time for what?" The man steps forward, leaning over the table and placing his hands on the surface, his left pinky on top of one of Brenda's pages. I see her glance at it and look away. I don't look away. I look up, into his dark black face, and wonder if he has a daughter, one my age. He's certainly old enough. That's gray in the sides of his hair.

"To fuck." I enunciate the answer and watch him flinch. I like his flinch.

"And did you?" the woman drawls out the question, without missing a beat.

I look away from the man. "I don't think so."

"It's not the sort of thing most women forget," he says quietly.

"No." I bite the inside of my cheek. "We didn't."

"Why not?" God, this woman was pushy. And nosy.

Yes, Deanna, why not? I remember stepping in the apartment, my hand in Jeremy's. Then…all I can remember is red. And Jeremy swinging. And…somewhere at some point…

Closing my hand around the butt of the knife, feeling the indents in the grip when I palmed it, a surge of pleasure at the illicit contact.

I swallow the memory and taste bile in my throat. "Sometimes," I say slowly, "you know…you just don't."

My bones crunched, like potato chips under the heel of a boot, and my fury, in that moment, exploded.

"Deanna? Deanna?" a hand waves before me and I focus on it. Dark palm, strong fingers, a wedding band. He probably *does* have a daughter. He should get home to her, and leave me alone. Brenda and I will be just fine.

"What?" I snap.

"You came home and did what?"

"He just dropped me off." If I say the words slowly, they will be more true. "Then he left."

"And Simon locked you in."

"Yes."

The man sighs. "Deanna, we've spoken to Simon."

This is news. I don't know why I'm surprised. Alibis need

to be verified, words can't be trusted. But it's as if the sentence opens up a new door of invasion. I suddenly remember Dr. Derek's call. They had spoken to him. And now Simon. Who else? How much of my inner circle had been touched? And what had they discovered in the process? I push back the handcuff on my right side. It's irritating, like a heavy bracelet that I keep forgetting I can't slide off. "So? What did he say?"

"He said he didn't lock your door last night. He said that you told him not to." The woman's eyes watch me closely, each dart of them quick and precise.

I frown. That's…odd. I've based so much of my innocence assumption on the fact that I was locked in. I wonder, a piece of my brain breaking off and skittering off on its own path of worry, if Simon mentioned, during this voice vomit, any other nights where he didn't lock me in. That could be problematic, a loose thread that, if pulled, could lead to…Wait, what? Could lead to me, sitting in a police station, being questioned? Could lead to my sins being exposed, my punishment delivered? I am already here, the house of cards has already fallen, my dam has broken and all of my safeguards are gone. I left the apartment. I got into a stranger's car and am in a strange room with a new fate. The what-ifs of my past…I can't worry about them now. I have bigger problems here. Like why I told Simon not to lock me in. "I thought you said that Jeremy fell from my window." Fell. Not pushed. Never pushed.

The woman nods.

"So…" I shift in my seat. "No offense, but why do you care if Simon locked me in? The lock on my door doesn't affect whether or not I pushed Jeremy from the window." *Fell. Not pushed.* I pinch the thin skin on the inside of my wrist as punishment.

"He was moved. After he fell."

I see the tension in the man's frame when the woman speaks, the quick turn of his head in her direction. He didn't want her to say that, to share that, to give me that piece of the puzzle. I want to join him, to go another step further and hold my hand over her mouth, shove back the words deeper down until they stay. *He was moved.* I close my eyes and try to remember if my bare feet had pricks of asphalt. Try to remember if my tennis shoes had moved, if my clothes had had anything on them other than the blood from my nose. I work through the layers, try to find my thought process though...when I'm red, there is often none. "So...you are saying that I asked Simon to not lock my door, then I pushed Jeremy out, ran downstairs, and moved his body."

"After stabbing him." The man interjects.

"I moved him after stabbing him?"

They look at each other, then at me. "Pretty much," Brenda says.

Pretty much. No, I wanted to say, not pretty at all.

❖

Throughout the questions I was strong. Cool. Collected. And there was a moment when I thought I might survive the interrogation. Then they pull out the photos and I break.

I recognize the Dumpster. That is my first thought. The

green slope of its front. The black lids of its top. I once stood, hands on hips, chest heaving, before this Dumpster and analyzed its feasibility as a body dump site. The funny thing is that I had discarded it. Deemed it too high in its top for me to heft a body over the side. Thought that its location, stuck behind the twenty-four-hour Quik Mart, at the end of an alley, was too public, the chance of a discovery before pickup too high. So I'd stretched before it, savored one last what-if fantasy, then jogged away. And now, here it is. In a glossy four-by-six, the photo pushed forward by one of Brenda's chewed-to-the-quick nails. I lean forward, look at the photo, and nod. "I know it."

"Here is where Jeremy was found." She pushes forward a second photo and I keep my position, expecting to see the lid open, a bird's-eye view looking down, an imprint in the pile of trash. I am surprised when I see the back of the Dumpster, in the space between it and the concrete wall. I am surprised when I see Jeremy's hat, lying on its side, the Sooners S half-hidden, the curve of its brim squashed.

When I pulled off the wall, he smiled at me from under the brim of his baseball cap.

He'd been wearing that cap, that day. I remember pulling it off his head and onto my own, when the whip of wind in the convertible had been too strong, my hair everywhere, my hair tie lost to the wind. At some point he'd gotten it back. I stare at the photo. "I was driving," I mumble. "So..."

What had been our plan? For him to stay the night? For him to take my car home? Had we discussed that? I didn't remember doing so. But he could have taken my car; it wasn't like

I was driving it. And I feel, in that afternoon, that perfect Sunday we shared . . . that we hadn't wanted to part, not even for the short half hour it would have taken to follow each other to my house. We had ridden together, and then . . . I look up and they are both staring at me. Waiting.

"Where's his truck?" I ask.

"At his house," Brenda supplies.

At his house. And my car was at my apartment, the three of us, just hours ago, standing next to it. So he didn't get home. He couldn't have. He was too busy falling, breaking, bleeding, and lying behind the Dumpster, waiting to be found.

Brenda pushes forward a final photo, and my world goes a little blacker.

When blood dries, it darkens. Not to black, that would have been more fitting, for Jeremy's face to be the color of my soul. But its loss of oxygen produces a darker hue, not the bright red cheer of fresh carnage. When this photo was taken of J, his eyes were closed, his cheeks bruised, his nose unnatural, blood caked and dried in rivers along and over his lips. He looks, in this photo, dead. And I feel, as it slides toward me, as if I am looking into his future.

One day, if something doesn't change, I will kill him. Maybe not intentionally, maybe it will be a side effect of my other actions, but he will, as a result of our union, die. It is a fact I am almost certain of, a truth I have run from since the first moment that I allowed him to kiss my lips and bring joy. I stare down at the photo and let reality fully sink in.

He deserves better. He deserves life.

She pushes another photo forward, this one showing more

of his surroundings, I can see the white of a hospital bed, bandages and stitches, the blur of a hand as it attends to him. I see the places the knife went in, six clear points of attack. The photo must have been snapped in haste, for no other purpose than to document. I glance back at the initial photo and wonder how long the blood sat before it was wiped clean. I wonder how long his eyes were closed, and if he gasped for breath or lay still as if he was dead. I wonder if, before the coma, he spoke.

I look away from the photos and up into her eyes.

He deserves better. He deserves life. I deserve containment. I deserve punishment. It doesn't matter if I don't remember it. Either way, innocent or guilty, I am dangerous—for this man and for everyone else.

I swallow and squeeze my hands together behind my back. "What do you want to know?"

"I want to know if you did it."

I stare at her chapped lips because her eyes are too sharp. "Yes."

"You did?" She sounds surprised and the man coughs, and I force my stare back to her pupils.

"Yes."

"You stabbed him?"

"And pushed him out the window." I filled in the blank.

"Hmm." I don't know why she doesn't like that. Doesn't every cop love a confession?

The man steps forward, his thigh resting against the table. "How'd you get him to the Dumpster?"

I look up. "Would you believe I carried him?" I smile; he doesn't. A shame. He smiled once during the invasive search of my property. It was a nice smile. I sigh and buy myself a few seconds. How did I get him to the Dumpster? I have no idea. I sigh again. Look down, like I am hesitant to say. "Someone helped me."

She leans forward and her breasts brush against the top of my boyfriend. Ex-boyfriend. Definitely. Relationships don't survive this. "Who?"

Yes, Deanna. Indeed. Who? "A black guy. I don't know his name. He was there, I offered money, he took it."

"A stranger?" David doesn't sound all that surprised, and he shouldn't. Not in my neighborhood. In my neighborhood it'd be odd for someone to walk from any cash, for any reason. In my neighborhood it'd be just as likely for them to help me carry the body to the Dumpster, then rape me behind it.

"Yes. I paid him five hundred bucks to help me carry him to the Dumpster."

"And no one stopped you guys?"

I look up with an expression that I hope accurately embodies my opinion of their intelligence. Brenda laughs. "Okay, ignore that. So this helpful black stranger shows up, carts away this body, and takes your cash. Then what?"

When I come to, the apartment is dark and I am on the floor.

"Then I went home and went to bed."

"Why'd you let him live?" David pulls out the ignored second chair and sits down.

"I didn't know he was alive. I stabbed until he stopped moving, then stopped." A rookie mistake I would never make. Or did I?

Brenda moves her chest off of Jeremy's face and sits back.

Taps her pen tip against the desk in an irritating fashion. "Anything else?"

I look at the photos. "Not that I can think of."

"So we can go ahead," she says slowly, "and charge you with the attempted murder of Jeremy Pacer?"

I lift my wrists and put my hands on the desk, the cuffs clanking loudly in the now-quiet room. "Go for it."

Jeremy deserves better. He deserves life. A life away from me. I deserve punishment.

❖

I killed him. Or rather, I attempted to. I pushed him to his death from my window. I stabbed him six times in the chest with my favorite knife. I dragged his body behind the Quik Mart's Dumpster and left it there. Then I washed down my apartment with bleach to hide any evidence.

I understand that I have broken the law.

I have not, nor have I ever been, mentally unstable. I was acting on my own accord and had full knowledge of my actions.

Statement: Deanna Matilda Madden

I sign the bottom, above my name, the pen biting into the cheap white paper. Then, I look up into Detective Boles's face.

She smiles. I don't. I may never smile again.

CHAPTER 60

Present

I ASSUMED, WITH a verbal and written confession, that the judicial process was, for the most part, over. That there will be some minor sentencing hearing, where the judge will pass over my sentence, then I will start my jail time.

I am wrong.

The process, explained to me by a large, dark woman who smells of lilacs, is for me to be booked first. A prosecutor will, within the next three days, decide what charges will be filed against me. Then I'll have an arraignment in court, where I will have the chance to plead guilty or not guilty. At the arraignment, my bail will be set or denied. I nod as she speaks, sign and initial when requested, and assist as best I can during the fingerprinting process. She asks me to step up to a black background and look at the camera. I stare into its eye, such a familiar eye, and wonder, in the second before the flash hits, when I will next cam. The possibility suddenly strikes that I may never cam again. I stare into its dark center. A Canon. I have a Canon. I had a Canon. In low light, when I moved quickly, it sometimes blurred. I am not in low lighting now. And I am still.

Very still. Does one smile in their mug shot? I feel suddenly like Ben Affleck in *Gone Girl*, the desire to produce a crooked smile maddeningly irresistible.

"Sit down on the chair and remove those shoes."

And my photo time is over. I sit down and stare at the black backdrop. Black draws light. Before I got ten thousand watts pumping in my apartment, I had black sheets on my pink bed. It lit my body, brightened my screen, almost better than the bulbs. I wonder if my skin glowed in the mug shot, if the black drew in the flash and distracted the viewer from my flaws. I may never again see my lights, my bulbs, my room. I may never again see my fans, my clients, my world. I may never again be Jess Reilly.

I sit down. Lean forward and pull at the laces of my tennis shoes. Pick at a knot, my mind going white and blank. Forget the pink bedroom. Forget my online world. This is the first step of the rest of my life. This is my new reality, and it is good and just. I think of the first crime scene photo, the reflective sheen, Jeremy's eyes closed. I shouldn't have called the hospital. I didn't deserve an update; I didn't deserve to introduce myself to his sister and to know about his status. I tugged the tongue of my sneaker out and worked the Nike over my heel, pulling my foot free and setting the shoe down, moving to the second. It comes quicker, and I scoop up them both and set them on my knees, looking up.

The woman holds out a hand, her nails long and bright blue against her chocolate skin. I pass over the shoes and she tilts her head. Studies me for a long beat. "You scared, honey?"

"At what?"

She chortles. "Jail. Prison. Loss of Freedom."

Ha. Scared? That thought hasn't even crossed my mind. Stir crazy? Probably. "No." How sweet of her to ask.

"You know, you're not like most of the girls in there." She tosses her head back, in the general direction of the jail. I shrug. Fitting in hasn't exactly been a concern of late.

She leans forward, lowering her voice. "Want some advice?" I don't. "Don't stick out. Cute little white girl like you will attract attention. You're going to have to deal with some rough-housing. Just keep your head down and color, you got me?"

I lean in, matching her pose, our two heads almost touching over the counter. "I gotcha," I whisper.

She sits back like she doesn't want to swap spit with a prisoner, swiveling her large body left and groaning as she bends at the waist and shoves to her feet. She moves to the door and waves at me. "Come on." I rise and follow, my socks hitting the smooth floor. Thank God I wore socks. She points to a white door. "In there."

Come on.

In there.

I come. I go in. She follows me into the room and shuts the door. "There's a camera up there." She points to the ceiling and I glance up, into a black curved piece of glass. "I got to search you now," her mouth turns down at the edges. "Everywhere. You understand?"

I nod. I understand. I pull Marilyn off my torso and unclip my bra, letting it fall down my arms. I unbuckle my jeans and sit on a plastic chair, working them over my hips and down my thighs. The room is quiet, the woman's breath soft, my own silent. Just the sounds of approaching nudity. No one has ever touched my skin, save Jeremy. I glance at the woman and her eyes are kind. She thinks the nudity bothers me. Ha.

I pull down my underwear and pull off my socks. Stand before her and spread my arms. "Go for it."

She is brisk and efficient, her latex-gloved hands skimming over my arms, shoulders, breasts. She picks through my hair, checks my ears, mouth, and throat. She asks me to lift one leg and I do. She pushes two fingers inside and I close my eyes. Turn around and feel the spread of my cheeks. I'd have let her fist it if she'd ended the exam with a hug. That was what, right now, I really wanted. A hug. She had asked me if I was scared. I am not scared; there is nothing inside of these walls that can hurt me. I am more afraid of what is in me that can hurt others.

She steps away and I lose the connection. Turns her back and I hear the snap of her gloves being pulled off. "You're clean. You can get dressed."

I look at my collapsed pile of clothes. "Back in those?"

"Yep. You'll stay in those until after the arraignment." The arraignment isn't until Tuesday. A long time to wear used underwear. I reach for the bra and T-shirt. Slide quick legs through the panties and jeans and pull them on. I take the shoes she passes me and sit in the chair.

"Anything in your pockets?"

I move forward and slide my hand into my back pocket. These jeans. I used to wear them once a week. Ice cream and lotto. That was when I was being stupid, when I thought I could rule the world because I was happy and in love. I pull out the last thing I put in there. A lotto ticket and my change.

Funny that I never pulled them out, never washed these jeans. They've sat, folded in my closet, like a dead child's preserved room, a memory of a life past lived. I look at the date of the ticket, almost five months old. Has it really been five months since I jogged down those stairs and crossed the street? Five months since I pushed on that door and had an interaction with the cashier? I pull the change out and count the bills. I'd supercharged the ticket, upping it from one dollar to two, wild woman that I was. And I must have, on that day, skipped ice cream, because eighteen dollars even unfolds. I skipped ice cream. That thought hits hard. I hadn't known that it would be my last night, hadn't known that Mike would call and things would go to hell and I'd have a lot bigger thing on my plate than cold delicacies. I hadn't known that, after that weekend, I'd change my habits completely. Withdraw. Put FtypeBaby in park and leave her alone. Settle into a cocoon of myself and hope the wrap of thin fibers kept me still. After that weekend, I hadn't allowed myself to leave the house. Not until that run last week. That grocery store trip. Then my drive to Jeremy's house. And look, now he's almost dead and I'm in a police station. So there. My cautiousness, my rules, my boundaries: justified. And it only took Jeremy dying to get me here. *Almost dying. Not yet dead.*

The woman's nails rattle against the counter and I push the cash forward. She counts out the money, blue nails fanning through the air like rainbows. "Eighteen dollars," she announces. "I'll put it under your name; when you get transferred it'll go in your canteen account." Eighteen dollars sounds like a small amount. What will I be able to buy in prison with eighteen dollars? From her expression, not a lot. She stacks the bills and puts them into an envelope. "Next time you get a visitor, have them put more in your account." She says the words matter-of-factly, like my stream of visitors will be frequent and may start any minute. I chew on my bottom lip, the fat muscle thick between my teeth, and say nothing. I will have no visitors. Of that, I'm certain.

CHAPTER 61

Present

I DON'T LIKE it." Detective Brenda Boles sucks a sip of coffee between her teeth, the wet sound of it conjuring up an image of brown-stained dental diagrams. She sets down the cup. Damn her dentist and his posters, cheerfully tacked up on walls, like anyone really wants to stare at gingivitis when getting their incisors scraped.

"Don't say that." David leans back in his chair, the front foot of it lifting up.

"You agree. You know you do." He better. Otherwise their whole camaraderie, the connection between them formed when two individuals share the same air for a decade, would be reduced to shit. Hell, a rookie could figure out right now that something smells wrong, the girl folding over so easily. Something changed in her eyes during the last hour, a glaze settling in at times, her mind taking her somewhere that was not the room, was not the questioning. Where had she gone? And what had she seen, in that place, to cause her to open her mouth and spew out that bullshit confession?

David's phone rings and he shifts, reaching a hand into the

front pocket. "Reuber," he barks. She listens, his grunts and mutters the type that traditionally lead to answers.

When he hangs up, she pounces. "What?"

"Jeremy Pacer's house exploded six months ago. He was supposed to still be in it. Barely escaped alive."

"How are we just now finding out about this?"

"The house was in his grandmother's name, over in Prestwick. He was looked at as more of a tenant; the case was determined, after speaking to Pacer, to be a home invasion gone wrong. They broke in, found nothing, and torched the place in retribution."

"Home invasions hitting Prestwick now?" Brenda asks skeptically.

He shrugs. "Blanchard and Jones took it." And that is all he needs to say. Two cops months from retirement. They probably didn't even ride out to the scene. She stands.

"Wanting to talk to Tom now?" He looks at the clock.

"Might as well. Could be a second attempted murder tacked onto Madden."

"Could be a coincidence." He holds the door open for her and she pauses, looking into his face.

"It's not a coincidence."

"Then why are you scowling?"

"Because something is wrong. I just don't know what it is."

"You know that three hours ago you were gunning for this girl with everything you had, right?"

She steps into the hall and moves toward the DA's office with purpose. "Yeah, well. Then she confessed."

CHAPTER 62

Present

I AM PUT in a cell with four others. They are spread out over
a room with six beds, two of them clearly unused, both top
bunks. I guess there is a point in life when you quit fighting
over the top bunk, and prison age seems to be it. I step inside
the door, am asked to turn, provide my wrists, and they unlock
my cuffs. Freedom. I rub my wrists and watch the door behind
me slide shut. Not free. I put my hand on the metal and stare
through the window. On the other side, the guard's impassive
face looks away, calls something to the other guard, and laughs.
I take a step back and turn to the room.

All four faces stare at me, slack and expressionless, as if the
prison walls have sucked out their souls.

I smile. No one returns the gesture.

❖

My lack of interaction with the outside world has spoiled me to
how annoying others are. Here, in a cell in booking, we are all
waiting for our arraignment, or bail to post, or for a transport.

A marathon before us of nothingness, no books, no magazines, no TV to break up the monotony. I lay in a top bunk against the wall and listen to things that annoy me.

The woman below me cracks her knuckles.

The woman standing paces, each step of her tennis shoes making a sucking sound that reminds me exactly how dirty this floor must be.

The woman in a chair, seated by the door, talks to anyone who will listen. She is here because some sumbitch at work jacked her wallet and got what he deserved. That confuses me, since in an earlier piece of the monologue, she rattled out that she works at her neighbor's house and takes care of a bunch of asshole kids. I close my eyes and picture the scenario. Kids. Sumbitches. Getting what is deserved.

No one, other than the sumbitch-getting woman by the door, has said anything to me. Which is a good thing, since I am too brittle right now. I feel as if my life has worn through my skin, like the skin has gotten thin and deteriorated, my elbows and hips beginning to poke through, the entire experience of the last two days a pressure cooker on my body, the air getting hotter and hotter, Jeremy getting farther and farther, the skin cooking like bacon under the heat, those worn edges curling up, the surface one hard push away from breaking open, my soul easing out like red-hot lava. If you poke, I will break. If I break, hell will pour out and I will not be able to get it back in.

I am just four hours in and I hate this place. Which feels familiar. Which feels right.

"Here's the key. Dumpster downstairs empties on Thursdays, and is normally filled by Tuesday, so get your trash down early.

Mailman comes in the afternoon, if you got anything to go out, have it in the box by noon." He rubbed at his nose, and a line of snot got smeared. I looked away. Trash? I hadn't even thought about that. Mail? Would I need to mail something? How would I do that?

"The utilities are already hooked up?" I was beginning to panic, I could feel the push of anxious blood, moving to my head and starting a mosh pit there.

"Yeah. You know..." He smiled and I saw a piece of pepper stuck in his teeth. "I'm right downstairs. If you need anything, you just swing by."

I nodded. I will not be swinging by. I will have to learn to not need anything. He had no idea, but this is the last time I intended on speaking to him.

He reached for the door and palmed the steel for a minute, testing it. When he turned back, he and the piece of pepper smiled at me again. "It was smart, getting a new door. You know I've been here three years and you're the only one who's had the door replaced? First off, I mean. Doors get broken all the time, need replacing. But no one ever uses a door like this." He knocked on the surface. "This thing is serious. Who you trying to keep out?"

I met his curious gaze and shook my head. "No one."

No one. Keeping out wasn't the intent. The door was for one purpose. To keep myself in.

I shut the door behind him and palmed the key. Walked to the center of the empty apartment and looked around. Too big for me, it dwarfed the size of my dorm room. Yet, when I looked at the space and thought about FOREVER, it seemed entirely too small. One year, I decided. I would stay in this place for one

year. *By then I'd come to grips with who I was. By then I'd figure out whether I was crazy or going through a phase. By then
I would find myself again, and she and I would move on to the
next phase of our lives. A good plan. I just, looking at empty cab-
inets, a lone mattress on the floor, boxes stacked with a hundred
cute outfits yet nothing helpful to a recluse...I just needed to
learn how to live it. I pulled my laptop from my bag and sat on
the floor. Logged in and found an unsecured Wi-Fi connection
close by. Brought up my bank's website and entered my creden-
tials. Stared, for the hundredth time, at the low balance.*

*Correction: I need to learn how to live as a recluse and make
money. Feed myself. Devise a way to keep myself inside no matter
what.*

*It would be hard, I knew that. I'd be poor, I understood that.
But, if this plan worked, at least I'd know that others were safe.*

*I stared at the door and already wanted to go out. One year.
How would I ever make it?*

I had moved into apartment 6E as such a confused girl.
There had been early nights when I had scraped holes in plaster, had screamed myself to sleep, not necessarily from the
crazy, but from the solitude. From the realization that I was
stuck there, staring at those walls, all by myself. For a nineteen-
year-old girl used to parties and normality, it was terrifying.

I stare at the ceiling now and think of the day I first logged
on. When I first became Jess Reilly. Dr. Derek would have a
field day with that transition. Would say I was sliding into the
skin of my old life, playing house to fool my mind into thinking
that everything was all right. And maybe that's what I've been
doing every day since. Maybe that's why the thought of leaving

camming, of leaving JessReilly19, is so terrifying. Maybe Jess Reilly has been the only thing keeping me sane this entire time.

I laugh and SumbitchWoman looks over at me, her jaw flapping shut. *Sane.* Is that what I think I've been? I sit up, rolling my legs off the side of the bed and speak to no one in particular. "Will they let me make a phone call?"

Beneath me a woman's face appears, white and pasty, her eyes mean, the folds of her eyelids cupping the hatred into place. This woman could smile, every piece of her face cooperating, and those eyes would still scream hate. "Shut it," she snarls, and her voice matches her eyes, the vowels asphalt black and scratchy, the next words harder to hear because I choose that moment to lift my foot up and smash it down onto her face.

I don't know why I did it. I've been told to shut up before. A hundred times, in fact. And this woman is no doubt stronger, wiser than me. She has to know people, have family who know people, has to have a hundred advantages over me in this space. What was it that other woman had said? Right before she bent me over and pushed her fingers inside? *Keep your head down and color.* That was it. I keep my head down as I push off the bunk, the howling woman's eyes following me from her position on the ground where my kick put her. One of my shoes landed on an outstretched hand, her scream almost loud enough to hide the crunch of her bones. Hand bones are so, so delicate. I color across her face with my heel as I give one last relatively gentle kick. I step off and away, moving forward, my view of her disappearing, the scrabble of her nails on this dirty floor the sound of a woman trying to get up. I hope she does. I hope she stands and brings that broken face closer. I hope she lunges out with that destroyed hand. I hope she tries to kick my ass. Really. Please.

I try again. "Will they let me make a phone call?"

SumbitchWoman just stares at me. I watch her jaw move, but nothing comes out. Finally, there is a wheeze of a breath from behind and I turn, looking past MeanEyes, her good hand pushing on the ground, her other lifted to her cheek, pain behind the blood on her face, a gash open on her right cheek, her nose similar to mine yet a hell of a lot worse. The fourth woman, her knees spread unladylike, her heavy girth comforting, the elbow she places on her knee thick and fat. "You could ask them," she huffs, her words hard and heavy, the effort made not lost on me, and I smile in thanks as I turn.

Oh, them. Three black uniforms at our door, one barking into a chest walkie, one unlocking the door, the other standing, eyes bouncing across the room, collecting details like trading cards. I walk to the door and wait for it to open. I speak to the only one who doesn't seem busy. "I'd like to make a phone call." I smile politely.

My smile must be broken, because in this place, no one yet has smiled back.

CHAPTER 63

Present

THE BEAUTY OF confessions is that they are one checkmark made. One task completed. One less case in a caseload of hundreds. Jeremy Pacer was avenged. When he, if he, wakes up, he will be happy to know that his attacker is behind bars. Brenda Boles can go on with her life and have one less bloodspattered crime scene to think about.

A confession. Beautiful. Except in this case, when it is not.

"I know that look." David stops before her desk, and she lifts her eyes.

"No you don't." He's holding two bananas. She reaches for one; he holds it out of reach. "No."

"You're telling me you're eating both of those?"

"Mattie says I need more potassium in my diet."

"Bullshit. You're punishing me."

"Damn right I'm punishing you. We closed a case, she's been booked, we're supposed to be celebrating over something fried and delicious right now."

"You're the one with the bananas."

"And you're the one with that damn look on your face." He sits down in the chair of the closest desk. "What is it? Is it the Henderson audio? 'Cause I told you the judge would—"

"No," she interrupts shortly. "It's Madden. The confession."

He frowns. "What's your beef with that?"

"It's wrong."

"But you said—"

"She's guilty but it's wrong."

He sighs and sets down both bananas. Her eyes follow them. The shit thing of it is, she doesn't even really like bananas. Yet withhold one and she's drooling all over the place. "Then we dig into the explosion. Go over it too."

"You know she only called one person? During her phone calls? *One.*" She holds up a finger and David nods.

"Yes, I know, you told me. The hospital."

"The hospital. She didn't even know what happened to him till we told her."

"So she's blocked it out. It's traumatizing to try and kill someone." He shrugs. Peels open his banana. She follows suit.

"I called booking. To get an update."

"And?"

"Waiting on a call back."

"It's booking. She's sitting in a cell trying not to get her white ass kicked. What are you expecting them to say?"

She takes a bite of banana. Too ripe. She eyes his. It looks better. "Maybe we should call the shrink."

"For what?"

She has a sudden recollection of his voice, the comforting

drawl in the tones, the way his voice had changed when she'd said Deanna Madden's name. "An update. Let him know his client has been charged."

"He's a shrink, what does he care? She's probably one of five hundred patients."

She pushes a boot on the edge of a file cabinet and swings the chair around. "He'll care."

"Then call him, let him know, and move the hell on."

Her fingers peel back the rest of the skin and toss it in the wastebasket. "I will," she says, pushing the final piece of fruit in her mouth. Spinning the chair straight, she reaches for the phone, brushing off her other hand before snagging the correct case file and flipping it open.

Dialing the number, she settles back in her chair and listens to the ring. Flosses her teeth with the edge of her nail. When the man comes on the line, she straightens.

"Dr. Vanderbilt?"

"Yes, is this Detective Boles?"

Oh, goody. He remembers her. "I'm calling about Deanna Madden. She's been arrested."

CHAPTER 64

Present

WHAT I DID to MeanEyes turns out to be against the rules. I absorb that information while, inside my head, a part of my brain does a little happy dance. Blood seems to do that to me. What is more disturbing, and what I muse over while I sit in a new room, by myself, handcuffs pinning my wrists together in my lap, is that the woman hadn't really *done* anything to me. As screwed up as my life has been, there was always, somewhere along it, a moral code. I killed because he was evil. I killed to save another. I killed or hurt *because* of something. But there, back in that cell, I had hurt for no reason at all. And I had enjoyed it. I have always dreaded jail. I may have been right to. This may be, after all, the most dangerous place for my brain to be.

The door opens and a new stranger comes in. He's a sheriff, not a cop, a brown uniform instead of black. I don't smile at him. I've noticed that the more I smile in this place, the more people look at me like I'm crazy. He stops before me, his hands on his hips, the buckle of his belt in my direct eyeline. "Three hours and forty-five minutes."

I don't look up. He moves his hands from his hips and places them on the table before me. Dirty fingers. I pull my gaze to them. Dirty fingers, short nails, hard hands. Has he been so busy that he hasn't had time to wash his hands? *Three hours and forty-five minutes.* I don't even have to ask what he's talking about. I already know. I know because I counted those three hours and forty-five minutes down. Every second, every minute, every hour in that room with those women was noted. "I didn't think you'd be a problem, Madden."

I sit back. God, it's hot in here. I can't be the only one who thinks so. This man, with his long pants, has to be hot too. I lift my eyes to his and realize that he's waiting on a response.

"I'd like to make a phone call."

He raises his eyebrows, twin caterpillars hopping on an ugly desert. "Oh, we all know about your need to make a phone call. I'm sure the EMTs tending to that woman's face are hearing about your precious phone call. Who you calling, princess?"

I suck a piece of my cheek between my teeth and test the gummy surface's strength. Look in his eyes and say nothing.

"You know, you look real familiar." He pushes off the table and stands, ambling around the table toward me. I watch him, the air around me infecting as he moves closer. "I couldn't figure it out, but that face... I've seen you somewhere before." He stops next to my chair and leans against the table. Lifts a hip and perches on the edge of it. I wish I were a unicorn and I could just tilt my chin down and impale this asshole with one hard headbutt.

"I thought it was from a prior arrest... but it looks like you've never been booked before." I blink slowly and wonder if he's inner monologued this whole bit. And if so, please God let him be close to the end.

"Then I spoke to one of the cops, who told me about your apartment." He moves a hand to his thigh, and I admire the way the hair on his knuckles brushes over his wedding ring. Sexy. "A camgirl, huh? *That's* when I put two and two together."

Oh. So *this* is where this asshole's thought process is headed. I lift my eyes to his face.

He's grinning like he just won something. I look at his rows of teeth and wonder how much it will hurt my fist if I punch him. "NascarGuy44." He raises his brows in eager expectation. I stare at him, my face carefully schooled into place. "That's me. Remember me?"

Is he kidding me? Not to brag about my client list, but I've cammed with thousands of men. This guy's probably a member of my fan club. Might have splurged once or twice and taken me private. A big deal for him, one of a hundred daily transactions for me. I sigh. "A phone call." At this point, I don't even know if I want the damn phone call. Not if it's going to mean more quality time between me and this asshat.

"Hey now." He has the gall to look hurt. Then he leans forward and I focus on his hand, the one lifting off his knee and reaching for me.

I don't move, everything in this world freezing as I wait. I can see my future very clearly right now. Can see the moment when his fingers touch me. Can see the moment that this space goes white and my body reacts. I reach inside, search for the place where I had just, moments ago, mused over control, morals, a bit of resolution to not be violent. I was going to control myself, learn to behave in this new place, find strength and peace in these walls. His finger connects with my cheek and trails across my cheekbone, tucking a loose strand behind my ear. I lift my eyes up to his, I can feel the heat of his breath near my eyebrow, a heavy exhale tickling the eyelashes of my right eye. I can do this. I can be stronger than this. I close my eyes. "Take your fucking hands off me."

His chuckle flips my eyes back open and I see his smile hovering in the place past his dirty wrist, a gold chain peeking from underneath his shirt sleeve, momentarily distracting me. "Now that isn't what you said to me in our chat." His hand drops down my hair and hits my shoulder, his breath heavier as his hand slides down the fabric of my sweatshirt. "You see, sweetheart, I know exactly what's underneath this—"

You know, I tried. Really I did. I can't help it that right now, my madness is stretched a little thin. I can't help it that when he squeezes my breast, hard and rough, I say *fuck it*. I can't help the fact that his small dick doesn't like the feel of my fists—he was the one who put it *right there* for me to rain down my linked hands on. I can't help it that when he wheezed and doubled over, I snapped my elbow across his scrunched face.

I've been in a few altercations with men, yet am still caught off guard when I'm hit. His punch lands on my stomach, my chair moving, falling back, my hands and feet left behind, my chest lifting forward, and that saves my head from a second interaction with a hard floor. Dr. Pat will be so pleased. I scramble out of the chair, spots in my vision, my chest struggling for some bit of air, but I can only wheeze, my feet skidding across the floor as I try to get *away*. Stupid, stupid, stupid.

Picking a fight I can't win, in a place where I shouldn't try. I close my eyes and manage one painful breath. Find footing and straighten. Open my eyes, my hands closing into tight fists, and meet my opponent's eyes. NascarGuy44 may end up kicking my ass, but I will drag hell into his life first. NascarGuy44. I'm gonna remember that username. NascarGuy44. I chant it in my mind, and raise my fists. Lift my chin and dare him to bring the fucking rain. NascarGuy44. I will personally bankroll Mike's research into and destruction of this man's entire life.

The door behind my future project opens, and I look past the asshole's face into the black woman's, the one who strip-searched me. Ms. KeepYourHeadDownAndColor. Her gaze narrows on my fists, then her head turns to the man. I can't help but smile when she speaks.

"You. Get the fuck out." He stares at me, a threat in his eyes, and steps over my chair, a big dramatic gesture that really isn't necessary, there's lots of room to just walk right by it, and passes her, his hand going to his face. Pussy.

I drop my fists and test my inhale. It doesn't hurt. She stands in the doorway, one hand on her hip, one on the door frame, her large body filling the space. "You don't follow directions real well," she finally sighs.

I shrug from the corner of the room. "Never have."

She shakes her head and looks at my overturned chair. "Shit. Paperwork." She pushes off the door frame with a loud huff. "Come on. We're putting you in solitary. Try to not pick a fight with the walls there."

I laugh and step out of the corner.

CHAPTER 65

Present

I EXPECTED MORE from solitary confinement. Padded walls, a dark place buried underground with a giant padlock on the front. A tiny slit where my meals would be slid through, three times a day.

Instead I'm in a normal-ass cell. Just like the other one but smaller, one bed instead of six. The same toilet and sink. Same walls. Same dirty white color scheme. Same smell, a combination of bleach and urine. I lie in the bed and stare at the ceiling. Wonder about that damn phone call. I should have let him cop the feel. Maybe if I had, I'd have the phone pressed to my ear right now. I practice breathing. One deep sigh, till my lungs burn and my cheeks puff. One long, long, long exhale, till my stomach cramps and my chest starves.

In. In. In. Hold.
Out. Out. Out.
In. In. In. Hold.
Out. Out. Out.

I cough. God. Six hours in and I'm bored. My master plan did not take into account the fact that I would not have a computer. Suddenly, the prospect of a year or five or ten seems impossible. What was I thinking? That I'd sinned, so I should be punished? That my apartment no longer seems to be working, so I'll take more drastic measures? I'd walked into jail thinking I'd be punishing my evil into submission. Yet, six hours in and I've already had a bloodshed fucking carnival. I reach up and touch my nose. Spread my fingers over the soft spots under my eyes. Tender. Probably both black.

In.

Out.

In.

Out.

I turn my head to the far wall where, wrapped in protective caging, the clock sits: 9:12 p.m. I close my eyes and decide to sleep.

In.

Out.

In.

Out.

This place will drive me crazy. More crazy.

In.

Out.

In.

Out.

Breathing is boring.

In.

Out.

In.

I wake when the darkness is interrupted, a bright light

flickering to life above me. I roll over, my back aching, my eyes searching for the clock on the wall. Six forty-five. Seriously? I roll to the other side and pull the lone pillow over my eyes.

I close my eyes but sleep runs a coward's retreat out from under the pillow and away. Six forty-five. These people should be shot.

❖

Sometime later, someone jiggles at my door, the sound loud and jarring, not that I was sleeping anyway. "Madden, you have a guest."

I sit up and yawn. Look at the new stranger, another sheriff's uniform hung on a person I've never seen. "A guest?" I push off the bed and stand. Maybe it's Jeremy's sister. Maybe he's woken up. *Maybe he's dead.* The second thought pushes past the first, its ugly voice loudest. "Who is it?"

The man holds up a set of cuffs. "Turn around and put your hands together."

I obey. "Who is it?" I ask again, this time nicer.

"No idea. He signed in with one of the other officers."

He. I can't think of a single He that I want to see. Except for Jeremy.

"Where are you taking me?"

"To an observation room. You'll meet him in there."

This is infinitely more exciting than breathing. I perk up despite myself, my feet speeding up in tempo, the man steering me down a hallway to the right. We stop before a door with a *4*

on it. The man pushes open the door and holds it for me. Chivalrous. I step through. "Thank you."

He nods. "Please sit down."

I sit, I am secured, then he speaks. "I'll bring him in."

I nod, a perfect picture of behaving, the room a copy of the
one with NascarGuy44. Same chair, same floor, same table.
In tiny ways different. A black scuff on the white table before
me. A break in one of the tiles to the left. The mirror to my
left is tinted blue instead of white. I lift one of my hands to my
back and try to scratch an itch, the entire production much
more awkward than it needs to be. I give up on the itch and
jiggle my right foot against the leg of the chair, and it makes
a soft tapping sound. A guest. I know a grand total of no one
in this town. Maybe it's the cop. David something-or-other.
TheOtherOne.

I flex my shoulders. Wonder how long I will have to wait.

Almost an hour later, the door swings open.

❖

The man is tall. Built but not muscular. He wears a cream
sweater with the sleeves pushed up, exposing tan forearms and
a thick watch. My eyes find his face, an aristocratic one, the
kind that took lacrosse blows as a teen and sips wine as an adult,
thick brows over intelligent eyes over cheekbones that perfectly
coordinate with a full, unsmiling mouth. Dark hair that is perfectly styled, every bit in place. He stands in the open doorway,
a hand still on the knob, the other by his side, like he hasn't

fully decided whether to come in or out. I sit in my chair, he stands in his doorway, and we say nothing.

Finally, my eyes having made the long journey across his strong forehead and down the crooked slope of his nose (a skiing accident? Or maybe polo?), I meet his eyes. Light in color, they sigh at me in studied disappointment and I know, before he even opens his mouth, who he is.

"Hi, Deanna." He doesn't smile, doesn't step forward, doesn't do anything but speak.

I swallow. "Hi, Derek."

CHAPTER 66

Present

HE STEPS IN and shuts the door behind him. Click. Steps two more steps closer, his hands reaching forward and wrapping around the back of the chair, his fingers settling around the metal, a breath of a pause, then he lifts the metal and swings the chair up, off its feet and around, setting it back down next to me. I turn my head to the right, toward him. I can't move more than that. My latest stunt has resulted in a new setup, my ankles shackled to the chair, my wrists now cuffed behind my back, the links also tied to the chair. If I go batshit crazy in this setup, the worst that can happen is that the whole chair, with me tied on, falls over. I know. I tested the limits during the hour-long wait. I flopped on the ground like a fish until someone was kind enough to come in and set me back up. Thank God Derek hadn't come in then. That would have been a horrible first impression, my cheek stuck against the filthy floor, my knees on the ground, my feet in the air, hands stuck up like a broken marionette doll.

He reaches forward, grabbing the leg of my chair and dragging me sideways, until my chair faces his. He leans forward, his forearms on his thighs, fingers tented as he stares at me. I sit stick-straight, my cuffs not giving me much choice in the matter.

"What's with the black eyes and the nose?" He moves his hands in a circular motion that brings in his entire face.

I shrug. Try to remember the last time I took a shower. It's been a while. I hate that this is our first meeting. Had I known, I'd have shaved. Perfumed. Worn makeup.

"Did it happen here? Or before?"

"Before."

His eyes narrow. I've imagined a hundred expressions on this man's face, yet I was so wrong. He looks nothing like I've imagined, yet is beautiful in fifty new ways. "Give me more."

I shrug. He chuckles. I stare.

"I was just thinking..." He rubs at his lips. "...of all of the times you are silent, on the phone. You've probably been shrugging." He smiles and it is beautiful. *Derek smiles.* I would have told you it was impossible.

"I do like to shrug." I smile back at him and we smile at each other and this is the weirdest conversation we've ever had. I think, sitting here, three tiny feet between us, that we need the anonymity of a phone line between us. This is too vivid, too personal, too much. I want to dig my fingers in his shirt and press my face into his chest, inhale his scent. Run my fingers along his forearms, along his collarbone, up his neck, through his hair, and mess up the pattern. Bite his earlobe and memorize the sound of his inhale.

"What happened to your face?"

I look at the room's window. "Is this conversation confidential?"

"Yes."

I keep my head turned. "I think it was Jeremy."

"Look at me."

I don't, strictly out of principle. When his hand reaches out for my chin, I flinch. Glare at him in offense. It's bullshit but it works. His face shutters, hand retracts, eyes drop. "I'm sorry."

"I don't have to look at you if I don't want to."

"I know that. I'm sorry."

I've known this man for four years. Have had hundreds of sessions with him. I don't think, in that course of time, that he has ever apologized to me. I look at him and repeat the answer. "I think it was Jeremy. I have a memory...of Jeremy hitting me."

"Why did he hit you?"

I frown. "I can't...I think I was out of control. I think he was trying to calm me. Or snap me out of it."

"Did it work?"

I smile sadly. "I don't know. The police showed up the next morning. They say he fell out of my window and was then stabbed six times."

He leans back in his chair and stares at the ceiling. Lifts his hands to his head and sets them carefully on top of his hair. I don't like that. I want to be worth messing up hair for.

"I thought..." His voice breaks. "I thought we had you under control. I thought you were manageable."

I close my eyes at the disappointment in his voice. Am just as quickly pissed. Pissed that I care that he is disappointed.

Pissed that he is making me feel guilty for something I'm not entirely sure I have even done. Pissed that he is convinced of my guilt. Pissed that I am something to be managed. I can't stop the words, they echo through my mind, a repeating record of what Not To Say, yet I open my mouth and say them anyway.

"You have never managed me. And you have no idea the things I have done."

His hands drop, then his chin, his eyes slowing opening and finding mine.

I sit before him, hog-tied to that damn chair, and beg him with my eyes for everything.

He looks back, his eyes dead, and gives me nothing.

I close my eyes and turn my head. "Please leave."

"I'm not leaving, we need to talk about this. *What* things have you done?"

Things I Have Done . . . what I had wanted to say was People I Have Killed. "I'm a little vague on visitation rules, but I'm pretty sure you can't force me to talk to you."

He sighs. "Deanna, I flew here to meet with you. Just talk to me. Please." The beg in his voice I like.

"Why did you come, Doc?" I turn my head back to him. He meets my gaze without flinching.

"You told me you lived in Utah."

I shrug. He's right, I do like to shrug. Goody for him. "I lied."

"Why?"

"It's a protection thing. It's not safe to share everything."

"Protect yourself? Or insulate yourself?"

"What's the difference?"

"I think you insulate yourself. Put lies between you and

others. They can't get too close if there are things about you that aren't known."

I stare back at him and wish I had full use of my arms. I'd reach out and dig my nails into his scalp. Mess up that mane of hair in a way that could never be put back orderly. Pompous prick. Good looks can't make up for being an ass. "I don't lie to everyone."

"Really?" He raises his eyebrows like he doesn't believe me. "Tell me one person who you are a hundred percent truthful with."

Mike. I think the name but I don't say it. It is my personal victory, made stronger by the fact that I don't have to share it, don't have to boast it. Plus, an utterance of his name will only lead to more questions, and I'm pretty sick of Derek's face right now. As a secondary concern, I'm not a hundred percent sold on Derek's proclamation of our conversation being private. The laws surrounding doctor/patient confidentiality have more holes in them than Marilyn Manson's body. The last thing I need to do is create a big red flag with Mike's name on it.

I look at his knees, clothed in dress pants. They look expensive. A random outfit to choose to visit a woman in jail. If I were Derek, I'd say he put on stiff business clothes to put a guard up between him and me, to hold me professionally at bay in avoidance of every moment we may have shared that wasn't strictly professional. Not that there have been many. There've been few, actually.

I stood at the window and looked out, my nail scratching absentmindedly on the paint of the frame. A sea of roofs before me, the moonlight reflecting off various metal tops. If I opened the sill, there'd be the faint scent of car exhaust, of city, of the musk of today's rain, the mist still heavy in the air, dots of the rain on the glass. A pebbled view of the outside world. I live in ugliness, but from my prison, it looks like freedom, and there is nothing more beautiful. I listened to the ring, a soft buzz that went eight times, then ended, his voice clipping through, the message swift and professional. I ended the call and redialed. Listened to the buzz repeat. A light in a building went out. One more soul put to bed. I pressed my hand against the glass and heard the faint sound of a siren. His machine answered again and I hung up. Redialed. Waited.

The third ring was answered, his voice gruff and scratchy, the confused hello and cough of a man roused from sleep. I bet he sleeps like a baby. No crimes to bemoan, no mistakes to lament, no demons to fight. He probably tosses a few times over a misplaced IKEA order, then sleeps the snooze of the perfect dead. I bet his life is boring.

"What's wrong?" He's reached out and flicked on a light. Was sitting up in bed and rubbing at his eyes, his vision adjusting on the clock. I reached up and undid a button on my sleep shirt. Paul bought me these pajamas. Said all the ones I wear on camera look incredibly uncomfortable. So I was in flannel. Flannel with baby kittens on it, because he said they reminded him of me. Stupid, yet I was wearing them.

"Nothing," I said softly.

"Deanna, it's three in the morning."

"I know." I undid another button.

He sighed and I heard a soft thud. Imagined him collapsing back against pillows.

"Are you alone?" I rested my forehead on the glass and looked down. The street was empty, the Quik Mart sign the only illumination on a road whose streetlight bulbs no one bothered changing.

"Yes."

"No missus, Doc?"

There is a long pause. "No missus, Doc," he finally responded.

"I'm lonely, Derek." I closed my eyes and felt a tug in my throat, in my swallow that was thick and painful. I pressed my lips together and took a deep breath.

"I know." The words were so soft. I let out the breath and opened my eyes. Looked out the window and stopped looking through it, seeing the reflection of me in the glass. A faint girl, wavy. Barely there. That was me. Barely here. If I disappeared entirely, no one would know. No one would care.

"I just want…"

"Everything?"

I laughed, the sound coming out as more of a sob. I sniffed in an inhale. "Yes." And that was the problem. Ninety percent of what I wanted I would never again have. My family. My freedom. My normality. "Who do you have, Derek?"

"For what?" I love his voice. Deep and safe.

"For not feeling lonely."

There is a moment when he says nothing. Breathes nothing. "My situation is very different from yours, Deanna. I have friends, I go to the office. I pull comfort and connections in everyday activities."

I undid another button. "That doesn't help at all."

He chuckled. "The truth rarely does."

"Then lie. Tell me what, right now, I need." I shifted my gaze in the window and saw myself, saw the thumb of my fingers across the last button, my shirt falling open, a window of pale skin underneath. I pushed the material aside and stepped forward. Reached out a hand and drew along the glass, the cool apartment's condensation providing an easy canvas beneath my index finger. I outlined the line of one breast as he sighed out a word. "Deanna..."

"Tell me about yourself. What does my doctor wear to sleep?" I lifted my finger and moved it right, stepped closer until I could see the detail of a pink nipple. Outlined its reflection in the glass.

He stayed silent, but I could hear his breath. Heavier. I smiled and lifted my finger off the damp glass. Brought it to my breast and dragged it across my chest, five fingers of contact smearing cool liquid, five tongues of Derek, across my skin, swirling down to one expectant breast, then the other.

"Good night, Deanna."

I heard the click of his phone and sank forward against the window. Held the phone to my chest and felt the cool spread of empty throughout my limbs. I shouldn't have pushed. But I needed, in that moment, more. I blinked hard and dug my nails into the unyielding cell.

It was a moment we never spoke of. A night that had, in the years since, faded like the aftermath of an orgasm, into a dream. Now, in the stark fluorescent light of the room, it felt like the slight break had never happened. Not with this perfectly put-together, disapproving psychiatrist.

"They may call me as a witness. In the trial." He picks an invisible piece of something off his pants and drops it off to the side.

"There won't be a trial. I'm pleading guilty."

The statement earns me eye contact, his head lifting sharply. "That's interesting. Have you spoken to an attorney?"

"No." I won't be speaking to an attorney. Another individual's involvement is the last thing I need.

"The detectives told me that Jeremy is in an induced coma."

I break the eye contact and look down. "Yes."

"He might come out of it."

I want to know so much more than I do, yet I'm terrified by the possibility of that information. Can I handle details of what I've done? I say nothing.

"I think you should talk to him. No matter what you did. You need that closure."

No matter what you did. "I'm not pleading guilty because I think I did it, Derek."

"But you do think you did it."

"I don't think he threw himself out the window." *My Spyderco. Yellow handle. Bloody evidence bag.* My guilt pushes down my throat. I wouldn't have. Yet, all the pieces are there, the only shortfall is that when I've stabbed in the past, my dead made it all the way to the finish line.

"I'm not understanding your logic."

"I'm pleading guilty because I believe, regardless of what

did happen to Jeremy, that I may no longer be able to control myself." *It's your fault. You brought up him leaving me. You put the crack in the stronghold that I had emotionally built.* The words never leave my lips, I swallow them and they die.

"So you think that jail can do it for you."

There is an itch on my collarbone that badly needs scratching. No wonder individuals in straitjackets are insane. "I'm willing to give it a few years to find out." Six hours. It's been six hours and I am practicing breathing. I search the room for a mental distraction but only find Derek. I wonder if he finds me attractive. I wonder if, in the last four years, he has imagined me as often as I have imagined him.

"This is a drastic mode of self-policing, Deanna." He leans forward, putting his forearms on his knees. If I could lean forward, I would. I try to pull my wrists apart and wince at the steel resistance. "I could have arranged a home, a facility that could have—"

"Drugged me." I'm sweating against this seat, my back damp underneath the two layers. I should have taken this fucking sweatshirt off.

"Drugs have proven very effective with psychosis."

"I don't want drugs, I want to be fixed." An old, tired argument we have had a hundred times before. I barely have the energy to say the words. I see the sigh in his shoulders, and he lifts a hand to his forehead and rubs the area there. "We..." He stops and I wait. "We were only four hours apart. This whole time. Four hours."

"So?"

"So I thought you were in Utah!" The statement is an explosion from his mouth and he jerks to his feet, my eyes lifting to follow him, decisive, angry steps taking him away, the room too small, his strides hitting a wall, and he paces, back and forth before me, his body a tight coil of tension.

"It didn't matter. Why would it matter if I was three hours away or thirty?" I wonder, as the words head in his direction, if he even hears them, his focus so absolute on the frustration he is experiencing. But I should know better. Derek is consistent in his unwavering love of listening, words his drug of choice. He stops and turns to me.

"It would have made a difference, Deanna."

God, I wish I could stand. Wave my arms. Stomp my feet. Grab his shirt and assert force. "No," I say strongly. "It wouldn't have." *There is no us; don't act like there was ever a chance of us.* "Jeremy may die." A reminder that shouldn't be needed, and I suddenly hate him for it.

A softening of his face, the fall of his brow, relax of his mouth, a hundred tiny motions that should have occurred but don't, the tension still there, greedy and selfish as he grips the top of his chair and leans on it, his forearms flexing as he stares at me as if he can force action from me. "You shouldn't be here. You don't deserve this. You are good, Deanna."

I laugh, and the sound comes out cruel and mean. I yank at my cuffs and push with my feet. The laughter grows legs and runs a fucking marathon. My wrists complain and I fight harder. Tip hard right, then left, Derek's face a blur as he reaches out but I buck away, my chair doing a mad dance of confusion as it skitters back before it tips too much and falls. He tries to catch me and gets there too late, my elbow catching the hard floor first, my laughter rolling out like an unending chorus that never ever stops.

You are good, Deanna.

I laugh harder and push the crazy out, to a place he can't avoid seeing.

I hear him fling the door open, hear him call out for help. I hope, through the next peal of laughter, that he never comes back.

You are good, Deanna.

He has no idea. All those smarts and still stupid.

CHAPTER 67

Present

THE PACKAGE COMES through FedEx. All of Mike's do. It's a principle thing. Having UPS knock on his door, earn his money... it feels like the equivalent of Tom Brady wearing a Jets jersey. It is supporting the other side, Jeremy's side, and that side doesn't need any more of anything.

Mike signs for the package, takes the box, and rolls back. Sets it on the kitchen counter, his hand hefting the weight and approving its bulk. He cracks open the lid and glances in. Leaves the box there and returns to his room. Logs back online and works.

Five and a half hours later, the engine of a lawn mower begins, and he straightens at the keyboard. Moves to the rear of the house, through a door he never uses, and flips the lock, rolls the knob, wheels down the ramp.

It takes ten minutes of sitting in his chair at the edge of his driveway, his hand raising in occasional attention-grabbing gestures, to get the man to see him. When he does, the lawn mower rolling to a stop, a slow click off, lazy dismount, and hesitant wander over, Mike is sweating, unaccustomed to the heat, the moisture in the air, the feel of sun against his T-shirt. No wonder Jamie is always pushing him to sit outside. He's becoming a vampire.

"Can I help you?" The man turns out to be a boy. Seventeen or eighteen, his baseball cap pushing up high enough to reveal a baby face, a pitiful attempt at a mustache, and a healthy scattering of acne. The boy's eyes avoid Mike's, avoid the chair, avoid the situation.

"I need a hole dug, then filled. When you're done here, could I pay you to do that?"

The kid scratches the back of his neck. "Where?"

"In my backyard." He twists his body and points, under the tree, in a shady spot that would make a suitable grave.

The kid nods. Slowly. As if great thought is occurring. "How deep?"

"I'll let you know when you come over. Forty bucks?"

The thought process stops, a smile spreading over the kid's face. Forty must have been too much. "Sure. I'll do it now." He starts toward his truck, a faded red dually with a landscaping trailer attached. "Gonna grab a shovel."

"I'll meet you in the back."

Easy. Not as easy as having the legs and doing it himself, but easy. Mike rolls back, forward, right, forward, and heads inside.

Thirty minutes later, he passes Deanna's box with great solemnity to the boy, who places it in the ground, fills in the hole, and lifts the headstone carefully out of the box, setting it atop the grave.

Rest in peace. Mike reaches out and shakes the hand the kid held out.

"I'm sorry about your cat. I had a cat once."

Mike nods somberly. "Thanks for your help."

"I'm gonna go back next door and finish up."

Mike reaches down and pulls two worn bills from his chair's side pocket and holds them out. "Thanks."

"No problem." Turning to leave, there is an awkward moment when the kid feels the need to pat his shoulder. He waits, settled into the chair, and listens to him leave. Closes his eyes against the sun and hears the catch of the lawn mower's engine as it fires back up.

The headstone had been simple, its fictional message still carefully thought out.

> ALLEYGIRL
> *You will be missed.*
> *Rest in Peace.*

The faceplate of the headstone was metal set on a granite stone. The plate would take the blame for any readings from a metal detector. And below the plate, below the stone, past three feet of soil, lay Deanna's box. Hopefully no one showed up for it. But if they did, if they tore apart his house, they wouldn't find it.

He raised his head off the rest and rolled backward, turning a rough path on the dead grass, his return to the house bumpy and uncoordinated. He had a lot of work to do.

❖

His phone next to him, he taps out a furious rhythm on the keys. She'll call. Soon. As soon as she gets the ability to make a call. And he'll be ready. Informed. He's already gotten into the Tulsa Police Department's internal site, pulled up the evidence log and the detectives' reports. Twenty-two documents so far associated with the investigation into Deanna Madden. While in their system, a new file posts from the lead detective, one Brenda Boles. He clicks on it, his eyes skimming over the fields. Prestwick Place. This is bad. He downloads the report and opens a new window. Dedicates it to the life and dirt of Brenda Boles. Then he renames the report, inverting a few of the numbers on the file and sending it into a corner of the department where it will never be found. Check.

There are seven members of the Tulsa Police Department who have a hand in Deanna's well-being. He opens a new window for each of them, each with a collection of tabs. Finances. History. Family members. Web history. A hundred places for skeletons, weak places, and pressure points. There will be an opening for each of them.

It's work he hasn't done in years, and never for a personal reason, always for a paycheck. One hand lifts from the keyboard, his other hand rapid-fire in its strokes, covering the full range of keys in the time it takes to scratch at his forehead, a smile crossing over his face. Because, despite the dire circumstances, despite the hurdles ahead, this is going to be fun. So, so much fun.

There is a moment of pause, right before the complete invasion into seven lives begins. A moment when he rolls right and hesitates, his hand slow as it reaches for the mouse and clicks. Clicks again. A string of keystrokes. Another three clicks. Refresh. The hospital records have gone online in the six months since Jeremy Pacer was last admitted. And that almost sucks, because it delivers the bad news so much quicker.

His status stares, unwavering, from the screen. *CRITICAL. Patient unresponsive. No AD.*

AD. Advance directive. Jeremy didn't plan ahead for this situation. Dating a girl like Deanna, he probably should have.

There have been a hundred times in the last year when he's wished to be Jeremy. Or wished for Jeremy to be gone. But now, with the man's life hovering above the dark precipice of death, he wishes fervently that he'll make it. Pull through. Open his eyes. Especially since, from all appearances, Deanna was responsible for his demise.

He closes the window and returns to the fun. Checks his phone for the twentieth time. She'll call. As soon as she gets the chance.

CHAPTER 68

Present

PRESTWICK PLACE HAUNTS Brenda. So does the girl's face, outside that apartment, when she put her under arrest. Utter surprise, then panic. Concern. The damn girl had had a party of emotions, all jostling for prime facial real estate. Something is wrong. Everything is wrong. Yet…everything is right, all *i*'s dotted, *t*'s crossed. It makes no freaking sense.

"Drop it." David speaks from the passenger seat, his hands busy with a piece of gum. He offers her the pack of Doublemint; she shakes her head.

"I can't."

"Sure you can. That triple homicide on Forty-Second. Sage's birthday party this Saturday. My irresistible good looks and the constant temptation. All things you could focus on instead of a closed case."

"The neighbor did the triple kill on Forty-Second."

"And Madden did Pacer."

"Maybe." She chews on her bottom lip. Tastes blood and stops.

He snaps his gum. "She confessed. What more do you want?"

She yanks the wheel hard left, the blare of a horn eliciting a curse from David, his hand gripping the center console as the patrol car whips around. She reaches forward and grabs at her cell, her eyes dropping down as she dials a number. "I want the truth."

CHAPTER 69

Present

MY LITTLE STUNT with Derek got me back in solitary. Just me and my boring breaths. But hell, that is better than staring at his face. Seeing the judgment, hearing the questions, feeling the lies of my past crawling over my skin. *You are good, Deanna.*

I still need my phone call. I don't understand the phone call rules. Either making calls is my right or it's not. Whether or not I had a bout of crazy shouldn't affect anything. After a hundred years in the room, I move from the bed to the floor. Lie on my back in front of the door and rest my shoes on the metal. Lift a foot and let it drop, the resulting noise a satisfying clang. Lift my other foot and let it drop. Clang. From the next cell, a man yells at me to shut up. I smile. Lift, drop. Lift, drop. I count, one number per foot. Twelve. Twenty-seven. Thirty-eight. At fifty-two, my door opens and Ms. KeepYourHeadDownAndColor looks down at me. "What."

I prop myself up on my elbows. "I'd like to make a phone call, please."

She sighs. Looks back over her shoulder for a beat, then looks back down at me. "Okay. Don't pull any shit."

I smile and hop to my feet, bouncing lightly on my toes. "I won't. Promise."

She points her finger to the ceiling and spins it. I obey, holding my hands behind my back and waiting out the cuffing process.

"You'll have to hold the phone against your shoulder and have me dial the number."

"Okay."

"Try to hit me and I'll lay your skinny white ass flat on the ground."

I smile. "Okay."

"I will."

"I believe it."

She huffs in response and swings me around, her hand settling on my shoulder and pushing me forward. We step as two, past three cells, and stop at a pay phone mounted in the wall. Twelve steps, maybe thirteen. I've been that close the entire time. I suddenly realize how small this complex is. Less than a dozen cells. Men and women grouped in close proximity. The same dozen officers keeping tabs on us. The jail will be very different. In jail, my outbursts would most likely carry heavier punishments, my requests ignored. In jail, I'll be one of thousands. In jail, NascarGuy44 will probably look angelic. I feel, waiting next to the phone, my first bit of trepidation. She looks at me. "The call will be collect."

"That's fine."

"Number?"

I tell her Mike's number, wondering—as I speak it—what call log this will go on, what attention will be brought as a result of this call. No matter, we won't discuss anything incriminating, but still. In my world with few friends, I like to protect the ones I have.

She finishes dialing and places the phone gently against my ear. I hold it with my shoulder and nod at her. *Thank you*, I mouth. She looks at me like I'm mental, then pats my back. "The call is recorded," she says. I nod and watch her step away, her large girth settling into the closest chair.

Mike's voice comes on quickly, and accepts the charges without hesitation.

"Hey, Dee."

"Hey, babe." I smile. Everything changes, everything stays the same.

"What's up?" God, I love him, giving me normal right now. I turn and try to settle against the wall, a position difficult when my hands are cuffed at the small of my back.

"Jeremy…he—"

"I know. Want an update?"

I close my eyes in gratitude. "Yeah."

"It's not good. He's on a ventilator."

"But he could wake up?"

"He has a subdural hematoma. It's a fifty-fifty thing. But if he does wake up, he could slip back under. The hematoma… it's blood built up around the brain."

I don't ask how he knows this. Or how he knew to check on

him. I listen to his words and wish I hadn't asked. *Fifty-fifty.*
"Thanks, Mike."

"No worries, babe. Just let me know how I can help."

"Just keep me updated. Also, I need you to keep up Jessica."
Jessica Riley. My online alter ego. Five days ago, she was an
Internet sex superstar, yet the Internet is fickle. A few more
days, or weeks, or months? She will fade into the black hole of
obscurity and be gone forever. And without Jessica, there is just
Deanna. Crazy, I'll-kill-you-before-I-hug-you Deanna.

"You mean status updates, Facebook, that type of thing?"

"And messages on the camsites and in my e-mail. Put an
auto-response on. Tell them I have a sick relative and will be
away to take care of them."

"Grandmother, sister...what?"

"Mom. Tell them my mom's sick." There is humor in that
statement. Ha. Ha. Ha.

"Done. Want me to pull some old files and run some nude
shows occasionally?"

"Umm...not now. But I might have you do that later. I'll let
you know."

"Anything else?"

"That was really it." I scratch the inside of my wrist. Try to
think of something else, a reason to extend this conversation.

"Need bail?"

I smile. "I pled guilty."

"Yeah, I found that interesting." I didn't say anything, just
rested the back of my head against the wall. "You don't belong
there, Dee."

"I did it, Mike."

He hisses through the line. "This is recorded, Dee."

"I know. And I'll tell you the same thing I said in my statement."

"You don't have to." Oh, of course. He's probably read my statement. Probably has video footage of my questioning. Probably is watching a live feed of me, right now, on the phone with him. I reach down and pick out an imaginary wedgie just to keep him entertained.

"Then you know I belong here. It's a good thing. I mean…" I falter. "Not about Jeremy. But I need a new place. One more secure than my apartment."

"No you don't. You just need a roommate. Or friend." *Or me.* I hear it through the empty line. I sigh. "My shrink already preached to me today, Mike. Please don't pretend I'm something I'm not. I can't take that from you."

"I won't preach at you. But give me one question, then I'll drop the whole thing."

I wait. Push on a crack in the tile beneath my feet.

"Think about the possibility, for one minute, that you didn't do it. That someone else pushed Jeremy out of your window. That someone else stabbed him, then hid his body. Then think of that person walking free. While you are babysat in prison for the next decade."

I lift my eyes off the tile. "But I did it." There is an invisible question mark at the end of the sentence.

When he responds, there are thoughtful lines in his voice. "No, I don't think you did."

I say nothing.

"Just think about it."

"Not much else to do here." The woman makes a *hurry it up* gesture. "Please stay on top of Jeremy's progress."

"I will. And that NASCAR thing... I'll take care of that."

I should have known my invisible angel would find out about that. "Thank you."

"Find the girl I know. Jeremy needs her."

I watch the woman stand, her wheeze of effort as she straightens her back. Speak quickly, before my voice betrays itself and shakes. "Oh, Mike. You know she never goes far." I hang up the phone and can feel his smile.

But I did it. Didn't I?

I wonder, on the walk back to my solitary cell. I wait patiently while my cuffs are undone, then step forward and listen to the door clang shut. Then I lie down, close my eyes, and try my damnedest to remember more, but all I feel is the fight of my mind.

CHAPTER 70

Present

I DECIDE, ONCE returned to my cell, my back on the mattress, fingertips drumming against my sweatshirt, that Mike may be right. No blood was on me when I woke up. There was whatever instance caused my broken nose. Maybe Jeremy didn't break it. Maybe someone else did. My mind really snags on the thought of me pushing him out the window, then traveling down six flights of stairs and still having the bloodlust to stab him. Me hiding his body and leaving it for dead. I killed individuals who deserved it. Not the guy who fixed me bacon that morning and looked at my face like I was *something*. I wasn't that girl, I can't be that girl. I am, in a thousand irreparable ways, broken, but I am not *that*.

And if, as Mike so obviously pointed out, I *didn't* hurt Jeremy, then someone else did. Someone who I, in my prison of solitude, can't punish. I lie there, stare at dark corners of the ceiling above me, and think. Dr. Pat had told me that I might have a concussion. That any additional head trauma in the future would make another much more likely. I tilt my head back, pushing it into the thin mattress, and feel the twinge of pain. I am actually ready for Derek to return. I have too many thoughts, too many fears. For once, I need his guidance, his questions. And besides all that, I am BORED. I am bored and hoping he will return. There is *nothing* to do in this space, I have no idea how I will handle five or ten or twenty years of it, and I am ready to deal with his disapproving faces and condescending sounds and even the whole "You are good, Deanna" bullshit. I'll deal with all of it and ask for seconds. Because if I have to listen to any more silence, I think I'll explode.

It's been lifetimes since my call to Mike. Long enough for the night to pass, the lights flickering on a few hours ago. I slept a couple of times, quick snatches of oblivion in between long periods of waiting, thinking, trying to remember. This shift's warden has walked by my door fourteen times since my phone call to Mike. Before this guy, Ms. KeepYourHeadDownAndColor passed four times. I sat there and waited each time for them to pause, their boots to stop at this cell, their hands to slide open the window and for them to say something. But they haven't. I've lain and waited and listened to the outside and none of it has had anything to do with me.

Another clop of steps, and I perk up. Roll the curve of my body up and move to the door, my ear to the cool metal. Clip, clip, clip, clip. They actually stop and I hold my breath. The slide moves, a harsh, metallic sound, and I scramble away. "Madden. Visitor."

❖

Be nice, be nice, be nice, be nice. I chant the words as I follow the guard. The nicer I am, the longer the visit. The longer the visit, the longer the distraction. "How long can a visit last?"

The man in front of me doesn't respond. The one at my back leans forward slightly. "Thirty minutes, max."

Thirty minutes. Too short, but I'll take it. It must be Derek, and our entire relationship has been thirty-minute chats so we have it down. We turn right and stop outside the same door as before. "Will I have to wait long?"

One shakes his head. "If it's his second visit, it'll be shorter." He opens the door and I am ushered in. Locked in like before, feet shackled to chair legs, wrists secured to the back of the chair. I guess my twenty-four hours of behavior hasn't impressed anyone yet. I don't blame them. I'm inches away from misbehaving just for personal entertainment.

The last hand drops from my cuffs and they leave. I roll my neck and wait. Sniff. I stink. Literally, stink. I try to think of the last time I had a shower. After Derek, that needs to be my next question. Where and how I can bathe. At this rate, my arraignment will consist of everyone holding their noses and running for the exit.

Twenty minutes, my concern over my odor passed, the door opens and Derek steps in. He's changed, probably got a good scrubbing in his five-star hotel's shower last night. The outfit of today is a white button-up shirt, sleeves rolled a few flips up, with dark jeans, a pair of sunglasses in one hand, the entire ensemble setting off his dark tan and once-again-meticulous hair.

"Good morning."

I nod in response, taking the moment to openly study him before smiling at him. I picked the smile out just for him, flipping through my reservoir of grins before deciding on fresh-faced innocent. It shakes him and his reach for the chair stalls, his eyes skittering over my smile before he looks away, pulling out the chair and sitting down before me. Not next to me like last time. Interesting. He sets his glasses down on the table between us and settles back in his chair. "How's it going?"

"Fine. Why'd you come here?"

The blunt question doesn't offend him. It shouldn't. He's had four years to adjust to my style. "I assumed you would need a psychological evaluation, or that I would be called to give my professional opinion as your primary doctor."

"Shrink."

He tilts his head in acknowledgment. I'll bet you a hundred bucks, right now, that he drives a Range Rover. A white one, which he vacuums out on Sunday afternoons and only uses premium gas in. His fuckin' jeans look IRONED. The tortoise-shell Ray-Bans he set carefully on the table are sparkling clean. You could drive this guy to insanity by just leaving your wet panties on his kitchen counter. He looks like he crawled out of a Banana Republic ad, then enrolled and got a master's in OCD.

"So now that you're here, you'll stay...what? Till the arraignment?" I ask.

"I'm not sure. If you don't have a trial, my purpose here isn't really clear. But..."

I wait.

"...an incompetent individual isn't able to plead their own guilt."

I stiffen, my wrists flexing out before the metal reminds them of their place. "Crazy can't tell crazy?" That's bullshit if I've ever heard it.

"There is the possibility that I can testify at the arraignment."

My jaw tightens, my teeth grinding together. "No."

"You don't even know what happened. How can I let you testify the inverse?"

"Let me?" Oh...that...that is kerosene poured on the fire of my irritation.

"You know what I meant."

"I know that I need every bit of control I can get right now, and you're stripping me of that."

"A normal woman would thank me."

"If you declare me mentally incompetent, they'll lock me up." I say the words so quietly, they are a whisper.

"It's not a jail, Deanna. It's a hospital."

"That I can't leave. Where I'll be drugged up twenty-four hours a day." I shake my head and a lock of hair sticks on my mouth. I blow out a huff of air and it falls aside. "I'd rather be in jail."

"You're not doing a good job of convincing me of your sanity right now."

I look down at his fucking glasses. "You don't understand." I wonder how much time is left.

"Let's talk about Sunday night."

"I can't remember it. I've tried."

"Deanna." His voice is soothing, it says my name like it is whipped cream being spread. I want to both eat the cream and vomit it out, all at the same time. "Just walk me through the last things you remember."

"I was in the hallway, with Jeremy. We were headed to my room." I had my keys in my hand, I can remember that fact. I remember, in the elevator, his hand rested on the small of my back, his fingers easing under the hem of my sweatshirt and just resting there, on the naked skin. It felt so good, so normal. I stop thinking.

"You know what happened."

"No." I shake my head, a frantic gesture. "I don't." This is a distraction; we need to return to the other conversation, deciding whether or not I will end up in a padded cell.

"You do. You've just blocked it out. Either you have residual effects from your stupid stunt during your fight with Jeremy or you have dissociative amnesia. It can happen when a person blocks out something, normally a stressful or traumatic event that they can't emotionally deal with."

"I don't know what happened." A thousand repetitions will make it true.

"Deanna, you don't have to be afraid. It is what it is. The unknown is worse than reality."

"That is, quite possibly, the stupidest thing you've ever said." Reality is a thousand times worse than a blank stretch of time. Reality will give me a clear vision of his pain, of my guilt, of the horrific moments that changed everything forever.

"Unless you're innocent."

"I'm not innocent."

"We need to find that out."

"That's the cops' job."

"You already pled guilty, Deanna. What could it hurt?"

"Another stupid question. You're two for two, Doc."

"Let's go through a quick meditation session. See what we can unlock."

"Let's not." I don't want to unlock hell. I've got enough going on without it.

"You need to at least try to remember."

I'm scared. That's the truth of it. Scared that once I know what I've done that I won't be able to move past it. How will I ever be able to forgive myself for that? At the moment, despite the psychological disaster that lies between my ears, I still love myself. Still think of myself as a good person. Can still look in the mirror in the morning and approve of the person that I see. But once I go into Sunday night, once I pull back that mask and see my actions underneath . . . I can't undo that discovery. And I don't think I can live with the knowledge of what is there.

"There's probably a reason my brain doesn't want to know it."

"I've never known you to be scared before." I hear it, in his calm and controlled words. The challenge that stands on a box and screams at me through the space.

"I don't want to be hospitalized, Derek."

"Unless you remember, I'm not supporting your guilty plea."

I stay quiet, my chin stubbornly set, my mind clicking through my options, the worst of it all the tiny speck of feeling that he is right. I know what happened that night. I know how Jeremy ended up in the hospital. I've seen the photos, heard the details. I just need to find that information inside of me. And, to be quite honest, I'm pretty sure I've hidden from that knowledge. In all of my mock attempts, I've boarded up that door and thrown a mountain of shit before it.

But maybe I should dig through that mountain. Pry open the door and look through. Stare into hell's face and suffer for my sins. I swallow. "We don't have long enough." Thirty minutes, max. That is what the guard had said. We've already eaten up fifteen, easy. Maybe more.

"Don't worry about that." When he speaks, it's a tone that relaxes, and for once, I yield.

"I'm scared." I don't look at his face.

"Do you remember your mantra?"

I don't want to do this. I don't want to do this transcendental meditation bullshit to relive hell. "It's the concussion," I object. "I think that's why I can't remember. Dr. Pat said it was possible."

"Close your eyes, Deanna. Just give me ten minutes. Start the mantra slowly." I hate this voice of his, this calm peaceful tone, melodic in its syllables, entrancing in its push. I think of Mike, I think of *what if.* And then I close my eyes, for no reason other than to drag vengeance to its rightful owner, and start the mantra.

CHAPTER 71

Past

I WAS SO drugged, at that moment, pulling Jeremy into my apartment, toward my bed, his laugh tumbling after me. Drugged with love, with lust, on a high from our date and our kiss and the moment that was about to occur. So drugged that I almost missed the box, tipped over at the foot of the bed. The kitchen drawers, two of the six open, their cheap guts exposed to the fluorescent light. The safe, which I may not have shut, its door open wide, my knives dumped unceremoniously out, like fallen chopsticks, the guns still tucked inside in neat order. But what I didn't miss was the person, by my window, the cardboard ripped off, the open sill letting in the night breeze yet doing nothing to clear the stench of violation.

Simon was *in my apartment*, his head whipping to me, his hair a wild mess of spikes, his eyes widening when it made the connection with mine. I stopped, a sudden motion that had the strong chest of Jeremy colliding with my back. I didn't have time to speak, to react, before Jeremy's hands grabbed me and shoved, his body pushing forward and in between me and Simon, his arms spread out as if to create a wall to protect me.

That irritated me, my surprise at seeing Simon replaced with an anger at Jeremy. I don't need protecting, especially not in my own apartment, my home. I did take advantage of the moment of protection, my eyes taking in the details I initially missed, Simon's search not missing an inch, disarray stretching from one mildewed wall to the other. Good lord, he even dumped out my dildo drawer. I'm sure *that* gave him quite an eyeful. My gaze paused on the pile of knives, my yellow Spyderco knife carelessly along the top of the pile, and something inside me clicked to the "On" position. I felt it happen, felt the switch of my mind, felt the closure of my focus, the flee of my sanity, the takeover of my mind. I felt it all and ignored it, ripping my eyes from the knife and ducking under Jeremy's arms, stepping closer to Simon.

"Explain to me, right now, why I shouldn't kill you." I spoke carefully, a thousand sensors in my body taking notice of my state. A thousand notices, all ripped from the walls and discarded by my current state of mind.

"I found them." Simon's eyes shone, a medicated shine, and when he lifted his hand, I looked, at the clear bag in his hand, duct tape still stuck to its top, the orange bottle inside. I'm surprised. Then again, it looked as if he'd taken a while with his search. My eyes flicked to the window, to the pile of cardboard shreds littered on the floor beneath it. He saw me look, and smiled. "Almost had given up. But who covers up a window, right? It drove me crazy, the longer I stayed in here. I don't know how to you do it. The damn thing was taunting me."

Funny, it taunts me too. Maybe the reason isn't my insanity. Maybe it taunts any living thing. I felt Jeremy's hand wrap around my arm and I shook it off. Held my hand out to him in a *cool your shit* gesture.

"So I ripped it off. Opened the damn window. Stuck my head outside. And that's when I saw it." He shook the bag and it began to swing, a pendulum before me. "Taped to the outside brick. You sneaky little bitch."

It is true. I am sneaky. I had also really, really wanted an excuse to stick my head outside, and that hidden place had offered it. I said nothing and wondered how hard I'd have to shove the blade to break into his chest.

I took a deep breath and stepped back. Smiled. Raised my hands in defeat. "You got me, you found them. Now please get out, it's almost nine." Nine, the deadline we had rushed home to meet, our schedule carefully organized in order to fit an hour of sex in before my curfew, an hour that was slipping from us with every second I dealt with this asshole. It was already dark out. The knives were behind me but I'd only need one.

"Oh . . . I didn't just find *them* sweetheart." Simon kicked out, and his tennis shoes collided with a book bag I hadn't noticed. A faded red JanSport. A piece of masking tape holding its front pocket closed, a carabiner hanging from its handle. Like Simon planned on hitting a rock face anytime soon. When he kicked, the bag shifted, and pills settled, a shake of sound like a giant box of Tic Tacs.

I was confused, then I understood.

My medicine cabinet. Three or four years' worth of meds that Dr. Derek kept sending and I kept ignoring. They'd stock-piled, one neat row before another, each new bottle marking the passage of time. Simon found them, thought he hit the drug mother lode, and shoved them all into this cute little backpack. His face seemed to think I'd care. I didn't.

"Don't call her sweetheart." The hard voice came from behind me, from the third party in this room that I'd almost forgotten. I turned to Jeremy. "It's okay." I smiled again. My cheeks were beginning to hurt. "He's leaving." I turned to Simon. "I'm sorry about the pills. I was upset because you didn't unlock me." I met his glazed, cocky stare, and dropped my eyes. He must have opened the bottle. Took a handful. He wasn't the shaky addict right now. He was high and confident. He needed to go. I lowered my head and turned my back to him. Walked around Jeremy and toward the door. Smiled as I heard Jeremy speak to Simon. Smiled as I heard them buy my act. Smiled as I bent over and wrapped my hands around the Spyderco.

CHAPTER 72

Past

JEREMY SHOULD HAVE known. That something was wrong, that something was off. But the whole situation was off. Walking into her apartment, his focus had been on one thing: getting her beautiful body naked and underneath him. Hearing her voice break as he pushed inside to the place that made everything sane disappear. There was nothing in life like the connection made when their bodies met. When she whimpered beneath him and took him, ran her fingers over his side and wrapped her legs around him. Whispered his name in the heartbeat right before she came.

He'd been so focused on that goal, the maddening tick of time passing...now only ninety minutes, now eighty-five... now sixty-four...that he hadn't been aware, hadn't been prepared. It had pushed at him, that nagging premonition that he always had when he twisted her unlocked knob, when he saw her enter and leave her apartment without hesitation. But by now, that feeling was second nature, easy to ignore, especially when her small hand was in his and she was pulling him forward, his cock already hard in his pants, her giggle a foreplay of things about to happen.

And then . . . that piece of shit. Standing there like he owned the place. Smiling and taunting her. The woman he knew would have tackled the man. Cut him to shreds with her words. But the woman before him did nothing of the sort. She bent, yielded. Ducked her gorgeous head and pacified. Used soothing words and gestures and asked him nicely to leave. A thousand warnings that he ignored, his heartbeat calming, his step toward Simon accompanied by all of the words he wished Deanna had said. *Get the fuck out. What did you take? I'm calling the cops. You worthless piece of shit.* He felt empowered, confident, more over Deanna's reaction than his words. It was his own high, an affirmation of everything he had, deep down, known about her. *She wasn't dangerous. She could control herself. She wasn't crazy, just passionate at times. It was all okay, they would be fine.* Simon's eyes had hardened, his mouth curling back into a snarl, and it was in that moment when the knife flew, straight and perfect, over Jeremy's left shoulder.

CHAPTER 73

Past

MY SECLUSION HAS led to a lot of obsessions, but knives have always been forefront. My first year, I learned to spin them in my hand. Flip a switchblade out, then in. Out. In. Out. In. I bought a dozen, cut myself fifty times, and eventually got to the point where the knife was an extension of my arm. I could flip out an arm, then return to a pocket a switchblade, pocket-knife, and tac blade with my eyes closed. My second year, I danced with guns, a difficult obsession when you're restricted to an apartment. My third year, I returned to knives, this time with a focus on throwing. I practiced with darts, then moved to knives, then stars. My fourth year, I refined and perfected the skill. My throw at Simon was the first time I took practical application of my skills.

Go figure that I'd miss.

❖

They didn't understand what the knife was at first, neither of them did. It wasn't until it pierced the bag, slicing through the clear plastic, the prescription bottle hitting the floor with a loud knock, that they looked at the wall, at the thud that had sounded, plaster giving easy way to the blade, the yellow handle sticking straight out of the wall. Jeremy turned quickly and was still too slow. I stood with my legs slightly spread, one before the other, my hand still outstretched toward the blade. I tilted my head and frowned, my tsk loud and hollow in the room. It's funny how everyone shuts up when knives come out. Too bad the Spyderco hit plaster and not skin. No worries. There were plenty more. I crouched before the pile, Christmas coming early, a grin blaring out, everything perfect, everything red, and this was my time, my moment, my victim. My fingers wrapped around a handle and I moved without looking, around Jeremy, toward the asshole by the window whose eyes were wide, fear coming and he had no idea. I broke left, avoiding the block, and when I lunged forward a hand wrapped around my arm and yanked hard and everything was broken, interrupted when I fell into the chest of Jeremy and heard his voice. "Deanna."

Deanna.

Deanna. I pushed against him, irritated. Simon. Simon is getting away, I need to drag my blade across his skin and bleed him dry. Jeremy holds me tight, repeats my name.

"Deanna."

Deanna. Fury rips through me, my vision blurring, my control and compartmentalization crumbling in one quick burst of anger. Fuck this man and his firm hands. Muscles can't beat blades. I see, in slow motion, the widening of his eyes, the change when he goes from attention getting to defense. But he is too slow, my hand jerking forward, my finger hard on the blade's release, the snap of the metal joyous to my ears.

"I'm sorry."

The words didn't belong in this space, in this moment, certainly not from my future victim. I heard his whisper and didn't understand it, didn't see his arm move, his body twist, wasn't prepared when my face exploded under the whip of his elbow. I only felt a brief moment of blinding pain, and fell backward, but I never felt the impact with the floor.

CHAPTER 74

Present

I SIT ON the edge of the bed, my hands fisting at the plastic mattress beneath me, Dr. Derek back in his Range Rover and out of this place. We have a gentleman's agreement: he won't declare me incompetent and we'll meet tomorrow before the arraignment.

I stare at the wall across from me, a slow rage rising through my chest, spreading down my limbs, festering in the pores of my skin. Simon. I've been torturing myself, literally *imprisoning* myself, and *Simon* was the cause of it all. Him and his damn pills. Him and his damn sister. Had she helped? Had she lifted part of Jeremy's weight when they'd moved it down the dark streets to the Dumpster? Had she been the one to think of using my knife, that cheery fucking yellow handle a giant blinking ARREST DEANNA sign? Simon. Chelsea. Simon. Chelsea. Punishment. Punishment. Now.

I am in here because of them. Or him. Or them. I'll get to Simon first. He'll squeal if she was involved. But of course she was. I couldn't open my door without seeing her face, then she'd vanished.

I am in here because of them. They let me lie on the apartment floor. They let me wake up with no idea of what had happened. They caused me to miss out on going to the hospital. Holding his hand. Looking into his sister's face. They caused me to doubt myself, to paint a giant-ass mural in my head of all the horrific things I'd done. They let me lock myself into a place where I can't kill them both. And that, after you shift through all the other bullshit, is my biggest issue right now.

I stand, walk to the door, and start to scream.

❖

It takes five minutes of screams to get a guard to my cell. My throat is exhausted when he opens the window, my lungs spent, breath short. I take in a deep breath and squeak out my request. "I'd like to speak to a lawyer."

My request doesn't impress the man. He eyes me for a long minute, his jaw moving in a slow chomp of gum, then picks at a spot on his face. "Okay," he finally says. "But shut the hell up. I'll call a PD for you."

"Thank you." I step back before he thinks about restraining me. Turn and walk to my bed like a good little girl. Sit on the edge and put my palms between my knees. He eyes me through the open window for one long final stretch, as if I am planning something, as if an extra minute of observation will change anything. Then he shuts the slider, and I hear his steps as they move down the hall.

A lawyer. I have the right to an attorney. They will get me out of this. I have to get out of this, to find my own answers and right Jeremy's wrong. And if I don't like their court-appointed attorney, I'll get my own. Use some of my millions to get Gloria Allred on *Nancy Grace*, screaming my innocence. But for right now, in this moment, I just need a face. Someone to spit my innocence to who can tell me the process and how soon I can leave this hell. I don't need a prison, I don't need safeguards. I was not the one who did that.

I roll my neck and think about my steps. I'll visit Jeremy first, then go to the apartment. Collect myself and get showered, dressed in clean clothes. Then I'll rain hell in Jeremy's name. I grin in the empty cell and can feel the walls smile back.

❖

It doesn't take long for my attorney. Less than an hour later, my cell door opens and I am escorted back out to the visiting room. There, I'm pleasantly surprised to see the attorney waiting, her navy suit patient in the corner of the room while I am secured.

"Ms. Madden, I am Dana Romansky, the public defender assigned to your case." She nods at the guard, who leaves us, gently shutting the door behind him.

"Nice to meet you." It was nice to meet her. A woman. I'm ashamed to say I'm surprised. I'd had visions of my court-appointed attorney, and he'd been short and male and stressed. She was tall and put together and calm.

"You requested me. Is there something you need?

To the point. Good. "Yes. I gave a confession because I didn't remember what happened. Now that I remember, I want to change my statement."

Her brow wrinkles. "So...you're innocent."

"Yes. Have you reviewed the case?" *Please say yes.*

"It's nine o'clock at night. I left a date to come here. You're lucky I know your last name."

Figures. The rosy cloud around her dims slightly. "What is the next step?"

"The next step is your arraignment, which is scheduled for tomorrow at two. At the arraignment we can have you plead innocent. A trial will be scheduled, and the time between now and then is when we, or whatever attorney you decide upon, can build your case. It will be difficult to overcome a confession, but it's not impossible."

"So...when would I get out?"

She smiles and I do not like her smile. It is smug and intelligent and carries a *you dumb little thing* in its smirk. "You won't get out unless you are found innocent at trial. Which is a very long way away."

"What about bail?"

"You've assaulted two people in the forty-eight hours you've been here. They tied you up just to talk to me."

"So...no bail?"

"Most likely not."

There is a long moment in which I digest the information. Stare down at the table and refamiliarize myself with the scratches in its surface. Line up the players in this game into a formation that I understand. "So...tomorrow afternoon, I go to the arraignment, where I'll plead innocent and be taken to jail."

"Yes."

"It doesn't matter if I plead innocent or guilty, I'm going to jail."

"Yes. Unless the judge, by some miracle, decides to set a bail."

"What are my chances of that?"

"Less than a percent. It's not gonna happen."

Well this sucks. "Can I talk to the detectives? Maybe if I convince them that—"

"You don't understand." She interrupts. "Once you are charged, it is put into the judicial system's hands. If you hadn't confessed, there is a chance that they wouldn't have had the evidence to hold you for more than twenty-four hours. But once you confessed, you changed everything. And that's not just something you can get a do-over on."

I let out a breath of air, and it comes out a lot harder and angrier than I had intended. She flinches and I lift my head to find her watching me warily.

"I'm sorry," she says carefully. "I wish I could do more."

I don't want her sympathy. I want freedom. I break eye contact and look down at the table. "Thank you for meeting with me. I'd like to go back to my cell now."

❖

This time, when they open that door and lead me out, I notice everything. The height of the knobs, the construction strength of the locks. The bars, the doors, the exits, the lighting. How many people we pass in the hall, how many guards look up when we walk, how many steps it takes, windows are present, keys jingle from belts. I notice it all. If I learned anything during that meeting, it was that I'll have to take my own freedom back.

CHAPTER 75

Present

IF I MADE a list of difficult tasks, breaking out of a prison would top the list. Thankfully, I'm not in prison. At the moment, I'm in booking, which...best I can determine, is fairly loose in its security practices.

But still, I'll need help. Mike, definitely. There is really no one else. I need to call him, plant a few code words that will somehow communicate to him my need to get out. But phone calls aren't permitted after lights-out. The big woman told me that, right after she said if I tried my foot-kicking-door routine again she'd put me in the straitjacket. I believed her. I'll keep my stomping to myself. Any minute the lights will go out and my opportunity to call Mike will end. I stand at my door and pray for a guard. The lights above me flicker, then go out. There goes my phone call.

I stay in place, hunched beside the door, and think. Mike knows I am here. Mike knew about NascarGuy44. Mike knew what I said in my statement. Mike probably has a finger on every single thing happening right now in this building. Mike, his level of prep far more advanced than my own, has probably been working his sexy little fingers to the bone since the moment I was arrested. Mike is probably just waiting to push "LAUNCH." I mentally cross my fingers and hope that I am right.

I step through the dark, my hands outstretched, eyes not yet adjusted to the change. Move cautiously, my hands patting at air, then walls, then surfaces. Running over anything and everything in search of one thing: a sharp edge. I am almost finished with the room, my chest tightening, worry peaking, when I find it, the underside of the left front foot of my bed, the corner of it sharp and unfinished. *Jackpot.* I lie on my back and shimmy under the bed, supporting the front end with my legs, both knees brought to my chest, feet lifting up the dinky metal frame. I dig the sharp metal point into my right index finger, then birdie finger, then ring finger, each prick hard and painful enough to draw blood. Then I do the thumb and pinkie, holding my bloody hand away when I finish. I scoot right, using my undamaged hand to support the frame, my feet moving, my body rolling out of the way as I drop the bed down, the sound loud against the finished concrete floor. Too loud. I pause, on my belly on the dirty floor, and wait a breath, then crawl to my feet, moving to the wall and raising my hand, softly dragging my first red finger over the white paint.

In the dark shadows, my letters slowly appear. Halfway through the third word, I run out of ink, squeezing of the pads not bringing any fresh blood to the surface. I roll back underneath the bed. Repeat the equation, subbing out my left hand for my right, a new series of pained hisses whistling through my teeth. Back on my feet, I complete the project. Then, I stand before the bloody wall and wait.

Almost an hour later, I hear the slide of my door, a face cutting into the bright white of the opening. Rounds. There is a moment of pause, then the light in my room bursts on, too bright, too white, too perfect. "What the fuck?" a woman utters. Oh. KeepYourHeadDownAndColor. Too bad. I'd hoped to spare her of this. She swings open my door and stands in the opening, feet spread, her eyes wide, darting from me, to the wall, to me. "You got some issues, you know that?"

My feet stay in place, twin roots into cement. The side of my face itches, probably due to the lines of blood, the sticky liquid drying into place. I must look mad, standing next to the words, their formation messy and crooked, the letters as large as I could make them. I lick my lips and taste copper. "You should probably file a report," I say softly.

She stays still, her head tilting. "We don't have a nurse here, if this is some big plan to get medical attention."

A drop of blood drips from my left index finger and hits the floor with a quiet *smack*. I wonder if she heard it. "No." I shake my head in case she didn't hear the quiet word. "I don't need a nurse."

Her eyebrows raise and show a hint of pink eye shadow. "Oh...kay." She steps back, shutting the door and locking it, her mouth moving to the open window. "You know you're going to be cleaning that up, right? So don't start smearing shit next."

Shit. I look down at my bloody and shredded fingertips. Shit would have been easier. Messier, but easier. I shrug and step back to my bed, pushing the edge of it until it was moved back into place. Then I sit on its edge and lean forward, my elbows on my knees, my fists underneath my chin. "Okay, Mike," I whisper. "Do your thing."

Before me, in all its bloody glory, my message dried.

GET ME OUT

CHAPTER 76

Present

MIKE'S FINGERS FLY, a blur of dexterity, the computer screens before him changing in rapid succession. He is side-tracked, shifting through a guard's financials, when a new file uploads to the Tulsa Pod 23's database. Fifteen minutes later, when he shifts back, he sees the report, double-clicking on it as he reaches for a fresh soda. The door to his mini fridge stays open, his act forgotten when he sees the name on the top of the form. Deanna Madden. He skims the report quickly, the short text making the job easy.

Female was seen standing beside the cell's back wall, facing forward. I turned on the light and saw graffiti painted on the wall in the inmate's own blood, the words "Get me out." The inmate does not need medical assistance and has not been questioned at this time. Incident will be reported to shift supervisor Markus Kumna. Inmate has had a number of issues while held, and her arraignment is scheduled for 14:00 tomorrow. ~ Dimarka Trible, 23:36 p.m.

Adrenaline surges. A message for him. And he is ahead of the game. This will be child's play. He wanted the go-ahead, and here it is. Clicking on windows, he minimizes all but the two he needs, Kavut Security's internal interface and Ned Millstone. Hunching forward, the strain in his back burning red, he goes to work.

◈

Ned Millstone was born to Frank and Beth Millstone in 1971. He graduated from high school in 1989, attended a technical college in Ohio for two semesters, then dropped out. He worked in the restaurant business for seven years, then enrolled in the police academy, after which he was placed into corrections. Ned Millstone is now an eight-year employee of the city and a four-year frequenter of the Sapphire Rose Gentleman's Club. He has a twenty-three-year-old girlfriend who, five months ago, was a patient of the Hillcrest Medical Center's maternity ward. His new baby is something his wife, Barbara Millstone, born Barbara French, sole heir to the French's electronics conglomerate, knows nothing about. Barbara is, according to her father's medical records, within months of inheriting a billion-dollar empire. A hundred pieces falling perfectly into place to make it one helluva bad time for his love child to come to the attention of his wife. Mike digs the last piece of the puzzle out, Ned Millstone's cell phone number. Then he leans back in his chair and types in the number, dialing via Skype, on a line that can serve an unlimited number of purposes and still never be traced.

"This is Ned." The voice sounds out of breath and irritated.

"Ned." Mike smiles. "You don't know me, but for the next few hours, we are going to be very good friends."

CHAPTER 77

Present

I SIT ON my bed, my back against the wall, and stare at the clock. Occasionally, my eyes drop. Two or three times, my head snaps down and I catch it, bringing my chin back up. Some minutes disappear but for the most part, I am vigilant. Mike will come through. Mike will help. Mike can do anything and everything.

If he could protect Deanna Madden and make her untraceable, he can get me out of here.

If he could track down a guy from his IP address and send me a digital copy of the guy's hard drive, he can get me out of here.

If he could steal a million bucks from me, give it away, then steal it back, he can get me out of here.

If he really cares for me despite knowing all that he does, he will get me out of here.

I hear the slow pat of the next round, a guard approaching, steps moving closer, then a slight pause at my door, one that has me leaning forward, my back leaving the wall, and through the dark I see movement along my floor. I am off the bed in a breath and on my knees on the floor, my hands catching the index card as it slides along the floor into my space.

It's a layout of the building, printed on paper and taped onto the card. The map looks to be from an outside source, the handwriting across its surface Mike's. On the left side, in tiny writing, a list of instructions. I start with the first instruction and examine the lines and arrows drawn on the map, corresponding times in clear print next to each X on the map.

I finish my initial read, then glance at the clock. Forty-two minutes. I read the instructions again. And again. Again. Again. Again. Again. Again. I read the list until I can close my eyes and see the building's layout. I read the list until I have mentally walked through every piece, every pause, every step. Three minutes. I fold the paper into a tiny square and stuff it into my pocket. If I have to, if this plan fails and I am again arrested, I'll eat the damn thing.

I stand before the door and take a deep breath.

One minute.

◈

Step 1: Your door will open. Head to #2. 6 mins left.

The door pops open with a quiet click and I step outside, not pausing as I turn right and walk through the dim hall, the red lights in the hall bathing the entire area in blood. The third door I pass, I see the man, out of the corner of my eye, standing in the dark, behind the open door, like a boogeyman of my childhood dreams. He is shirtless and I stop, looking into his cell, his face in the shadows, and it takes a full heartbeat for my mind to catch up and to realize that my cell is not the only that Mike has opened. This will be interesting. I continue forward, seconds counting down, the map in my head, the steps on the list, pushing me on.

Forward, then left, then down, then right. I stop at a door, a lit office to my left, its chair empty and turning slowly, the crawl of movement creepy. I don't touch the door's handle, I wait. Behind me, like the foul odor of an exhaust, a presence. I turn and see the bare-chested man, his face pale red from the lights, his eyes on me. "Hey," he says.

"You fuck with me or fuck this up, I will kill you."

He smiles and there is a black hole where a front tooth belongs. "I'm getting out tomorrow anyway," he says. "Just along for the ride."

I hear his sentence but all it says to me is that he is stupid. It doesn't matter. Stupid is easier to control.

Step 2: The lock will turn green. Move through it and the next door, then hurry to #3.

Like a maze. A simple maze. Except now I step through the door and I'm in the booking area. I move quickly, my new toy following behind, and see three officers in the open room, two at their desks, one at a Coca-Cola machine to my right. The soda buyer—my large and friendly Ms. KeepYourHeadDownAnd-Color, glances up, then down at the machine, then her head jerks back up, her feet in motion as her mouth opens wide, a scream of hell-raisin' bellowing out. And here I thought we'd become friends. I jerk forward, hearing the screech of chairs against linoleum, a man two desks over falling as he lunges for my shirt. But I am quick, I am ready, I came prepared, and they are off guard and all I have to do is get across this room and into the next, all I have to do is shut that door behind me and Mike will lock its mechanisms, and these three will be locked in, captives. It's humorous, really. I dart around a seating area and shove on the door, its keypad already green, and I glance up at a security cam as I slam my back against the door and lock all of them, including my new toothless friend, behind me.

Except the door doesn't lock. It hits a hand, the collision of bone and muscles and gristle, a hand that moves and flexes, a hand attached to a voice, one that barks in pain. I lift off, then come back down, my feet planted on the floor, my body turned sideways, shoulder against the door as I use every muscle I have to break through the appendage. It flexes, shakes, and in the moment it jerks back, I slam my shoulder again, the door moving past the place where the hand had been and clicking into place.

The door will lock behind you. I will be watching.

LOCK. The lock turns red a second before a chorus of unknowns attack its surface. And just like that, I lose my human pet. I take a deep breath and push my shoulder off the door, wincing slightly. Sometime, I'll need to ice it. Once all the ass kicking is over and precious seconds are in greater supply. I roll the shoulder and turn. Before me, a long hallway, one final sprint, the exit door before me in full metal glory, the red sign above it a beacon to my fate. Only one issue stands before me, his legs spread in a fighter's stance, halfway between me and the hallway's end . . . a hulking giant of a man. I don't move, I don't advance. I just stand, my breath heavy as it breaks from my chest, and I stare.

I have fought many men in my lifetime. If I ever get through this moment, through this chapter in my life, if I ever avenge Jeremy and escape a prison sentence, I will learn how to do it properly. Because although I have fought many men in my lifetime, I have won very few times. And never without a gun or a knife, a weapon or an advantage. And right now, in this interaction right here, I have only one card to play and it is Mike's instructions, and I square my shoulders and put all of my trust into the man I have never met.

Step 3: Fight. Take the keycard attached to his shirt.

That was the whole step. The map stopped at this hallway with its X, then continued out to the parking lot, the gate which I would open with the keycard. Why Mike could unlock every internal door yet needed me to fight this heap of muscle to get out of the parking lot made no sense to me. Should I survive this, I'll be sure to give him a piece of my mind.

I stop dicking around and step toward the man. A few feet from him, I stop, the fluorescent light above our heads beaming down on the man's features, his face hard and set, his hands raised and already clenched. I sneak a peek at his fists and my confidence withers. Muscular and strong. I have to lift my chin to look up at him. Maybe sexuality will work. I pull at the bottom of my sweatshirt, pulling the material up my stomach and over my breasts. When his eyes drop, I lift my knee and go for his balls.

Weak. Cowardly. I know. But you stand face-to-face with Goliath and see if you fight fair. Besides, any morality issues dissolve when one of his big meat hooks blocks my knee, his balls effectively protected, my sneak attack card gone, just like that.

"Not there," he grumbles. He points, and my eyes wander up his outstretched finger, to his face. "Here." Our eyes meet and his are blue.

"Really?" I frown.

"Hurry." He closes his eyes and tenses. I don't hesitate, widening my stance and throwing my sore shoulder into the jab, barreling the heel of my hand up, right at the underside of his nose, the connection of my hand and the delicate belly of his nose loud, bloody, and delicious. He staggers, a hand going to his nose as he swears loudly.

I don't wait for a recovery, I see the green light hit the exit door and I step forward, yanking at the clip on his shirt, his identification coming off in my hand, a quick *thank you* whispered. I start, then stop, digging my nails into the guard of his holster, the pop of metal sharp and beautiful, my hand wrapping around the textured grip and pulling. Goliath doesn't like that, he drops his head and hand and spins, reaching for me, but I am sprinting down the hall, the push on the door yielding me my first cool and perfect kiss of freedom. I spin and shove against the door and hear the slam of his head against the metal, his face bloody and furious in the thin window. I mouth an apology and then rip away from the door and into the freedom of the night.

The sky is clear, the parking lot small, our slice of prison surrounded by the buildings of the city. I jog down a set of steps, sliding the gun into my sweatshirt's pocket, an unfamiliar unease stealing over me. A gun wasn't on the list, wasn't on my directions, but in this moment, I have nothing. No cash, no connections, no phone. I am free yet hunted, the night air terrifying in its openness. I zigzag through a line of cars, the bright lights of the parking lot shining down. And then, like clockwork, they all turn off. Mike. I look up and manage a smile, a wave of endorphins pushing through my system in the newly created dark. I am not alone. I can do this. I can force my life back into order, find my way back to good. I reach the gate and hesitate for a moment, staring at the bars before me, the one last guard between me and the outside world. Then, the photo of Jeremy's battered face coming to mind, I swipe Ned Millstone's card through the reader and jog on silent feet through the crack of the opening gate. I need to, in this final chance at freedom, at least find the truth.

Step 4: Go five blocks west to the McDonald's and wait by the pay phone.

I flip the hood up on my sweatshirt and begin to jog, the weight of the gun slapping a hard and tempting beat against the knot in my stomach.

CHAPTER 78

Present

WHEN A PHONE rings in the night, you answer it. Especially if you're on the force. Especially if you're a mother with kids. Especially if you have thirty seconds before your husband will wake and any spousal love will go to shit.

Brenda sits up in bed and hunches forward, over the cell, the BLOCKED screen familiar and, at the same time, depressing. She'll have to get up, go somewhere, do something. Probably uncover a dead body and knock on some mother's door. "Hello." She whispers the word.

"Boles, this is Eva Aransoti, dispatch number one eighty-nine. There's been an incident at the Fourth Street booking station." The crisp female voice is that of someone fully awake, with no regard or sympathy for anyone soundly sleeping.

Fourth Street. Deanna Madden. The case that won't stop giving. She slides out of bed and walks to the bathroom, closing the door quietly behind her. This woman was a disaster. Lock her up and she was assaulting every person in sight. "I thought Madden was in solitary." Maybe she won't have to go anywhere. Maybe she could knock out this chat and then crawl back into bed. Still three good hours of sleep left before breakfasts and showers and lunch money and backpacks.

"She was. Something happened at the station and all of the inmates were released."

Her eyes fully open. "All of them?" What kind of thing releases an entire pod of criminals?

"We need you and Reuber there."

"Okay. I'm fifteen minutes out." She feels along the wall and flips the light's switch. "Wait." She rubs her forehead. "Why me and Reuber?"

"Deanna Madden is the only one who escaped the booking compound. The others were redetained."

"But Madden is free."

"Yes. You can review the footage at the station."

"I realize that." Brenda stands, yanking down flannel pajama pants and digging through the dirty clothes basket for yesterday's khakis. "Thanks," she adds as a polite afterthought, before hanging up the phone, flipping the light off, and tiptoeing into the dark bedroom.

In the car, without coffee or a breath mint, she calls David. "Did you hear?"

"Yep. I'm walking out right now. Think she'll head to the hospital?"

"I'm gonna call them next and have a plainclothes posted by his room. See if she shows."

"All right. I'll be at the station in ten."

"See you there." Reaching down, she flips on her lights and pulls out onto the quiet street.

CHAPTER 79

Present

THE GRIM REALITY of my situation looms larger as I run. I have nothing. My weapons, shipped to Mike. My apartment will have a new lock on it, crime scene tape stretched across its front. I cannot go to see the man I love, for I am a fugitive, with a name I can't use, money I can't access, and no one nearby to call on for help.

He was pushed out the window.

He was stabbed six times.

He was left to die.

Jeremy is my person; I only have two of them in the world. You do not fuck with my people; I will fight you to your death to protect them, I will climb buildings to kill you slowly over a drop of their blood. Jeremy's blood was a flood that has gone unpunished, and I feel the hot prickle of vengeance push at my psyche, a tempting chorus I stop midsong, my hands covering useless ears, my breath hard and fast when I stop running and break, wheezing out a few exhales. I cannot do this. I cannot go red, not when everything else is falling apart.

I hear a siren and sink into a doorway. Stand in its shadows as a cop car, then a second, screams past. Then, my heart thumping in my chest, I step out and run farther. One more block. I see the golden arches ahead of me. They haven't changed much in four years. Same fluorescent yellow, same billions served. I see the pay phone, installed against the building's exterior brick, and slow to a walk. I don't like it. Too brightly lit, exposed to anyone who drives by. I stop on the opposite curb, seventy-five feet from the phone. Debate Mike's instructions, though I have nothing else to follow.

Against the restaurant, the phone begins to ring. I hesitate, the sole of my tennis shoe bending over the curved edge of the curb, then step forward, rolling off and across the asphalt and into the bright light.

"Hello."

"Hey, babe."

I have to smile at his tone, so warm and relaxed, like we didn't just break a dozen laws together. "Hey. Talk quick, this pay phone has a freaking spotlight on it."

"There's an Uber car in the back of the parking lot. It's a red Taurus. I paid with a credit card, the driver will take you wherever you need to go."

I grip the phone. "Any change in Jeremy?"

"No." His voice drops. "I'm sorry, Dee."

I nod without speaking. It's been too long, too many days. If he doesn't come back... I try to refocus, bits of my psyche floating loose like flaking skin. "Thanks for getting me out. I don't know how you did it, but I appreciate it."

"No problem. One day, over beers, I'll brag to you about the complexities of it all. Whenever that day comes, ooh and aah a lot for me."

One day. "Deal. I'll call you when I can."

"Get a cell phone when you can."

"I need cash, that's my first issue."

"Don't have any friends in town?"

I bite on my bottom lip in response. The silence on the line grows, each second another embarrassing weight on my solidarity. I shrug, a motion he never sees. "I'll call you when I can. If I can."

"Be safe."

I smile sadly. "Always."

Then, before he has a chance to say anything else, I hang up the phone. Glance around and head to the back of the parking lot. See a red Taurus idling beside a Dumpster, and step toward it.

I stop beside the driver's door and bend over. Look into the face of a woman, one in her midfifties, her white hair styled in the short-haired manner favored by grandmothers everywhere. I blink in surprise. She rolls down her window. "You Jessica?"

Jessica. I smile the friendly smile cams.com's most popular coed. "Yes."

"Hop in."

I open the back door and slide into the middle of the backseat. She locks the doors and shifts into drive. I stare at the lock and run my hand along the handle. "Where to?" she calls back, her eyes meeting mine in the rearview mirror.

"For the moment, please head south."

She nods and doesn't comment. I run my hands over the top

of my jeans and try to think. I'd kill for some cash right now, no pun intended. I feel naked and unprotected. I turn my head and watch dark houses move past—catching myself seriously considering breaking into one of them. At three in the morning, how do I differentiate between an empty house and a sleeping one? I know of one house that's empty, its new owner hovering between death and life. But I can't go there, I can't step inside the house where, just four days ago, I had so much hope.

"Mulholland Oaks. It's an apartment complex on Greenvale Street. Please take me there." Inside my chest, my heartbeat quickens, pushing blood to every vein, my hand trembling against the armrest until I grab it with my other hand and force it still. Forget planning or weapons or cash. I can't wait any longer, both for logistics purposes and for my own control. The police will come looking for me. And I can't not find out the truth.

I am unprepared, this is stupid and reckless, but I need it and I need it now. I feel a familiar tightening of my body, my brain, a loss of intelligent control, and I close my eyes, inhale deeply, and let it happen.

Four a.m. Smack-dab in the middle of my witching hour. Inside, a prickle of excitement flares. I am going to Simon for answers; that is what I need to remember. And if his answers are wrong? Well. I push aside that thought for now.

I reach out and tap the back of her seat, two blocks away from my complex. "This is fine. You can let me out here." The car quiets, rolling to a smooth stop and I step out, she leaves, and I'm alone on the street. I flip up my hoodie and head home, a moving smile in the darkness.

CHAPTER 80

Present

PLEASE WALK ME through how this happened." Brenda stands in the small office, David taking up valuable real estate next to her.

Before her, the station chief settles into a chair, waving them down. They don't sit. "The short of it is, the manufacturer of our locks, the ones on the cells, internal and external doors... it's a Russian company called Kavut. Their system was hacked and it went haywire."

"Other stations had problems?"

"Nope. Just us."

David shifts forward. "You talked to Kavut? Find out how many of their clients were affected?"

The man rubs his forehead. "Yes. It looks like it was just us."

"Us, the TPD or us, this booking station?" Brenda prods.

"Us, this booking station."

"I'd like to see the security footage."

The chief props an arm on the armrest of his chair. "So would I. But it's gone, was wiped out about a half hour after the incident."

"Kavut glitch also?" David guesses, a pained expression on his face.

"No, our video system is an internal one."

Brenda waits for the explanation but nothing comes. "So what happened?" She pulls at the front of her shirt. It's so hot. God, she's too young for menopause, it can't be menopause. She stares at the chief and is perversely pleased to see a bead of sweat roll down the side of his face. It's not just her.

"Tech guys are trying to figure it out. All video from the last thirty days is gone." He waves a hand in the air. "A thousand hours"—he snaps his fingers—"whoosh."

"And Deanna Madden is the only detainee missing."

"Yeah." He nods. "Another two got out into the parking lot, but couldn't get over the razor wire. Madden took a key from a guard, caught him by surprise in the exit hall, and that got her through the gates."

"Who was the guard?"

"Ned Millhouse. He's not an easy guy to overcome." He taps a finger on his desk with a laugh. "She broke his nose. He heard a noise behind him, turned around and *pow!*" He pantomimes the jab, then points at them, his face growing serious. "If you see him, give him hell. We've all been ribbing him about it." He coughs, his face sobering. "There's another issue. She took his service weapon."

Ouch. Ned Millhouse would have greater hell to pay than just ribbing. David glances at her, and they share a silent moment of communication. The stakes to find Deanna Madden just quadrupled. A gun, a hacked security system, and wiped camera footage with no logical explanation. Twelve hours before she goes to jail and the stars align for her to just waltz out. Beside her, David's cell phone buzzes and he glances at it, opening the door and stepping out. She glances at the wall clock. Four thirty-five. Hopefully news of some sort. She'd issued an APB for Madden, which, at this time of morning, will go largely unheeded. This is Tulsa. Officers have bigger fish to fry then a missing camgirl, and it doesn't matter who she had or hadn't tried to kill. "We'd like to talk to any inmates and officers who've had contact with Deanna Madden."

"No problem. I can make a list and round them up, if you want to . . ." His sentence dies as David props open the door and sticks his head in.

"Brenda?" He jerks his head toward the parking lot, a smile on his handsome face. "Jeremy Pacer is conscious and talking."

The best news she's gotten at four in the morning in a very, very long time. She beams a smile at the chief, who raises his eyebrows. "We'll be back," she promises. Then, she grabs the door and escapes into the hall, her boots slapping on the linoleum floor to keep up with David.

CHAPTER 81

Present

ON THE FOURTH floor of Hillcrest Hospital South, there is a moment of quiet, the two nurses working in tandem on the left side of Jeremy's bed, his sister on the right side, his hand gripped in both of hers. A doctor is coming, is still minutes away, but all will be fine because he is awake and is speaking, even though his face is twisted in pain and his hand is trembling between hers.

"I love you." She leans forward and lowers her mouth, kisses the top of his hand.

He smiles weakly. Moves his lips and staggers out a single-word question. "Deanna?"

She blinks back tears through a broken smile. "She's in jail, sweetie."

He frowns, a thousand questions asked through his eyes, his mouth struggling to work. "She was arrested, J. She confessed. You might not remember but she tried to…" She swallows. "She stabbed you."

He shakes his head roughly, a gesture that has all three women springing forward, their hands holding him still.

"Please stop talking to him," the first nurse snaps. "We need to keep him stable."

Lily nods, breaking a hand from his to wipe at her eyes. He glares at her, a grimace breaking into a sound as he lifts his head from the pillow. "Simon," he hisses. "It was Simon."

Four short, tiny words. The machine next to him flares to life, the numbers on it jumping erratically, and his head rolls to the side, his eyes still open, still stuck on Lily, a tortured plea that doesn't stop as a vessel in his brain reopens, flooding the area with blood, his mental system shutting down in protection mode. Squeezing his limp palm tightly, she looks at him in panic.

CHAPTER 82

Present

I AM NOT a normal individual. I've known that for quite some time. And tonight, with my nerves humming, my worry over Jeremy cresting, my night demons kicking, I calm myself the only way I know how: by planning. And my plans align in agreement that it costs at least ten bucks to properly kill someone. I've determined that after wandering up and down the eight rows of the Quik Mart. I stand by the convenience store's front window and watch my building.

There are four good options on the shelves of this store, my calculator of death rattling up totals in my head like jackpots.

Zip ties, one gallon of gas, and a lighter. Total: $8.52 + tax *Burn, baby, burn.*

Or zip ties, one gallon of antifreeze, and a funnel. Total: $9.32 + tax *Poison, baby, poison*

Or zip ties, a razor, and (optional) aspirin. Total: $9.29 + tax *Bleed, baby, bleed*

Or duct tape and plastic bags. Total $7.98 + tax *Choke, baby, choke*

All four options would allow me to keep the gun's safety on, the chamber free of bullets. I don't know if I can handle a gun tonight. Scratch that. I know I cannot handle a gun tonight. Put Simon within range of a loaded weapon in my hand and I won't get the first question out, won't get the first truth revealed.

"Need any help?"

"Nope." I don't turn to the store's attendant, the nerdy one whose eyes have undressed me three times in the last ten minutes. I pushed up the sleeves of my sweatshirt five minutes ago, and his interest increased tenfold. I really don't want to rob this guy, especially not over a handful of items that adds up to a large box of tampons. I stay in place, hidden from the street, standing behind a postcard carousel, and watch the road. Ten minutes and no one has passed more than once. I walked past all of the cars on the street twice before coming in here. No bodies in the cars, no stakeout, best I could tell. But I'll give it two more minutes, just to be sure. I tap my fingers against a postcard of Niagara Falls, an inventory item that makes no freakin' sense in Oklahoma. "Any cops come in here lately?" I ask.

"No." A normal person would be suspicious of my question. A normal person wouldn't choose to work the night shift in this neighborhood, especially not with white skin and acne that screams underage. I glance over at him for a moment before returning my gaze back to the street. I can't pull my gun on this guy. It'll ruin the boner he's spent so much time and effort adjusting. Maybe I could offer to flash him, sex over violence, a new page for me to turn. What American male won't pay a few bucks to see breasts? I count over windows till I get to my apartment. The lights are off. How considerate of the cops for my utility bill. Too bad that Simon's is on the opposite side of the building, no hint as to its life from this angle. No matter. If he isn't up I'll wake him up. And her. Please let her be there.

My two-minute sentence ends and I turn, half-excited by my future, half-irritated by the steps needed to get there. I face the man and watch his eyes move to my face. Gun or sex, gun or sex...the kaleidoscope of options rolls through my mind. An easy decision, though sex feels dirtier, for some reason, than violence. I tilt my head and let a slow smile spread over my face, as my hand unwraps from the gun. I step across the store over to the crowded counter and lean on it, my elbows pressing into the hard edge, a glass mat of lotto tickets my stage. "Daniel..." I drawl the name off his name tag, and he shifts in his ironed khakis. "I have a proposition for you."

❖

Five minutes later, I move through the Quik Mart's door, my sweatshirt back on, hood up, feet quiet, a tossed wave given to Daniel, who flashes an enthusiastic smile in my direction. I step outside and jog across the empty street, my feet hopping over the curb and along the broken sidewalk. I tug at the sleeve of my sweatshirt and cover my hand, use the protection to tug on the door's handle. Then, just like that, I am inside Mulholland Oaks and thundering up the stairwell steps.

Second floor. If they are both there, I will go for him first.

Third floor. Maybe I'll play nice in the beginning. Get their guard down while I look for extra weapons. Wait, answers. That's what this is about. The plastic bag in my hand swings as I climb higher.

Fourth floor. I will burn this sweatshirt when this is all over.

Fifth floor. I can't burn the sweatshirt. He gave me the sweatshirt. He may never have the chance to give me another. Assholes.

Sixth floor. I would have loved to shower but there is no time. I round the final bend in the stairs and stop on the landing, my chest aching. I wait, shaking out my limbs while my breathing calms. Jump a few times in place because I've seen guys do that on television before a fight and it looks badass. My breath quiets and I let out a long, controlled exhale. Then I quietly climb the last seven stairs and stop. I set the bag on the floor and crouch before it, pulling out my stash. I pop the plastic off each item, leaving a sea of plastic wrap and price tags on the ground. Sweet Daniel. Should my life ever return to normal, I'll send him a thousand bucks. He rang up each item on the register, carefully and precisely. It had totaled $9.57 and he had even given me the forty-three cents of change. I start with the zip ties, pulling out a few pieces and linking them together, a foot or two of chain, both ends left open. Then I grab the duct tape, ripping off five long pieces and sticking one end of them to the backs of my legs, their loose tails fluttering down like fly strips. I keep the zip tie chain in one hand and put the rest of the unwrapped items in the plastic bag, snagging it off the ground. Moving to the door, I press softly on the door handle. Crack it a hair and peek down the hall. Empty. I push the door the rest of the way open and step into the hall.

I am not a physically imposing person, I don't have a wealth of martial arts skills, I am horrible at taking a punch, and strangling others really takes it out of me. But all that being said, I am intelligent and I have studied the art of killing for the last half decade. When the creative minds at Survival Life posted instructions for a makeshift grenade with a PVC pipe, baking soda, and vinegar, I tested it out in the north stairwell one chilly December night. When Gizmodo explained the harmful effects of the Bleach Bomb and warned readers to "never ever create one," I printed the recipe out and taped it to my fridge. Did you know you can create napalm by stirring Styrofoam in gasoline and scooping out the resulting goo? I don't have to be a black belt or have my weapons arsenal to be dangerous. All I really need is to be smarter than my opponent.

I am smarter than Simon. I suspect I'm smarter than Chelsea. I am definitely, at this moment in time, more awake, prepared, and motivated than either of them. I walk down a hall I've lived on for a thousand days yet walked down less than fifty times. Pass my door and eye the new lock. Go down two more doors and stop before Simon's. The last time I knocked on his door, I had almost killed someone. I had been a barely contained mess of emotions. Funny how, this time, I am falling apart in a thousand different ways. The madness in me, it is pushing, stretching, filling my body down new and unique paths, my skin growing accustomed to its heat, its darkness. I reach up my hand to knock, and realize, it hovering in the air, that it is not trembling. I frown, unfolding my fist and rolling it over, looking at it for a moment. *I am in control.* I am here, with instruments to kill, a plan of attack in place, and I am in control. Is this the madness, my hereditary push toward the darkness? Or is it just me, is this the person I am becoming, a person with full faculties and awareness of the actions she is about to take? That thought, that realization...I step away from Simon's door for a moment and take a deep breath. Right now, my world breaking apart at the seams...I can't do what I need to do and be in control. In control means responsible. Responsible means that, if I go batshit crazy and everyone inside dies, that I, Deanna Madden, in full control of her actions, was responsible. Not the demon inside, not the loss of control. I close my eyes and search for the deep, scary part of myself, the part that I've run from so often. I search for it, I find it, and I dive into the cool pool of its depths. I push further, imagining my kills, the thirst I had had, the feeling I had gotten, the high I had experienced. I plunge into the past, make it my present, and inhale the sexy stench of evil.

When I open my eyes, I am the girl I never wanted to be but have been for a long time. I am the madness, the demon, the insanity. I step forward with purpose and pound my fist on the door.

CHAPTER 83

Present

ALL IS NOT lost; it will be fine. There was a rebleed, but he'll come out again. Lily knows it. She stands in the doorway and watches the nurses work. Everyone quiet, the monitor behaving. The doctor left a few minutes ago but said he'd be back. *This is a good sign*, he'd said. *His brain is tired*, he said. *We'll give him some time to recoup, then pull back the drugs in a few days. See what happens.* See what happens. Like it was Olivia's softball practice and they weren't sure if it would be rained out. She doesn't like the doctor. He fidgets and doesn't ask her name and doesn't look her in the eye. Like he doesn't want to connect with someone who might get hurt. She told him, what Jeremy said, those five little words that brought everything crashing down. He blinked down at his phone and then took Jeremy's pulse.

It's not fair, that he came to life for a few minutes and uttered only five words. Even more unfair that every single one of them were about *her*. The girl that, just hours earlier, Lily had been cursing to an early grave. She had literally spent all of last night planning out and practicing the speech she would give jurors, the stories she would tell about Jeremy, and the final dramatic moment when she would gasp back a tear, point toward the bitch and scream, *She took it from him! She took everything from him!* before collapsing into an inconsolable mess, right there, on the stand. It had played out very nicely in her head, a potent nail that would push every juror to decide, in their final deliberations, to send Deanna Madden to Death Row. That, Lily Ortiz had decided, was her rightful punishment.

Granted, she hadn't always thought that. She had actually believed in her innocence. Had scoffed a little at the detective's questions about Jeremy's girlfriend. Yes, Deanna seemed weird. Antisocial. Yes, Lily had been irritated and put off by Jeremy's resistance to introduce them. But why would his girlfriend try to kill him? Jeremy wasn't the type to piss off a girlfriend. If anything, he'd always been too nice, too forgiving, too willing to overlook a flaw or two. So she had pushed that option from her mind. But then the girl had confessed and everything, in that quick line of news, had changed in Lily's mind. A dark, venomous hate had grown in her gut and eaten every bit of compassion and understanding in her heart. She had sat in that hospital room, stared at his still form, and begun to hate Deanna Madden with a black madness previously reserved for any person who would think of harming her child.

I love you, she had sobbed to Jeremy.

Deanna, he had responded.

She's in jail, she had said.

Simon. It was Simon.

Who the F is Simon? Not one of his friends, no one he worked with... She digs deep and comes up blank. She turns away, toward the hall, and takes a few steps, then stops, leaning her back against the wall. She cups her hands around the cell phone and unlocks the screen. Stares for a long moment at the home display, the time changing as she watches it, one more minute lost forever, one more minute she will never get back.

Simon. It was Simon.

Slowly, she scrolls down the call log, her finger hovering over the number of the detective, their last chat a couple of days ago, when Deanna Madden had confessed.

Simon. It was Simon.

Who was to say that Jeremy was coherent? That he even knew what was going on? That he even remembered what had happened? Who knew if Simon was a real person or just a figment created by a morphine-high brain? Why should she listen to him?

Simon. It was Simon.

He'd only managed five words during his journey to the surface. It only makes sense that she should listen to what he said, damn the validity. She presses on the number and lifts the phone to her ear. Hears the ring and worries, for a moment, about waking the woman.

When Brenda answers, there is the rush of road noise in the background, and Lily breaths a sigh of relief.

"Detective Boles? This is Lily Ortiz, Jeremy Pacer's sister."

"Lily, we're headed to you now, we're about twenty minutes away." She says something to someone else, a muffled conversation occurring out of Lily's earshot.

"There's no point in coming." Her voice cracks and she swallows hard, forcing her vocal cords into submission. "I mean...

he's back asleep. He probably won't talk again for another twelve hours or so."

"Oh." The disappointment in that one word is clear and pronounced.

"But he did say something. Right before he fell back asleep." Asleep, that's all it was. The heavy medication, his injuries... he was asleep. Asleep with his eyes open, that's the part she can't erase from her mind. That's the scene that, if this doesn't end well, she will never ever forget.

"Yes?"

She squeezes a chunk of hair in her fist, her nails biting into the pad of her palm. "He said it wasn't Deanna. That it was someone named Simon. Do you know who he could be talking about?"

There is a long pause, the hum of background noise the only thing verifying their connection. "Simon?" the woman says warily. "That's what he said? Are you sure?"

A stupid question but she'd asked the nurses a hundred of them that day alone. *Will he be okay? Is he thirsty? Will he wake up? Is that medicine helping?* "Yes." She says shortly. "I am a hundred percent sure. He said the name twice."

"Yeah," Brenda says carefully. "We know a Simon. Thank you for the information, Mrs. Ortiz. Please call me back if he wakes up again."

"When he wakes up again." She can't help the snap.

"Of course. When he wakes up again."

"Who is Simon?" She blurts the question quickly, before the woman can hang up.

"At the moment?" the woman's voice is wry, her response quick and unpolluted. "Our new suspect."

"But how does he—" Lily stops her question midstream. It is too late, the background noise gone. When she glances down at the phone, the "Call Ended" screen blinks up at her.

Simon. It was Simon. So Simon is real. And Deanna may be innocent after all. She locks the cell phone and lowers her head to her knees. Replays the conversation for a second, then a third time. Hopes fervently that she did the right thing by calling the detective.

CHAPTER 84

Present

I SEE A light come on beneath the crack of the door, and step back. The asshole himself opens the door and stands before me. From the darkness behind him, I hear her mumble his name and see a pile of blankets move on the right edge of the room. *Good.* We'll make a threesome. So much fun.

"Hey..." Surprise in his greeting. He is not happy to see me. I can see it in the dart of his eyes, his hand's nervous play on the knob.

"Hey." I smile and it's a good thing I've had four years of smiling at clients because I am damn good at it. He has never seen a Jess Reilly smile from me before and he hesitates, caught off guard. I lift a hand to my mouth, the index finger pointed up, the universal *shh* sign, and giggle softly. *Come here* I mouth, stepping back, against the opposite wall, the plastic bag in my hand bumping against the plaster with a seductive *swoosh*. I crook my finger and the idiot follows, pulling the door behind him. I sway a little sideways as if I am drunk, and drop the bag on the floor.

Shh..., I shush and giggle, though he has said nothing

and this is too easy, his hands coming out and supporting me, his body close enough that, if my breasts were knives, he'd be impaled with one step forward.

"I thought you were—" I cut off his sentence with my mouth, pushing my pelvis forward and grabbing the back of his head, pulling him to me, his mouth stiff then softer on mine, his hands settling on my hips and his hair is spiky and unwashed and his mouth tastes like pot and kissing this prick is absolutely worth it as I stop the passage of his hands up my shirt and grab his wrists, wrapping a giant zip tie around them, threading one end into the other and yanking hard. The handcuffing is done without a break in our mouths, his attention captured while his freedom is taken. Then I break the kiss and kill any mood by pulling the gun from the small of my back. I drag back the slide, pop a bullet into the chamber, and level the barrel at his forehead. SimonTheAsshole freezes still, the dim hallway light bright enough for him to understand the situation. He tries to lift his hands in surrender and struggles, the tight grip of the tie making the act awkward and—from the grimace on his face— painful. Oh, Simon…The poor boy has no idea what is ahead.

I hold the gun with my right hand and grab a piece of duct tape, yanking it off my jeans and slapping it over his eyes. Another piece for his mouth.

He flails in the sudden blindness, his cuffed hands reaching for me, and his shoulder hits the wall with a loud thud. That's bad. Any minute Chelsea will be opening that door. I put the gun at his temple and lean forward, close enough to smell his scent. "Be still and go where I push you, or I will pull the trigger. Nod slowly if you understand." He nods and I kick at the cracked-open door, shoving him in and turning right, holding the gun out and steady at the bed where I had heard Chelsea's voice.

Before, she was under the covers, a shadow moving in the background. Now, she is propped up on her air mattress, an Iron Maiden T-shirt on, an irritated look on her face when we crash into the room and I level the gun at her. To her credit, she doesn't react, doesn't scream, she just sits there, her eyebrows raised, and glances from the gun to me, to Simon—who trips over a recliner and falls—to the gun. "You look like you know how to use that."

"I do. And I'd *really* love to smear your brains across that cheap comforter, so please. Make my fucking day and try something."

"You know you tried to kill me already. It didn't work." She adjusts the neck of the T-shirt as if we are sitting in Starbucks, waiting on our Frappuccino order to be called.

"Second time's the charm."

"What are you doing here, Deanna?" She sounds tired, like this midnight meeting is inconvenient but not life threatening, and I want to shoot off a body part just so she shows me some respect. "I thought you were in jail."

"I was. Move to the end of the bed and kneel on the ground before me."

She is too sluggish, and I am half-giddy with bloodlust, half-irritated by her attitude, and half-anxious for answers, so I decide to screw plans and shoot some respect into this bitch. I grab the closest pillow, shove it down on her thigh to muffle the sound, and pull the trigger.

❖

"Here is the plan, Chelsea." I nod toward the floor. "Kneel."
She kneels. "Good girl." I listen to Simon moan something
unintelligible, and smile. "I'm going to give you some zip ties,
and you are going to tie your ankles together, and then your
wrists. You are going to do it tightly or else I am going to shoot
off whatever appendage is being lazy."

"Are you going to miss again?" Her voice sounds hard but I
see the shake in her eyes. She's lucky I missed, that the pillow
hid the quick movement of her skinny leg and the air mattress
got the bullet instead of her. It was almost better it worked out
that way. The mattress deflated, she got motivated, and I finally
have some freaking respect without having to worry about her
bleeding to death before I am done. I smile and pull out a handful of ties from my pocket.

She looks down at them, then up at me, her blue eyes study-
ing me as if she could see her future in them. "The faster you
move, Chelsea, the quicker I'll be gone. Answer all of my questions and I'll leave you two unhurt." It was a lie but I smile as if
it were true and added the one word that makes everyone calm.
"Promise."

She rolls onto her butt, her bare feet before her, and I can
see the hot pink of her underwear. Her toes are painted dark
purple, a shade that is seriously going to clash with the yellow
ties she picks up. I stare at her toes and try to remember the last
time I painted mine. Thursday? It feels like five months ago.
"Tighter." She glares up at me, pulling on the end of the tie, her
skin squishing out a little around the plastic tie. I smile. For a

skinny girl, she has fat ankles, and that makes me happy. "Now your wrists."

"I'm not coordinated enough to do my wrists."

"Make the loop really big, slide your wrists in, then use your mouth to tighten it."

She sighs like it is an enormous task. For a woman who is still alive, she's extremely ungrateful. I step right as she works, putting Simon fully in my vision, the skinny druggie on his back, his hands tied before him, with apparently no plans for escape or heroism. I think of him, in my apartment, his face triumphant and cocky, and my world turns a little redder, my control shifts into a lower gear, my plans take on a more fluid state. I glance back to Chelsea, her mouth on the end of the tie, her lip curling at me as she bites down on the end and tightens the plastic around her wrists. "Stop." I pause her movement before it's too late. "Face your palms in the same direction. Not palm to palm, one palm on the back of the other one's hand." She hesitates, then flips over one hand, putting her wrists in a position that is pretty much useless. She looks up at me and I nod in approval. She replaces her mouth on the tie and tugs on it, cinching her wrists together. "More," I prod and smile when she complies. *Power.* I sometimes wonder if it is that, more than the blood, that I crave.

CHAPTER 85

Present

THE PATROL CAR is silent yet filled with sounds. The chomp of gum in David's jaw. The tick of the engine as she accelerates. The drag of wipers as she tries to clear fog off the windshield.

"Think he's protecting her?" The click of bullets as David loads his clip.

Brenda shakes her head. "I don't think so."

"The kid seemed clean to me. Messed up, sure. A druggie, sure. A killer?" He snaps the loaded clip into his gun. "No."

There is a static burst of radio chatter and he grabs the mike, giving their location and ETA. When he hangs the mouthpiece back on the dash, he looks over. "You got your vest?"

"It's in the trunk." Chelsea Evans will probably be there. Human Resources couldn't, at five in the morning, confirm whether she has moved. This might be messy. They need to prepare for anything.

❖

I grab my bag and sit on the pleather sofa, the focal furniture piece in Simon's apartment, the massive entertainment center its crown jewel. I set the gun on the coffee table and eye her. Pull items from the bag and set them down on the table before me, dusting off the surface with one aggressive swipe, weed flakes fluttering into the air, his rolling papers following suit. I catch a Zippo before it slides off the table and set it upright, next to my container of antifreeze. Reach down, to the bottom level of the coffee table, and steal a razor out of a glass bowl.

Duct tape.

Antifreeze.

Eight remaining zip ties.

Two plastic bags, thrown in for free by the wonderful Daniel.

The Zippo lighter and razor, courtesy of Simon's coffee table.

Questioning. That's what this would start as. Entertainment for my madness, a drink of something violent to calm my world, answers for Jeremy. I can feel the flutter of things in my world returning to normal and it will be here soon, as soon as I figure out the truth. I clap my hands in anticipation and smile at Chelsea. She sits in the same place, her wrists hanging off her knees, her eyes on the table of items before me. "Unharmed," she repeats. "You promised."

"Dee-Dee!" Summer's face scrunched into that of an old woman's, wrinkles popping up everywhere. "The park! You promised!"

"Oh yes, I promise," I reassure her and smile again. My face is starting to hurt but soon I will know, soon he will have justice, soon this breakdown of my world will come to an end.

"I'm not going to the park, Summer. It's a thousand degrees out."

"But you PROMISED!" She stretched out the final word, giving it four syllables instead of two.

I shrugged, flipping the magazine's page. "I lied."

The two of them sit before me, like a matching set of salt-and-pepper shakers—Simon the Salt, Chelsea the Pepper—back-to-back because I said so and I hold the gun. They are handcuffed together with zip ties, Simon's bare back pressed against Chelsea's T-shirt, her long blond hair probably tickling the hell outta his vertebrae. I take the tape off Simon's eyes at some point. He needs to see this. All of this. I stand up from the table and grab one of the trash bags and the roll of duct tape.

"Let's talk about Sunday night," I instruct, and step closer. I'll pull the bag over Chelsea's head and duct-tape it tight. Let her suffocate until Simon talks. Then I stop, think of Jeremy, and walk to the kitchen. Pull open the first drawer, then the second. I glance over at the pair.

"The police told me Jeremy was stabbed six times."

There is no response from my quiet charges. I pull out a paring knife and wrap my fingers around the handle, rolling my wrist a few times to get accustomed to its feel. I look over and see a tear drag quietly down Simon's cheek. There had never been a question of who would break first, but I am pleased to see my hypothesis proved true. I walk over and crouch before him, my touch with the knife's blade gentle as I run it from ear to ear, teasing his beautifully exposed neck.

"Did you stab my boyfriend?" I whisper, watching his eyes, watching them jump to his sister. I would have protected Trent. I wouldn't have let a psychotic girl handcuff him and play tic-tac-toe with his skin.

"No," he whispers and I smile. Push the tip of the knife gently against the heave of his ribs and lean forward, the sharp tip breaking through, pushing harder, blood appearing at the same time that his mouth opens and he screams, a beautiful, long, pained scream, the kind my orgasms are built around, the kind that make Chelsea twist her head in panic, her eyes on mine, her own mouth opening and protests spilling out.

I jab harder, the paring knife buried to the hilt, then yank out. "That's one, Simon. I owe you five more. Unless, that is, you have a confession to make."

"I didn't stab him!" he screams, his voice high and tinny, like a child's. "It was an accident, it was all an accident!"

"Bullshit," I growl, my next stab neither slow nor gentle, hitting quick and hard into his bare shoulder, his body bucking back, against Chelsea, her scream at me to *stop you crazy bitch* hitting dead ears and a broken soul. Jeremy was my person. You kill him and so God help your soul I will take all that you love. I leave the knife in, straightening to my feet and pull out the gun. Hold it against Chelsea's forehead, her mouth falling silent, our eyes glued to each other. The cocky woman who tried to seduce my man is gone, and suddenly there is fear in her eyes. Respect in her silence. I don't think, until this moment in time, that she truly realized what I am capable of.

"Talk." I grit out the word and I can feel the edge of my world as it is destroyed, my control slipping, this interrogation one shaky step away from being a full-blown bloodbath for no other reason than my personal enjoyment.

Chelsea swallows hard and opens her mouth. "It was—" The door bangs open behind me, a sharp crack of sound and a series of spotlights bounce over the kitchen, zeroing in on our trio, my shadow thrown against the wall and I look *huge*. I stay in place and hear a series of clicks, bullets being chambered, guns cocked. It sounds like a brigade, like death in a marching band, but I ignore them all and look down at the woman with the answer to my soul.

"Me," she whispers, the sound so soft that Simon and I are the only ones to hear, but I have my answer and I believe the word and when Brenda Boles says my name, I break my gaze from Chelsea's and drop the gun. I can't go back to jail, can't be locked back up, I tried it and it is nothing like 6E, it is boring and long and will only drive me even more insane. This is not what I wanted, this is not how it should end, and I lift my hands in surrender, my eyes dancing over the nasty fridge, the bare countertop, and then I see my answer and *run*, my arms pumping, legs quick, and

jump my feet lift up together, my hands on my head, elbows creating a protective frame around my face, the coordinated bulk of me crashing into and through Simon's sixth-floor window.

I loved him. No matter if it was twisted and deceitful and false, I loved him. Without him, it's all broken.

It's stupid, it's dumb. I know what that fall can do. I know the chances of my walking away are nil. But as I fall through the air, my arms flailing out, I only feel free. I will not be harnessed, I will not be kept; I am freedom, and my name is Deanna.

The ground comes much, much sooner than I expect, and when I hit it, I feel death.

CHAPTER 86

Present

EXCRUCIATING PAIN, WORSE than any I could ever imagine, from every piece of me that I didn't even know existed. I lie there, on my back, and break, my eyes struggling to open, the sky lighter now, pink and pretty, and it is a view I haven't seen in a very, very long time. Through the pain, through the ragged gasp of my breath, every other sound mutes, my effort to live competing with the hammering of my heart that—at least—tells me I am still alive...I hear her steps. I flick my eyes right and see, upside down, the sprint of Brenda Boles. She skids to a stop, bending before me, her face a blur as it moves in dizzying swirls above me.

"Madden!" An unnecessary yell as I am right here.

I cough.

Yes, I am alive. No, I will not let you take me. I will shrug off this stitch and stand. Run. Faster than you. Get in FtypeBaby and drive to heaven, where I will spend my millions. Alone. I have learned one thing, and that is that I am dangerous. I am my mother, and I hurt those that I love. I will not hurt him anymore.

I will get up and leave Brenda behind because I am young and she is old and there is

Everything goes dark.

CHAPTER 87

Present

THE NEXT TIME I make a dramatic exit through a window, I should look through it first. I'd looked out my own apartment's window a hundred times, enough to know that my side of the building, which faces the street, is a straight shot down, a plummeting fall that, if you're lucky, lands you on grass. It turns out that Simon's side of the building has an extra lip of one-bedroom units; they stick out and run up to the third floor. So my leap took me only three stories down. Good for my life. Bad for my theatrics.

When I fully gain my faculties, I am in the hospital. The blanket over me is pink, the television before me is on. There is a sitcom on, a trio of strangers laughing on its screen. I test my neck, turning my head, and see the tray next to my bed. A cup with water, a bent straw perched in its icy depths. I lick my lips, and they are cracked and dry. There is also red Jell-O there and a bag of chips, opened. I stare at the chips for a long moment.

The door opens and a woman walks in, her hair pulled back in a ponytail, her white tank top tucked into designer jeans. This must be the bitch who ate my chips. I watch her casual entrance, her toss of the phone onto a chair, her gaze sweeping over me and then stopping.

"You're awake."

I nod.

"Let me get the nurse." She holds up a hand as if she's worried I'll scamper away. "Just a second—"

"Wait." My voice croaks when it comes, and I swallow, a hard and painful process. "Wait a minute."

She steps closer, her hands smoothing at my blanket, tucking the edges into the bed, and that must be why they are so freaking neat. I don't like neat blankets. I like mess and disorder and killing people. I go to link my hands and find out I can't move one of them. "What's wrong with my arm?"

"It's broken." She perches on the edge of the bed.

"What else?"

"You're banged up a bit, you've got some sprains and a pretty nasty cut on one knee, but that's it. You landed on a weak section of the roof. I think it had some give."

That's it? On one hand, I feel super-tough. On the other hand, those injuries don't sound bad enough that I couldn't have hobbled away. "But I passed out?"

"A bone broke the skin." She picks up the bag of chips and peers into it, pulling one out and chomping on it. "They said it was shock."

A bone broke the skin. Well good. That sounds alarming enough to faint for. I want to reach for the bag of chips but it's on my bad arm's side and I don't want to reach across and come up short. "I'm sorry, who are you?"

"Oh." She sets down the bag of chips and brushes her greasy

hand off on her jeans. "I'm Lily, Jeremy's sister. We spoke on the phone."

Oh. I shake her hand numbly. And...she's really here. Sitting in my hospital room. Eating my chips. "Where's Jeremy?" Half of me doesn't want to know the answer. The other half wants to rip it from her throat.

"He's on the fourth floor; you're on the second. Want to visit him?"

"Is he awake?" My heart seizes in a dozen different ways.

She swallows and puts down the bag. "No. Not yet." She picks at the inseam of her jeans. "But he will be, the doctors are really confident. He's on a ventilator now." She peeks up at me and it is our first moment of full eye contact. She looks like J; I see it now. Same eyes. A few minor tweaks of the face I would never have picked up on unless given the link. "Did they tell you he woke up?"

I lean forward and feel a pull of pain in my back. "No." I wonder how long I have been out. I wonder if, right now, there is a chorus of police outside this room. I wonder if, if she pulled back this blanket, I'd see my ankles shackled.

"Yeah. Last night." She pulled at her ponytail to retighten it. "That's how the cops knew." She looked back up. "That you were innocent."

"What?" I need a hundred details, and this woman is feeding them to me through a freakin' cocktail straw.

"He told me it was Simon." She reaches out and grips my casted hand and it feels like a violation. "I'm sorry." She stares at me as if her eye contact alone does something. "I'm sorry that I thought, for a minute..."

"That I did it." *No worries, Lily. I was right there with you on that thought process.*

"Yes."

I pull with my shoulder, and the casted arm moves away. She looks hurt and for a moment, I regret the action. "It's fine. Thank you for talking to me when I called. I appreciated the update."

When her cheeks flush, she looks younger, and I wonder how old she is. "It was before you confessed. I was—well, anyway." She stands. "I should get the doctor. And then get back to Jeremy. I just wanted to have something to tell him—" Her face breaks and she looks away, letting out a huff of breath. "When he wakes up."

I am my mother, and everyone that I love dies. I look up into her red face and smile. "I'll be up there once they clear me."

She takes my lie and swallows it with my smile of sugar. "Great. Thanks."

I watch when she opens the door, but do not see a cop.

CHAPTER 88

Present

SO IT WAS all you?" David settles into the chair, the metal creaking from his weight. Across from him, Simon Evans glances nervously up at Brenda.

"That's right. But I told you, it was an accident."

"The push out the window."

"Well...everything." He raises his hands, and the cuffs clink loudly, the boy jumping just from the sound. He lowers his hands to the table and she watches the tremble in his fingers. Not an essential tremor, not nerves, this was something more. Drugs. She steps forward.

"You don't accidentally stab a person, then drag his body to a Dumpster, Simon."

He swallows, his eyes darting away, his mouth flipping his lips in and out in an obsessive cadence. "Yeah."

She leans on the table and stares at him. "Unless you start talking right now, we're going to book you, take you down the hall, and lock you up in one of the cells. Whatever habit you have going on, you're going to go through weeks and months of withdrawal. Your skin is going to crawl all night, your head is going to turn inside out from insanity, and you'll be Big Earl's ass bitch within hours just for a snort of some backwoods shit that will cause you to piss blood."

His eyes flip to David, his face paling. "It's true," David says quietly, and he always can manage to communicate more with a calm tone than she can with screams. "It'd be in your best interest to just tell us the truth."

Simon swallows, his eyes dropping to the table, his fingers dragging a slow set of lines across the wood. "When he fell...I didn't know what to do. Deanna...she was just lying there, for all I knew she was dead. And he..." He lifts a hand to his mouth and chews on the edge of his finger. "He was down there and it was an accident! I was just trying to get him away from her—"

"Yes, Simon. We know that part."

His eyes twitch up to her. "So I called Chelsea. And she came."

"And did what?"

His shoulders rise, his fingers spreading slightly, a shrug that stretches into unease. "She fixed it. Like she always does."

Brenda is out the door, her shoes slapping on the floor, Simon's final statement ringing in her ears as she fumbles for her phone, dialing into dispatch, then requesting the head of crime scene. *Chelsea Evans.* She should have known. She should have freaking known. "*She fixed it. Like she always does.*"

Like she always does.
Like she always does.
Like she always does.

CHAPTER 89

Past

WHEN SIMON EVANS tackled Jeremy, it was an act of chivalry. You don't hit a woman, especially one like her. A man who made that mistake deserved to be beaten to a pulp.

That was how it began: chivalry. Chivalry paired with 800 milligrams of oxycodone and a line of coke. The drugs pushed the chivalry into hatred, three years of animosity pushing him further further further until he was swinging at the man's face with wild abandon, chivalry a forgotten stimulus that was already packing its bags and taking the next bus.

Poof. When the deliveryman's fist connected with his stomach, it hurt, the breath whooshed from him, stars dotting his vision for a moment before he staggered back, his hand out, asking for a moment from the man. Remarkably, Jeremy straightened, wiping his mouth, and stopped. Rested his hands on his hips and turned his attention back to Deanna, who remained on the floor, still and silent.

They both saw the knife at the same time, Jeremy's head turning the wrong way, then right, Deanna's outstretched hand acting as an arrow to the blade, which had skidded over to the wall, still open. Simon lunged for the knife at the same time Jeremy stepped toward it, the reach suddenly a race, Simon's jump over Deanna's body awkward, his boot landing on something delicate that gave beneath his heel, his body pitching forward and once again plowing into Jeremy. Only this time he hit Jeremy's back instead of his side. And this time Jeremy was in the act of leaning forward for the blade. And this time there wasn't empty floor behind him, but an open window. Jeremy fell, and Simon expected a scream, but there was only silence and the occasional whistle of the night air.

He hadn't wanted anything more, had dry heaved when Chelsea had pushed the knife into his hand. "We have to do it right," she had instructed. And then, when he couldn't do it, couldn't stab the man just to make sure he was fully dead, she had taken over. Punctured his chest a half dozen times with quick and efficient strokes, then called him a pussy as they'd lifted his body, one of Jeremy's arms around each of their shoulders, their drag across Glenvale and behind the Quik Mart fairly painless, if you ignored the fact that it was a dead body in their arms.

Simon had felt a sigh come from Jeremy, a twitch in the hand that he gripped around his neck. But he hadn't said anything, had prayed a silent prayer that the man may live, had hesitated before his body once it was pushed into place behind the Dumpster.

His sister was right; he was a pussy. But not for the reasons she thought.

CHAPTER 90

Present

WHEN MY HOSPITAL room phone rings, I pick up.

"Hey, killer."

I smile weakly, the nickname suddenly sour. "Hey, Mike."

"Ready to get out?"

"Am I clear?"

"Babe…" His confident drawl makes me smile. "I got you out of Alcatraz. You think I can't handle an overworked hospital?"

I laugh. "It wasn't exactly Alcatraz."

"Easy. You don't want to offend the hand that frees you."

"Good point. And yes, I'd love to get out of here."

"I'm putting in discharge instructions for you now." I can hear a chorus of keystrokes, the sound of freedom with a new ring.

"Am I heading back to jail?"

"God, they don't tell you anything in that place, do they?"

"Meaning?" I pull at some lines leading to my cast and wonder if I can remove them.

"Simon confessed, blamed the psychotic shit on his sister, some chick named Chelsea. You know her?"

I forgot the cast and sank back against the pillow. So the police got the confession I was gunning for. I should be happy, but a part of me feels cheated. "Yeah. I know her. But I'm still in trouble, right? I mean…I did break out of Alcatraz." *And stab Simon.* That pesky little detail.

He laughs. "You're in a little bit of trouble. You've got to report for a hearing, and you might have a short stint in for assaulting an officer, that type of thing. But we're talking weeks, not months. And if you hire some hotshot attorney, they can probably get most of that gone."

"What about what happened at Simon's apartment?" *My next stab was neither slow nor gentle, hitting quick and hard into his bare shoulder.*

"Well, I don't know your side of it, but Simon and Chelsea declined to press charges. Apparently Simon is saying he stabbed himself, though no one is believing that. I think the detectives are more focused on pinning the attempted murder charge on them right now, and will deal with you later."

Surprising. Christmas has come early for psychopaths this year. I glance toward the windows and wish that I had asked Lily to open them. "Can I ask you a favor, Mike?"

"Anything."

"I need a new ID. And a credit card attached to it. How long would that take?"

"I've got those I made for you back in the day. There's nothing wrong with them; they've been collecting dust waiting for some excitement."

"What are the names?" I reach for the ice water and come up short. I scramble for the bed control and lift myself closer.

"Damn you are picky." His voice drops away for a moment. "Just a second, let me pull them out." I can hear movement and picture him walking through the house. "By the way, are you gonna want your stash back?"

I succeed, the edge of my fingers dragging the cup closer, until I can wrap my hand around it and bring it to my mouth. My stash? I think of the knives, all carefully picked out during late-night fantasies, the sadistic thoughts that pushed me to each and every purchase. My guns, some of them with sins already to their credit. "No. Not right now."

"Good." He huffs out a breath. "'Cause they're in a place that's a bitch to get to. Okay, let's see…I got a Mindy, a Whitney, and a Marisol."

I wait, because surely he has *something* else. "And…"

"And…what?"

"That's it?"

"God you are high maintenance. Who needs more than three backup aliases?"

"The names suck." I huff out my own breath and set down the water. "What real-life individual is named Marisol?"

"You don't have to go by Marisol, you can go by…"

"Mary?" I finish. "I'm twenty-three, Mike."

"Actually, you're twenty-six on this batch of IDs."

I grunt out a laugh. "You are worthless. Not that I'm complaining, mind you, I just want to put that in as a side note."

"Pick one. Mindy or Whitney, since you hate Marisol."

"Whitney. Can you overnight it to me?"

"Yeah. Are you running?"

I smooth a hand over the blanket. "I can't go back, Mike."

"It's only a few weeks, Deanna. Jail isn't so bad."

Says a man who has never been. "Just send it, please."

"Anything, babe. You know that."

We say our good-byes, and I hang up the phone.

"I can't go back, Mike."

"It's only a few weeks, Deanna. Jail isn't so bad."

I hadn't been talking about jail. I'd been talking about my life.

CHAPTER 91

Present

THERE WAS A time in my life, a very short one, when I thought that my sickness might be a gift. At that time, I had just saved a little girl's life and killed a very bad man. I thought that maybe all of the self-imprisonment and urge suppression had been building up to some greater purpose. I had driven back to my apartment with peace in my soul, and had closed the door and returned to my life with warmth in my heart.

But then, the cold came back. And the two people closest to me in the world suffered. And so I closed further off. Removed any element of freedom, scaled down more, plucked away temptation points until there was just Jeremy and me and Jess Reilly. That layer of sequestration didn't stop anything. Jeremy still, for all intents and purposes, died. Because of me. Because of my ridiculous systems and connections and the world I built with a thousand sharp edges and safety nets with predesigned holes, because, let's face it, I like to fall out.

Jeremy is the first man I have ever loved. But our love is a safety net riddled with holes.

I love him because he looks at me like I am normal. He looks at me like I am normal because he doesn't know the whole of my depravity. He looks at me like I am normal because he doesn't know that the reason my box spring was missing was because I used it to carry out a dead body. He looks at me like I am normal because he doesn't know that I once chopped off a man's finger and mailed it to Mike as a cute little joke. He looks at me like I am normal because he doesn't know that I killed my own mother and then drove back to my grandparents' house.

I love him because he has shown me a life outside of 6E. He took me on a first date where I tried not to stab him. He drove me to buy a car and I came home and called my shrink. He gave me a taste of freedom in outside foods, outside experiences, in the scent of fresh air, in the rumble of fireworks, in the sound of *I love you*. I became a freedom addict and he was my pusher. I loved seeing him because every moment included one more push for *more more more Deanna* and I yielded to him and ripped my fragile world open wider and wider.

I love him because in our relationship, I see a normal future. I cried in his bed and thought about the possibility of more fuckin' bacon. About a life where I might forget my old memories and make new ones. About a life where we watch cartoons and go for walks and he pulls me to him and laughs into my neck then makes love to me on the floor of our house. I picked up a photo on his mantel of him and his niece and thought about having his child. I love him for a future that can't exist, that isn't possible because fuck all the other roadblocks, *I am not normal.* And staying with him will mean a hundred more lies to myself, omissions of thought, excuses of self, a house of cards built to justify an existence that will never be.

I love him for a hundred reasons that are paper thin, an illusion I've created and he's bought into. He is my finest Jess Reilly moment and he has no idea. He is my knight in shining armor made of tinfoil. I cannot be rescued; there is no Happily Ever After because, at the end of all this, Cinderella isn't allowed to kill the prince.

I should have, from the beginning, run from him. Run from anyone. I can't take back that mistake. But I can, right now, end the madness.

This isn't about whether it's true love. It's about whether the love is true. And it's not. My love for him is selfish and wishful. His love for me is pure and naïve. He may never wake up. But if he does, I won't be here to break any other pieces of him. He doesn't deserve that, not anymore. I've been too unfair to him as it is.

And right now, I'm going to give him the only thing that he does deserve.

The truth.

I unfold my letter to him and read it one last time. It's my third draft of the letter. The problem with confessing all of your sins is that you try, for some perverse self-preservation, to paint yourself in a good light. I did that with the first few drafts. I was ending things, confessing my sins, but I was trying to retain his love, trying to justify my actions. It was great for me, I was practically beaming with pride by the end of it, but it was useless for the purpose I was trying to accomplish. So I sat back down and wrote a fourth, then a fifth draft. This one is as close to perfect as I can do. And by perfect, I mean ugly and real. He will not love me by the final word but he will know me. And that is what he deserves, to really know the girl that he, at one point in his life, loved. And I can only hope that one day, that is all he will think of me as. The girl who passed through his life. The girl he loved, then got over. The girl who was a pain in the ass until the day when she wasn't. The girl who lied more than she told the truth. The girl with the brown hair and all the web-cams. The girl in 6E.

I close the letter back and slide it into the envelope, addressed to him, care of Lily. She seems to think he will wake up once the swelling on the brain goes down. I'm glad she has hope in her heart, I'm glad that he has someone like her in his life. I like to think that, if Summer had grown up, she'd be like Lily. She'd have been the one waiting in my hospital room, eating my chips.

I stand and look around the sea of boxes. It is funny that boxes are what brought Jeremy into my life and now, with my largest delivery, a stranger will take my life away. Everything that once sat in this apartment is now in cardboard. It took nineteen hours. In some ways, that seems long. In retrospect, it should take longer to pack up a life. Now the boxes are in three piles. One is for Goodwill. They are scheduled to pick up my furniture and donations tomorrow at ten a.m. I will not be here but the super will let them in. The second pile is for FedEx. I couldn't bear the thought of another man in brown picking up my packages. FedEx will deliver those boxes to my storage unit back home, where I've arranged for them to join all of the pieces of my childhood, boxes with my webcams and sex toys slid next to photo albums and Summer's art projects. Maybe one day I'll return and go through the unit, maybe I won't. The final stack, a small cluster by the window, is trash. The super will cart it downstairs and throw it away. His wife will clean the place and prepare it for the next tenant. I hope the new resident treats it well. I hope they understand and appreciate its beauty, its sanctuary. I will miss this space, these walls. If I didn't have so much to run from, I'd stay here forever. I was happy here. Through the screams and the breaks and the crazy, there were whispers in time when I was happy. Times when I laughed. Times when I smiled and meant it.

There is a knock and I run a last, slow hand over the top of my boxes, then step to the door. When I open it, it isn't FedEx, and I blink in surprise and angle the door to block any view inside.

"I'm sorry to bother you."

"It's fine." I scratch an itchy spot on my neck. "Is everything okay? My attorney said my hearing isn't until next week."

Detective Brenda Boles waves her hand dismissively. "Everything's fine. I just saw these come through and wanted to return them to you." She holds out a plastic bag and my eyes drop to the contents.

"Oh. Thanks." I grab the bag with the meager items from my intake. Eighteen dollars, the lotto ticket, and my watch. Yippee.

"You have to sign this." She holds out a clipboard, a form attached to the front. "It's a receipt."

I sign my name *Deanna Madden* and pass it back. *Whitney McTucket.* That is my new signature.

"And here." She reaches in her blazer pocket and pulls out something small, holding it out to me. "It's the key to your car," she says unnecessarily. "We never impounded it, but Evidence had the key from the day of the warrant search."

"Oh." FtypeBaby. In all of this packing, all of this preparation, I'd forgotten all about her. My beautiful wild child. My getaway girl. I lift my chin and smile at Brenda. "Thank you." She drops the keys into my palm and I close my hand around them.

"I'll be at your hearing. I'll see you then." It's a threat, though I don't know if she intends it to be. I smile politely.

"Thank you. You didn't have to personally come by. I appreciate it."

"I was so sure that you were guilty." She shakes her head and laughs a little. "I'm not wrong very often."

I say nothing and she steps back. Turns a step later and faces me. "That night you jumped out the window…I have enough just from what we saw to charge you with *something.* We don't have to have Simon and Chelsea file assault charges to arrest you."

I shrug. "You have a job to do. I understand that." *But I won't be here if you come back.*

I watch her walk down the hall, then I step backward into my apartment and shut the door. Drop the bag and the keys onto the floor and press my forehead against the door. *Freedom.* It is almost here.

I hear the familiar wheeze of a delivery truck outside, a sound that has so often brought me joy, and I blink back tears. I stay in place, the cool metal of the door comforting, and let the tears drip free. When the knock sounds, I step back and wipe my face. Open the door and smile at the two men who stand there, nodding my way through their introductions. When they mention the pickup, I step to the side and swing open the door.

"Come on in. You have a cart?"

"Yes, ma'am."

"Great. It's the stack in the kitchen." I take the package the first man offers and scrawl my signature across his pad. I carry the thin parcel to the kitchen and rip the top of it open, shaking out its contents. A passport, birth certificate, and social security card. I open the passport and see my face, a gold credit card tucked in between its pages.

My name is Whitney McTucket. My birthday is February 16, 1989. My parents are two names I will memorize later. My passport photo is a good one, and it looks like I've already been to four countries.

"Ms. Madden?"

"Yes?" I glance up and set down the passport.

"We loaded up everything in that stack. Is there more?"

Loaded up everything? I thought it would take three trips, maybe four. But the two of them have stacked the boxes in neat order on their cart and there are fewer than I remember, only ten or eleven boxes, all of my life that's worth keeping and 80 percent of it is sexual. I glance at the other two piles and shake my head. "No, that's it."

"Here's a receipt for the pickup." The shorter of the two steps forward and passes me a thin slip of paper.

"Thank you."

"Have a nice day."

Ha. I smile, they smile, and then they leave. I look at my suitcases, two of them, next to the door. Nothing to do now but leave.

CHAPTER 92

Two Weeks Later

CAN I SEE your ticket?"

I straighten and dig in my pocket, pulling out the yellow square and handing it to the man.

"She yours?" the man asks, tilting his head toward FtypeBaby.

"Yep." I kick a tennis shoe up on the railing of the barge and lower my sunglasses. I could suffocate him with enough of those tickets. Stuff them down his throat like pushing batting into a pillow.

"She's a beaut. You'll certainly turn heads on the island."

I force a smile and hold my hand out for the ticket. He passes it back. "When we land just get in and idle. The attendant'll wave you forward. Welcome to the Cayman Islands, Ms. McTucket."

McTucket. A horrible last name. "Thanks." I stuff the ticket back into my pocket and close my eyes, resting against her side, the ocean breeze bringing the scent of salt with it. Two weeks of freedom down. I took the scenic route, driving south through Texas, then across the border into Mexico, spending a night here or there as I skipped across the country, my foot heavy on

FtypeBaby's gas, the top down, music up. Mike was my guardian angel, watching Tulsa PD for any sign of alarm, but they didn't realize I'd left till the hearing and I was already in Mexico by then. As Brenda said in an e-mail to her boss, I turned myself in for an attempted murder I didn't commit. Who'd have thought I would run from a misdemeanor? I bought a gun in Monterrey, and a knife in Tampico, both only for protection. And now, my baby's first boat trip, one that would take us to our final destination and to the rest of my funds: two and a half million dollars, transferred from Deanna Madden's accounts and now in Whitney McTucket's possession. It's enough for a small house on the beach and a new life.

There, in the sun, the car's warm curves against my back, I almost feel hope.

Dear Jeremy,

I did love you, that is the one truth I ever told you. You are a man who deserves to be loved. You are a man who is honest and good, one who protects the weak and sees the best. You are a man who works hard and thinks harder. A man who deserves a woman by his side whom he can be proud of, one who can be a mother to his children and a partner in life.

I never really told you about my mother. I know that you know what happened, that she killed my brother and sister and our father. But I didn't tell you that there was a piece of her mind that was broken, and that she passed that piece on to me. Maybe it was in me all along, but I didn't discover it until I was seventeen. Until the night I walked in and found my dead family, my mother in the midst of it. I killed her that night, J. It was me, not suicide. I *killed* her.

That first night, the start of our relationship? You brought me flowers and I asked to borrow your truck. I never told you where I went that night and you never asked. I killed my first man that night. I got back in your truck with his blood on my clothes. He was a horrible person but his life wasn't mine to take. And I took it because I wanted to, because my hands shake and my blood pulses and I get *motherfuckin' excited* at the thought. I drove back to Oklahoma and slept for three days because I was hungover from killing. Because my body was spent and my mind was reeling. And, for a short while, I was fine.

The first time you almost died? In the hospital you told me you didn't want to know, in case the police questioned you. I didn't get to you in time because I was getting rid of a body. Because after I killed him, I lay on his body and slept. I didn't kill him because of you; I didn't even know about you. I killed him because I wanted to. Because I had a free pass and a sliver of motive and I grabbed hold of it and unleashed hell. I risked your life because I was cocky and too badass to just be *normal* for once in my life.

And now, you lie in a hospital. I didn't kill Simon and Chelsea for you, but I would have. You can thank Lily for their lives, for her calling the cops when she did. I'm not going to thank her. I'm pissed at her for taking that from me. A double kill...it would have been so beautiful. But I do believe that Simon's actions were, at least initially, an accident. You should forgive them. You *will* forgive them. I know you; it's what you do. It's what a truly good person would do.

Don't forgive me, Jeremy. Understand me. Understand that there is a part of me that is broken and it can't be fixed and it doesn't want to be fixed. It is how I was made; it is how I will be until the day that I die. I am not the girl that you fell in love with. You fell in love with a girl I played, a part I do so well that I can sometimes escape to her place and pretend that it's real. That is what I did with you: I pretended. I pretended until the day when the game stopped being fun. I pretended until the day that my plastic world crumbled around the hum of a ventilator.

My game killed you, J. And I'm sorry that I ever asked you to play. I'm sorry that I ever stood in my doorway and let you see me. I'm sorry that I lied. I'm sorry that my heart is black and I didn't let you see that until now.

It was a fun game. And now it is over. I pray that you one day get a chance to read this letter. You deserve life. You deserve happiness. You deserve truth and someone who doesn't have to hide it from you.

Sincerely,
the girl in 6E

AUTHOR'S NOTE

I know there is a large group of you, dear readers, who will be upset with me. I don't have a response for you, except to say that Deanna is a big piece of me and she spoke very loudly in the writing of this book. One day, should you ever decide to write a book, you will understand that I, as the author, have very little say in the direction that my characters take. It was a very emotional journey, the writing of this book, and I still—even after five rewrites and three editing sweeps—tear up when reading the final chapters. Please know that as emotionally attached as you may be to the characters, I am even more so. I have lived and breathed these souls for over two years.

As far as whether I will write another book in this series—I think that I probably will. I want to explore Deanna's journey further and see where she goes and what happens to her. And I have a few surprises still tucked up my sleeve that want to be pulled out.

To all of the readers, bloggers, and other authors who have loved Deanna and experienced this series: THANK YOU from the bottom of my heart. Thank you for embracing this wicked girl and taking her under your wing.

With love,
Alessandra Torre

ACKNOWLEDGMENTS

Thank you to Maura Kye-Casella, my angel of an agent, for embracing my little self-pubbed evil child and growing her into this franchise. Thank you to Susan Barnes for seeing her beauty and making her into so much more. Thank you to the entire team at Redhook for perfecting her and then sending her out into the world to be read. A special thanks to Lindsey Hall, Alex Lencicki, Ellen Wright, Laura Fitzgerald, Wendy Chan, Andromeda Macri, Rachel Hairston, Anne Clarke and Tim Holman.

A second giant thank-you to Kiki Chatfield with The Next Step PR and to Tricia Crouch—the greatest assistant an author could ask for. You ladies are amazing. Another thank-you goes out to Perla Calas, whose sharp eyes helped make this book shine.

To Joey—thank you for taking my crazy and pouring kerosene on the fire. I love you so incredibly much.

And to the readers and bloggers. Without your support, these books would never happen. Thank you for reading them, reviewing them, and recommending them to others.

MEET THE AUTHOR

Photo Credit: Romona Robbins Photography

A. R. Torre is an open pseudonym for Alessandra Torre, an award-winning *New York Times* and *USA Today* bestselling author of eleven novels. Her books primarily focus on romance and suspense, all with a strong undercurrent of sexuality. Torre has been featured in such publications as *Elle* and *Elle UK*, as well as guest-blogged for the *Huffington Post* and *RT Book Reviews*. She is also the Bedroom Blogger for Cosmopolitan.com.

You can learn more about Alessandra on her website at www.alessandratorre.com, or you can find her on Twitter (@ReadAlessandra) or Facebook.

INTRODUCING

**If you enjoyed
IF YOU DARE,
look out for**

THE GIRL IN 6E

A Deanna Madden Novel

by A. R. Torre

My life is simple, as long as I follow the rules.

1. Don't leave the apartment.

2. Never let anyone in.

3. Don't kill anyone.

*I've obeyed these rules for three years. But rules were
made to be broken.*

CHAPTER 1

I HAVEN'T TOUCHED a human in three years. That seems like it would be a difficult task, but it's not. Not anymore, thanks to the Internet. The Internet that makes my income possible and provides anything I could possibly want in exchange for my credit card number. I've had to go into the underground world for a few things, and once in that world, I decided to stock up on a few fun items, like a new identity. I am now, when necessary, Jessica Beth Reilly. I use my alias to prevent others from finding out my past. Pity is a bitch I'd like to avoid. The underground provides a plethora of temptations, but so far, with one notable exception, I've stayed away from illegal arms and unregistered guns. I know my limits.

The UPS man knows me by now—knows to leave my boxes in the hall and to scrawl my name on his signature pad. His name is Jeremy. About a year ago, he was sick, and a stranger came to my door. He refused to leave the package without seeing me. I almost opened the door and went for his box cutters. They almost always carry box cutters. That's one of the things I love about deliverymen. Jeremy hasn't been sick since then. I don't know what I'll ever do if he quits. I like Jeremy, and from my warped peephole view, there is a lot about him to like.

The first shrink I had said I have anthropophobia, which is fear of human interaction. Anthropophobia, mixed with a healthy dose of cruorimania, which is obsession with murder. He told me that via Skype. In exchange for his psychological opinions, I watched him jack off. He had a little cock.

While I may go out of my way to avoid physical human interaction, virtual human interaction is what I spend all day doing. To the people I cam with, I am JessReilly19, a bubbly nineteen year old college student—a hospitality major—who enjoys pop music, underage drinking, and shopping. None of them really know the true me. I am who they want me to be, and they like it like that. So do I.

Knowing the real me would be a bit of a buzz kill. The real me is Deanna Madden, whose mother killed her entire family, then committed suicide. I inherited a lot from my mother, including delicate features and dark hair, but the biggest genetic inheritance was her homicidal tendencies. That's the reason I stay away from people. Because I want to kill. Constantly. It's almost all I think about.

Over the last three years, I've learned how to optimize my income. From 8 a.m. to 3 p.m. I use a site called Sexnow.com, which has a clientele of mostly Asians, Europeans, and Australians. From 6 p.m. to 11 p.m., I'm on American turf, on Cams. com. In between shifts, I eat, workout, shower, and return emails—always in that order.

Whenever possible, I try to get clients to use my personal website and also make appointments. If they go through my website, I make 96.5% of their payout, plus I can hide the income from Uncle Sam. The camsites only pay me 28%, which officially constitutes as highway robbery. I charge $6.99 a minute. On a good month, I make around $55,000 and on a bad one, about $30,000.

Camming makes up seventy percent of my income; the rest comes from my website, which allows men to watch my live video feed. I broadcast at least four hours a day and charge subscribers twenty bucks a month. I wouldn't pay ten cents to watch me masturbate online, but apparently two hundred and fifty subscribers feel differently.

The $6.99 a minute grants clients the ability to bare their sexual secrets and fantasize to their heart's content, without fear of exposure or criticism. I don't judge the men and women who chat with me and reveal their secrets and perversions. How can I? My secret, my obsession, is worse than any of theirs. To contain it, I do the only thing I can. I lock myself up. And in doing so, I keep myself, and everyone else, safe.

Sometimes I allow myself to be delusional. To daydream. At those times I tell myself that one day I will be happy—that I am banking all of this money so I can move to the Caribbean and lie on the beach. But I know that if I did that, the sand would be covered in blood soon enough.

I try to sleep at least eight hours a night. Nighttime is when I typically struggle the most. It is when I thirst for blood, for gore. So Simon Evans and me have an agreement. Simon lives three doors down from me in this shithole that we all call an apartment complex. He has, over the last three years, developed a strong addiction to prescription painkillers. I keep his medicine bottle filled, and he locks me up at night. My door is, without a doubt, the only one in the complex without a deadbolt switch on the inside.

I used to have Marilyn do it. She's a grandmotherly type who struggles by on the pittance that is her social security. She lives across from Simon. But Marilyn stressed out too much; she was always worried that I would have some personal emergency, or fire, or something, and would need to get out. I had to find someone else. Because I worried over what was coming. At night, my fingers would start to itch, and I would come close to picking up that phone, to asking her to unlock my door. And then I would wait beside it, wait for the tumblers to move and my door to be unlocked. And when I opened it, when I saw Marilyn's lined and tired face, I would kill her. Not immediately. I would stab her a few times, leaving some life in her, and wait for her to run, to scream. I like the sound of screams—real screams, not the pathetic excuse that most movies tried to pass off as the sound of terror. Then I would chase her down and finish the job, as slowly as I could. Dragging out her pain, her agony, her realization that she had caused her own death. I had gotten to the point where I had picked out a knife, started to keep it in the cardboard box that sat by the door and held my outgoing mail and various crap. That was when I knew I was getting too close. That was when I picked Simon instead. Simon's addiction supersedes any concern he has for my well-being.